Down and Out in Kathmandu

A Backpacker Mystery

Jennifer S. Alderson

Traveling Life Press
Amsterdam

Down and Out in Kathmandu: A Backpacker Mystery
(Adventures of Zelda Richardson Volume 1)

Copyright © 2015 Jennifer Stacey Alderson
Traveling Life Press
First Edition, published December 2015
Second Edition, published July 2016
Third Edition, published May 2017

ISBN-10 number: 1519365903
ISBN-13 number: 978-1-519365-90-3

www.JenniferSAlderson.com
www.facebook.com/JenniferSAldersonAuthor

Cover artwork by Philip Derijcke
Cover design by James, GoOnWrite.com

To my father, for always being there

PREFACE

Tommy could feel his bowels draining as his legs went limp. Harim's sidekicks pulled him back up, wrenching his shoulder blades.

"Better be careful, Tommy. Nobody would think twice about yet another stoner hitting his head against a wall or – better yet – falling out of his five-story hotel room after smoking illegal drugs. You really think the Bangkok police are going to waste their time on your sorry ass?" Harim's left hook emerged out of nowhere, slamming into Tommy's stomach.

Tommy spit up bile. He tried to find the words to beg for his life, to make his boss take pity on him and let him live. If only Harim would stop hitting him, maybe he could catch his breath and explain it all. The diamonds, the money, the traveling, none of it mattered anymore. He just wanted to live. He had to see his mother one more time. And to make peace with Chantal. He'd had no right to kill her cat, let alone string it up like that. Tommy was only twenty-five, much too young to die. He still had so much to do, to see, to experience. How could he make Harim understand?

"Where are my diamonds?" his captor roared.

Fear robbed Tommy of speech. Only air bubbles and groans escaped his lips. The Greek slammed a chair into the wall above Tommy's head. Shattered wood rained down…

CHAPTER ONE

Compact soldiers fidgeted with their machine guns as the newest arrivals entered the airport. Zelda joined the visa queue and took out a paperback. As the long line nudged forward, she noticed the owner of the backpack behind her seemed to have disappeared. Begrudgingly, she dragged the lonely luggage forward with her own. The stocky, dreadlocked man soon returned, apparently not noticing his bag had moved.

"You should really be more careful," she said.

"Pardon?"

"You should really watch out more, you know. Be more careful. There are probably pickpockets and thieves all over the place just waiting for a chance to grab your bag."

"What?"

"Your backpack! If you haven't noticed, it's pretty chaotic in here, and I can't be held responsible if anything happens, so you should watch out for your own stuff. I could have stolen from you twice now, and you never would have noticed."

"You can do what you like, but it's not bloody likely that you'd get too far, in case you hadn't noticed those blokes with Uzis," he replied, gesturing towards the armed men dotted around the hall. "Besides, I don't recall asking you to watch my bag."

Kicking herself again for not getting her visa ahead of time and now starting off so badly with the ruggedly attractive stranger behind her, Zelda took a deep breath and began again. "I noticed you getting on in Bangkok. Where did you connect from?"

The man let out a deep sigh, followed by a long stretch and a yawn. "Australia. Man, what I wouldn't give to be on a sandy beach smoking a joint right about now." He started doing upper-body twists, his springy dreadlocks dancing around his bronze face. "Say, do you know how much the visa is gonna cost?"

"Twenty-five dollars for one month."

"American dollars?"

"Uh, yeah," replied Zelda sarcastically, not realizing Australians used dollars too.

"Oh. Don't suppose customs takes traveler's cheques, do they?"

"No, but there's a currency exchange right back there. I'm sure they'll be happy to help you."

"Fantastic! Would you mind watching my bag just once more? Cheers..." He was already walking towards the booth, digging a passport and traveler's cheques out of his money belt.

"What a jerk," Zelda mumbled. Unable to concentrate on the book in her hand, she glanced around the crowded arrivals hall, purposefully avoiding setting her eyes on the man's bag. It seemed like every available surface was covered with paintings or carvings of fierce-looking demons and other strange creatures she vaguely recognized from her guidebooks. She knew she should be excited to finally see these things in real life, but an overwhelming sense of fatigue outweighed her fascination. All she wanted to do was to get to her hotel room and lie down on a real bed. The weather certainly didn't help her mood. Nepal was a heck of a lot warmer than she'd thought it would be, and the airport didn't seem to be air-conditioned. After pulling her long brown hair into a ponytail, Zelda carefully wiped the sweat off her face with a Kleenex.

A few feet later, the bubbly blond stranger returned. "Cheers for that! You're a sport. Do you need to change money yourself? I'll watch your rucksack for ya..."

"Thanks, but no. I've got everything under control." Zelda twisted back to face the slowly shortening queue. She pulled out her wallet anyway and silently counted her cash. It wouldn't hurt to get more rupees while she had the chance, she thought. The exchange rates here had to be better than at Seattle-Tacoma International Airport. A few moments later, she turned to face the Australian again. "Actually, I would like to get some more money, as this line isn't really moving very fast. If you don't mind?"

"No, not at all. I'll be here."

Zelda sprinted to the currency exchange, changing greenbacks for rupees in record time. Racing back, she was relieved to see her bags still safely in line and seemingly unmolested. Sure, there were armed guards everywhere, she thought, but those bags were filled with gifts for the families she'd be staying with, and that guy was a complete stranger. Zelda muttered a "thanks" while casually checking the zips on her bags.

"No worries," he replied cheerfully. "So how long are you going to be in Nepal anyway?"

"Oh, about three months or so, I think. Everything's open-ended at the moment." Zelda couldn't help chuckling for the first time in days. After thirty-two hours of flights, bad food, and long layovers, she was actually in Kathmandu, well, at least technically. She could feel a smile spreading across her face. The months of preparations – subletting her apartment, quitting her job as a computer programmer, getting several rounds of vaccinations, and arranging all the tickets – finally seemed worth it. Everything was going as planned, and soon, very soon, she would begin her own amazing adventure. She was sure of it. Somehow the delays at the airport didn't count.

The man behind her slammed one hand into his forehead and thrust the other towards her chest. "Where are my manners? G'day, the name's Ian."

"Hi, I'm Zelda, my name is Zelda," she said, her own hand extending automatically to grip Ian's right palm.

"Goodtameetcha. This is my first time abroad, at least by myself," Ian confided. "I'm planning on traveling around the world – so long as my money lasts anyway," he announced with a big wink and a grin.

Before they could continue, Zelda noticed the armed guards were motioning for her to move. "Oh, it's my turn! Good luck, Ian," she sang, while throwing on her biggest smile for the customs officer and the two soldiers flanking his sides. A few flurries of his brown wrist and she was charging downstairs towards the baggage claim.

"Where the hell are my bags?" Zelda demanded from no one in particular. Even though she had spent the past forty minutes crossing the arrivals hall inches at a time, the luggage from her plane had still not been unloaded. Other western tourists who had smugly breezed through the visa holders' control point now sat slouched and folded in frustrated heaps along the rusty conveyor belt. Zelda took a seat and began waiting semi-patiently, tapping her foot on the bare concrete floor. In America she never had to wait for luggage.

A few minutes later, Ian bounced into view. His face was split open by a set of teeth that would make an oyster envious. "Beauty, ain't it?" Smiling at his passport's freshly violated pages, he didn't seem to notice Zelda rolling her eyes.

The conveyor belt grumbled to life. A large group of well-equipped Asian tourists – cameras at the ready – shuffled forward *en masse* and retrieved their matching bags, before reassembling around a plump woman furiously waving a pennant on a stick. The two frosty pieces of glass marked "Exit" slid open. On the other side, a squirming mass of human bodies convulsed towards the pack of fresh arrivals. Shouting men in long tunics waving signs announcing hotels, tours, and guides competed with each other for lucrative tourist dollars. Thin barricades and more armed guards lined both sides of the exit. The doors slid shut before the crowd's screams could register as anything other than primal.

Zelda's eyes felt as if they were going to pop out of her head. An overstuffed blue backpack, jerking towards her on the conveyor belt, snapped her back to reality. She rose, grabbed her heavy bag, and returned her attention to Ian.

"Sorry?"

"How exactly do you get to the tourist district from here anyway? Do ya reckon there's a bus?"

"You mean Thamel, right? That's where most of the backpackers head to, according to my guidebook. I know you can take a taxi. I'm not sure whether there's a bus or where you'd catch it. I don't think you can walk there from here, though. I have my travel guide in here somewhere, if you want to take a look."

Ian refused her offer with a wave and a grunt. "How are you getting into the city?"

"I have a ride waiting for me." Zelda's words reverberated in her head. She wouldn't have to fight with *that* crowd for transport or shelter. Immediate relief swept over her, amplified by the sight of her second piece of baggage – seventy-two pounds of donated schoolbooks – heaving towards them on the visibly straining conveyor belt.

"How's that? You have a ride waiting for you? How do you reckon?"

"I'm here to volunteer. The director is picking me up and taking me to my hotel. That's why I know I have a ride." Zelda looked around the hall, noticing that while they'd been talking, everyone – save a few concerned-looking souls – had emptied out of the baggage claim area. "Speaking of which, I really should go out and find him. Almost everyone from our plane has left already. I don't want Ganesh to think I missed my flight!"

"Bloody hell! Did someone steal my rucksack?" Ian swore under his breath as he followed her gaze around the empty hall. "Listen, I'm sure your friends are used to the airline being delayed. Do you reckon you can wait around a few more minutes?" Before she could answer, Ian darted over to the lone Royal Nepal Airlines representative, already surrounded by a small mob of angry, well-dressed Europeans. Momentarily interrupting their heated conversation, Ian asked, "Sorry, whom do I ask about lost luggage?" The uniformed man pointed tiredly at himself. Ian raced back towards Zelda.

"I reckon I'll be a while. I have to see that bloke about my bags. Where are you staying?" Ian asked distractedly, watching for any escape attempts from the airline's representative.

"The Royal Guesthouse…or Hotel, something like that. It's supposed to be just outside Thamel proper. I have the address in here somewhere if you want it, but I really need to get going."

"Right. Don't worry about the address. If you can wait outside for me, that would be bloody brilliant, otherwise I'm sure the taxi driver will know where it's at. See you soon." He was already trotting back to the small Nepali man and foreigners, now swearing in French.

Zelda shrugged the books and backpacks onto her shoulders and arms. Once balanced, she moved slowly towards the exit. As the doors slid open, her nasal cavities were assaulted by a wave of feces, unknown spices, and body odor. Piercing, unintelligible screams echoed off the high concrete roof. The kaleidoscope of colors, languages, and noises overwhelmed her. As the doors to the airport closed swiftly behind her, Zelda repressed an intense urge to jump back through and declare this experiment a huge mistake.

She pushed her way through the seething crowd, exiting onto the open parking lot unharmed but sweatier for the experience. Wiping her forehead off with the back of her hand, Zelda squinted against the unrelenting afternoon sun and took her first real look at the scenery around her. Blinding light reflected off tin-roof shacks. Swirling brown earth thickened the already heavy, humid air. It looked as if the city center was far off in the distance. Where were the snow-capped peaks and serene monasteries? Why was it so hot; weren't they at the top of the world? She wasn't sure what she should do next; Ian was already a memory. The chaos she had just witnessed wasn't part of the plan. Zelda had assumed that when she got off the plane, someone from the volunteer program would be patiently waiting for her at the gate.

Rifling through her daypack for her program coordinator's phone number, she did not notice the well-dressed man rapidly approaching her.

"Excuse me, Miss Zelda Marie Richardson?"

His welcoming grin and moisture-free appearance affected Zelda more than him knowing her name. "Mr. Ganesh Pundam, I presume," she exclaimed. "I am so pleased to meet you!" She shook his hand fervently, melting with relief. No wonder he'd wanted passport photographs *before* she'd arrived.

"I am pleased to meet you also! Tell me, did you not see the sign?" he asked, gesturing behind him towards a young boy sitting on the hood of an old taxi, holding an enormous sign stating her full name.

"Sorry, I didn't see it. I guess I was a bit overwhelmed by all the people," she replied sheepishly. Zelda certainly hadn't expected Ganesh to be waiting for her in the parking lot.

"Yes, yes. It is not a problem. Please to come with me." The large grin was back in force. Attempting to be gentlemanly, Ganesh nearly dislocated his shoulder when he lifted Zelda's box of books. "Oh my gods. May I inquire, what is inside this?" he rasped, carefully setting her oversized luggage into the undersized trunk.

"Books," Zelda replied, beaming. "Donated by a few elementary schools in my old neighborhood for my school's library. My school here in Nepal, I mean."

Ganesh looked up at her – clearly astonished – but said nothing, only wrestled further with the trunk, finally using a piece of rope to tie it closed.

A few minutes and strained muscles later, Ganesh hopped onto his bright red motorcycle, promising to meet them back at the hotel. The shy young boy – "my cousin," Ganesh reassured her – would guide the taxi to the hotel. As soon as his uncle sputtered off, the boy jumped into the front left-hand seat, ready to follow. Zelda was about to protest – there was no way he could have been more than ten years old – before realizing that the steering wheel was on the other side of the car. Hugging her backpack, she braced herself for the drive to Thamel, wondering what else was going to be backwards here.

Zelda didn't know whether the manufacturer of the tiny automobile she was jammed into intended the car to be driven so quickly over the incredibly narrow and potholed streets. Insane motorcyclists, belching buses, three-wheeled breadboxes, kamikaze bicycles, and brightly dressed women competed with her cab for room. Whenever she dared to look ahead, another vehicle would be hurtling towards them, darting back into place at the very last moment. Zelda didn't like being part of this constant game of chicken, but she figured she would be worse off walking then riding. At least the car would absorb some of the impact.

As they approached a major intersection, Zelda saw a flustered policeman perched atop a raised cement circle, angrily motioning traffic into the city center. Thankfully the drivers heeded his whistles and waves. So far Zelda couldn't remember any part of the road being straight; their cab was continually winding around ornate squares, pools of water, and colorfully decorated temples.

It was so exotically different that Zelda was having trouble processing it. She tried her best to relax and enjoy the scenery, but her body seemed to be shutting down. Her head started to droop as they approached a heavily guarded building, towering high above the thick stone wall protecting it. She was trying to figure out whether the Royal Palace was supposed to look like a series of melting snow cones, when she crashed out on her backpack.

Rap, rap, rap. "Miss Zelda? Excuse me, please to get out now." Ganesh was peering into the backseat. Her box of books and daypack already sat on the hotel's steps. Wiping the drool off her hand, she stepped out of the cab and into a quiet, tree-filled courtyard. Only the chirping of birds and whisks of brooms filled the air.

"Come, come. This way," Ganesh said, encouraging her with a wave of his hand to get out of the cab.

She followed her program coordinator and his cousin into the guesthouse. The group climbed three flights of stairs before the hotel owner produced a key the size of his forearm and jiggled the creaky lock open. He motioned for the tall foreigner to enter her temporary chambers. Zelda was pleasantly surprised by the large mustard-colored room and two single beds. A vase filled with flowers stood on a small writing table, filling the room with a glorious scent. The four of them dragged her luggage inside before returning to the hallway for a brief round of goodbyes.

"I will return in three days' time. We will have tea in the garden and talk more about the program. Then you will meet your first family!" exclaimed Ganesh.

"Fantastic! How many volunteers are there in total? Is anyone else here already?" Zelda asked.

"There are only four of you. It is a small group this time, better for you. One volunteer arrives tomorrow and another a few hours before we meet again. The fourth is an American lady – like you – staying two rooms down," he said, gesturing towards the end of the brightly lit hallway. "But she is not here now. I made a program for her to go to Dhulikhel. She will return in two days' time! Would you also like to see Dhulikhel before beginning the volunteer program? It is not difficult to arrange."

"Thank you, but I want to explore Kathmandu before we begin. I won't be volunteering in the city, right?" Zelda replied, not really sure what or where Dhulikhel was.

"That is not a problem. The American lady did not like Kathmandu, but she arrived one week ago. Perhaps she had too much time to explore on her own," said Ganesh, laughing. Zelda didn't get the joke. Before she could push him for details, he continued. "Tomorrow there is a transportation strike; none of the taxis or tempos will be working. It is of utmost importance that you take caution when you go out in the city. Perhaps you should only walk around the city center? Durbar Square is quite beautiful. There are many temples for you to see there," he offered.

"Oh, okay," Zelda replied slowly, processing his words. "Wait, the taxi drivers aren't mad at foreigners, are they? How is the other volunteer going to get to the hotel then?"

"No, no. Foreigners are not the issue. I will meet the lady from New Zealand at the airport and bring her back here on my motorbike. It will be great! It is not a problem," said Ganesh, clapping his hands together with a loud crack. The small group snapped to attention for his final words. "So Zelda, we will leave you now to rest. Enjoy Kathmandu. Welcome to the kingdom of Nepal!" With a deep bow and palms pressed together, Ganesh bid her the first of many dramatic farewells, taking his shy cousin and the hotel owner down the stairs with him.

Zelda closed the door and twisted the deadbolt. Lying down on one of the feather beds, she closed her eyes and within seconds was fast asleep.

CHAPTER TWO

Two hours of forms, declarations, and sworn statements later, Ian finally found himself speeding towards Thamel, or at least to a hotel his cabbie told him was in Thamel. Too physically exhausted to barter with the manic crowd, he jumped at a hotel sign dancing centimeters from his face promising "cheapest price" and a free ride. Dropping his meager possessions into the taxi's torn backseat, he did ask about the Imperial Guesthouse, but the driver swore it was full, and Ian didn't care enough to push.

He clambered seven floors up the midget-sized stairwell before finally being able to right himself again in the narrow hallway. The lock practically fell open to reveal a tiny concrete room and two fold-up army cots. Cheap? Yes. Comfortable? Not really, but he hadn't come to Nepal for the accommodations. Noticing a large family of red ants crisscrossing the shower wall, Ian decided to skip cleaning up and hit the streets in search of something native to smoke.

His mates back in Darwin told him it was dead easy to find hashish and sometimes weed in Thamel. It was their stories about pipe-smoking priests and temples dedicated to ganja that had sent Nepal shooting to number one on Ian's list of countries to see. He knew well enough that drugs were easy to come by in other Asian countries; he just liked the idea it was worshipped here. And besides, all of his mates had been to Nepal before and had their own stories to tell. He was tired of being the odd man out.

Ian stepped out of his hotel and immediately into the chaotic heart of Thamel. All around him he heard whispered calls beneath high-pitched touts: "Green sticky bud, hashish, brown hash cakes, Shiva's best mar-u-ana." Ian smiled broadly; his mates hadn't been putting him on after all. Walking slowly up and down the main drag, Ian checked out which little boys were selling what and noted where the policemen were hanging out. Casually approaching a kid wearing a faded *Are You Experienced?* T-shirt, Ian made eye contact, grinning widely. The boy smiled back.

"Oi, can I get some –"

Shaking his head violently, the boy put two fingers over his lips, his eyes lingering on a group of policemen congregating around a water

11

spout. He motioned for Ian to follow. At the next intersection, the boy looked up at Ian expectantly. "You want?" he asked.

Ian nodded yes.

The boy whispered, "Then you follow me." He darted off into the crowd, expertly weaving his way through the throngs of tourists. Just a few meters ahead, Ian could see his would-be dealer turn left. Ian sprinted to catch up. Rounding the corner, he almost knocked over a group of soldiers busy moving street beggars along. Ian grunted his excuses while keeping his head down, but they didn't seem to take any notice of him. Heart racing, he speed-walked through the masses, frantically searching for any sign of the Jimi Hendrix T-shirt. He caught sight of the kid just as he disappeared behind a screaming street vendor. Ian pushed aside carpets and bracelets in time to see the boy pause at the head of a narrow alleyway. His dealer made eye contact, nodded, and then disappeared.

Ian forced himself not to run. At the alley's entrance, he hesitated – it was so dark and quiet. His instincts told him to walk away, leave it, and try again later. But curiosity and a need for weed got the better of him. Besides, he was three times the size of his dealer. Squinting, he could just make the boy out a few meters farther ahead, walking very slowly. Ian charged on into a maze of alleyways, the boy always staying just in front of him. When Ian finally caught up, they had reached an intersection of sorts. Three other alleyways met here, creating a small, poop-filled square.

The boy turned to face him, illuminated by a cobweb of light. "You want the mar-u-ana or hashish?" he asked.

Ian wiped the back of his hand across his forehead. "Marijuana, please. One hundred rupees' worth."

Peals of laughter erupted from the young boy, quickly replaced by an intense businessman's calm. "One *thousand* rupees, not one hundred. Too little. One thousand rupees for everything." He shook a black film canister in Ian's face.

Ian pretended to double-check his wallet. "All I have is…five hundred, that's it. I don't have any more."

"No, no. One thousand rupees, not five hundred. One thousand for everything."

"Look, I said all I have is five hundred. See? Five hundred." Ian waved a handful of rupees in the boy's face.

The boy spat in disgust, gesturing at Ian's chest. "You have more, yes?"

Ian was momentarily taken aback by the boy's savvy but finally raised his shirt, revealing an apparently belt-less chest, nothing more. Man, was he glad his money belt was riding quite low on his hips.

A deep sigh emerged from the little dealer. Apparently used to bargaining, he held his palms up to Ian. "Okay, okay. You go over there," the boy said, pointing to a filthy corner of the square.

Obediently Ian turned to face the mud-brick wall, slyly watching the boy divide the canister's contents into two. The mere thought of kicking back with a joint and a beer got him salivating. They'd passed plenty of bars along the way, but where could he light up? His room didn't have any windows, but there must be somewhere nearby where westerners could smoke in peace. He chided himself for not scoping out his hotel's rooftop terrace before he left or asking his mates in Darwin more.

Something broke his train of thought; Ian looked around distractedly. His mind registered human voices refracting off the brick walls. He couldn't tell how near they were, but it seemed like they were closing in fast. Ian looked over at the boy, but he was still bent over the film canisters. Ian didn't know what to do. Should he just walk away or say something first? He hadn't given his dealer any money yet; he could bolt, and nobody would be the wiser. But then where would he be?

The voices were definitely getting closer, and the boy didn't seem to notice. Ian could feel his heart pounding as sweat began pouring out of him. He wanted to score but not get caught doing it. "Oi, I'm gone," Ian mumbled to himself, turning to walk away just as the boy briefly touched his sleeve.

"Okay, five hundred," the young drug dealer said, shoving a black canister into one of Ian's hands and grabbing the rupees from the other.

The voices rounded the corner: a group of street children appearing just in time to see the final transaction. The tiny gang crushed around Ian's legs, screaming incomprehensibly. His little dealer high-tailed it, running off into the darkness. The boys tore at his clothes and chest, pulling on his pockets. Ian could only make out "Rupee, rupee, rupee!"

"Hey, stop that! Bugger off!" Ian swatted at hands and legs, kicking himself free of his mini-assailants. Adrenaline propelled him through a crossing and down a darkened passageway. He looked back to see five boys in hot pursuit. Ian heard only the beat of his heart as he tore down the alley. Blinded by panic, he tripped over a pile of rubbish while rounding a corner, sending rats scurrying. His screams, as they scrambled over his body, masked the boys' approach. He didn't notice the rocks until they sailed past his head.

"You shits!" Ian turned to see his assailants rearming themselves with loose bricks. His legs kicked into overdrive as reddish-brown chunks shattered on the walls penning him in. He hung a right, launching himself down a light-filled alleyway. Thamel was just ahead. Another brick exploded behind him. Ian focused on the white faces and large backpacks at the end of the alley, not daring to look back. He sprinted the last meter, knocking over a woman covered in Gore-Tex.

"Hey, look out, buddy!"

"Sorry," Ian panted, helping her up.

She brushed off her pants. "No harm done, just watch where you're going next time, okay?"

Ian nodded, grabbing his sides as he tried to catch his breath. The woman looked at him strangely but kept walking.

Ian glanced back down the alleyway and saw two boys still running towards him. "Bloody hell! Why don't you just give it up?" Ian screamed at his pursuers as he jumped to his feet, running up the crowded road. A few meters farther on, he saw a large sign announcing the Trekkers English Language Bookstore and dove inside.

He stood by the front door panting heavily, willing his heart to slow down. He peered cautiously out the window but saw neither children nor police racing towards the store. Ian took a handkerchief out of his pocket to wipe the sweat off his face, almost spilling his expensive purchase onto the ground. Looking around quickly to see whether anyone had noticed, Ian realized that no one would find a sweaty, poorly dressed backpacker with film canisters strange in this tourist-oriented shop. White faces speaking a multitude of languages surrounded him. A plethora of standing bookshelves was crammed into the single-story structure, with maps and souvenirs filling the gaps in between. The sweet smell of chai tea wafted through the aisles. Turning his nose to the source, Ian could make out a cafe towards the back of the store.

He glanced over their exotic selection before sauntering over to an extensive collection of coffee table books. Many were adorned by the unmistakable Mount Everest. The gorgeous moonlit photos of that mysterious triangle of black granite captivated Ian completely. He picked up a weighty volume and began flipping through it, when the overwhelming scent of pot attracted his attention. He instinctively grabbed for the film canister before noticing a far likelier candidate. A skinny, similarly dreadlocked man stood next to him, searching through a bin full of maps outlining treks through places with incomprehensible names. After a few moments, he stopped and looked over at Ian with a bemused expression.

"Can I help you?" the stranger asked.

Ian didn't realize he had been staring open-mouthed. Here he was freaking out about purchasing a small quantity of weed, and this guy was walking around smelling as if he'd just put out an enormous spliff. Ian couldn't help but bust out laughing. "No, sorry for staring, man. How are ya? Name's Ian." He offered his hand to the stranger.

"My name's Jake. I'm fine, thanks, and yourself?" he responded politely.

"Doing fine now. Say, I'm going back to my hotel to smoke out. Care to join me? I just landed in Kathmandu and suspect you already have a few stories to tell."

The stinky American laughed out loud. "Why not? I've got some time. Let me grab a map and we can head out. I don't know where your hotel is, but there's a 'kind pub' across the way."

"A what?"

The stranger smiled warmly. "A kind pub, a place we can smoke out, without trouble."

"Brilliant. Take your time, eh? I'm still absorbing all these crazy book titles." Ian returned his attentions to the volume in his hands. Realizing the store had probably saved him from the police, Ian got behind Jake in line at the counter. He purchased the coffee table book and a set of Buddha postcards from a heavily bejeweled woman wrapped in a fancy bedsheet.

Jake, so far a quiet companion, waited patiently for Ian to sort through his rupees and collect his purchases. "Shall we?" he asked, holding the door open for the Australian.

Ian paused before setting foot outside the shop's walls. He took a long look down both sides of the busy street, hoping his drug-dealing friends had already forgotten about him and moved on with their prosperous day. No cops were waiting outside to jump him. He sidled up alongside Jake, following him willingly to the kind pub.

Two quick twists and turns down the main street brought them to another dark entryway. A colorful sign above the doorway promised cheap, late-night happy-hour drinks and appetizers, but the building looked more like run-down apartments than a bar. Most of the windows were covered by shutters carved out of a dark brown wood, their intricate patterns casting trippy shadows across the alleyway. From the lower stories, a few dirty-faced children peeked out over tiny balconies, staring curiously at the strangers below.

It was only two in the afternoon, but Jake ducked inside and began climbing the stairs anyway. A slight ripple of paranoia washed over Ian; he wondered whether this was some elaborate setup or just normal for Nepal. He wasn't sure he could find this place again or get out in a hurry if he had to. Too fresh off the plane to know any better and dying to smoke some herb, Ian followed, albeit slowly. Two flights of stairs later, another sign appeared, this one featuring large marijuana leaves. Ian smiled and picked up his pace.

Jake was waiting on the fifth floor. They entered into what Ian could only imagine a modern Turkish hash tent would look like if set up indoors and decorated by a rebellious sixteen-year-old. The entire top floor had been converted into a series of small rooms, each decorated with an assortment of pillows, low couches, and long tables. Ornate hookahs and water pipes lined the walls. Black lights revealed fluorescent Bob Marleys, Jamaican flags, and Pink Floyd prisms tacked to the ceiling. Trails of scented smoke wafted from cones of incense scattered around.

In the center of the club, a beach cabana had been reconstructed for serving drinks. As Jake and Ian entered the inner chamber, a voice announced, "Welcome to the Sherpa Club! Is it time for a safety break?"

Ian correctly assumed the disembodied voice meant, "Do you want to smoke marijuana?" and nearly cried with relief. *Meeting Jake must be some kind of omen*, he thought; this was bound to be a great trip. His new mate walked up to the bar and ordered mango lassis with vodka for the two of them, after greeting the bartender affectionately. The man behind the bar was a short, stocky man who had seen his share of bar brawls. A jagged cut, visible just under the collar of his T-shirt, was still healing.

Jake grabbed an enormous silver hookah off the cabana counter, gesturing for Ian to follow. He moved to a low table and stuffed a large sticky bud into the hookah's vertical stem.

When Ian sat down, the film container pushed into his leg. He suddenly remembered he'd never looked at his own supply. It was so dark inside the club that Ian had to dump the can's meager contents onto a paper menu and walk it over to a crack of light emerging from the shuttered windows. He didn't need much illumination to see it was not exactly high quality. More like crappy desert weed – dry and crispy with little green sticking to the thin stems. No wonder hash was so popular here. Ian tried to hide his disappointment in his recent purchase as he meandered back to the table and carefully refilled the black container.

Ian's new friend handed him a snakelike tube fitted with an ornate silver mouthpiece. Snapping open a Zippo, Jake held the flame to the large central bowl while sucking on his own hose like a vacuum cleaner. Ian joined suit, knocking his mind out of commission for the rest of the afternoon. He could feel the jet lag leaving his body with every exhale. He let his body sink into the fluffy cushions, becoming one with the room. Above him a Pink Floyd prism pulsated in time with the heavy bass pumping out of hidden speaker boxes. At some point, the bartender set the drinks on their table and disappeared behind a tapestry with "OHM" embroidered on it.

After a few minutes of meditative contemplation, Ian sat up and began stuffing some of his dry shake into the hookah's wide stem. Jake, previously motionless, grabbed the bowl and dumped its pathetic contents onto the table.

"That's okay. Go ahead and keep your stash," he said, stuffing another sticky bud into the hookah.

"Fair enough," Ian replied, giggling like a tipsy schoolgirl. "Least I can do is buy the next round of drinks, eh? This mango concoction is brilliant," he said, taking another frothy drag of the yogurt-based drink.

"Don't worry about it." Jake waved his offer away, stretching out on the thick Persian carpet. He relit the bowl. "So when did you get here anyway?"

"Dunno, few hours before I met you, I reckon," Ian replied, smiling at the thought. That's what he loved so much about traveling: Less than twenty-four hours ago, he'd been pounding beers and bowls on the beach; now he was chilling with a like-minded brother in Kath-man-fucking-du.

"Wow, that's a record! You must have scored as soon as you got in. Too bad about the quality. It's kind of a grab bag with the kids here."

"Ah, no worries. I took my chances," Ian answered quickly, not ready to share his recent experience. "Mind if I ask where you got that?" he said, pointing at Jake's sizeable ziplock bag. "It looks better than the weed I buy back home."

"This?" Jake responded with a quick grin. "I harvested it myself over in the Annapurna range. Most of the places we trekked through had healthy crops growing out in the wild, unattended. I picked a few buds here and there as we walked and wrapped 'em up in newspaper to dry them out. Some of the plants were taller than the locals."

"Right! Where is Annapurna?"

"Man, you did just get off the plane. Have you heard of Pokhara?"

Ian shook his head slightly.

"It's a day's bus ride to the west, a sweet little village right on the shores of Phewa Lake. It's kind of like a base camp for the Annapurna mountain range."

"Sounds right to me."

"Yeah, it's pretty damn nice. You can do all sorts of treks out of Pokhara. I did the Sanctuary Loop. The trail is pretty crowded right now, but the scenery is so beautiful, it's easy to ignore the others. A buddy is flying in from the States in a few days, and we're going over to do Everest." Jake, sniffing his sleeve as if noticing his strong scent for the first time, blushed slightly before adding, "I, ah, just got back this morning and obviously haven't done laundry yet."

"No worries! When you came up next to me in the store, I thought maybe my pocket had caught fire. If you didn't smell like a pothead, I never would have said anything to you." Ian smiled as he handed his new friend one of the mouthpieces, repeating the American's actions. "Nothing better than a hookah," he said, lifting the tube to his mouth.

"Hey, so you're Australian right?"

"Full-blooded Ozzie at your service." Ian attempted a seated bow, just missing knocking over their empty glasses.

"Where's home exactly?"

"Darwin, up north."

"Oh yeah, I know the place. Me and a buddy did some hikes out of Darwin, to Kakadu National Park I think. You know, with all the crazy rock paintings and moon landscapes. And there were these little gray kangaroos jumping around everywhere."

"Wallabies."

"Oh yeah, right, wallabies. Probably the best bit was a two-day bush hike in this gem called Litchfield. Swimming with crocodiles and shit. Wicked, man. Truly wicked."

"I could have been your trip leader! I mean, I used to lead tours through Litchfield and Kakadu in the summers to earn a bit of extra cash. A mate back in Darwin runs an outback tour company."

"Wow, man, what a great way to earn a living. Pretty hard-core, right?"

"I dunno 'bout that."

"Now yeah, the meanest things we have to worry about back home are cougars, or maybe getting frostbite. It seems like everything in Australia could kill you."

"Cheers to frostbite then."

After a few more vodkas and bowls, Jake stood up and stretched. "It's time to find a laundromat; this stench has to be rectified."

"Okay. I'll see you later this week then?"

"Maybe. We're probably heading out in a few days. But if I don't see you again, the Sanctuary Loop is totally worth doing."

"Cheers for that, and this." Ian held up his film canister, now filled with some of Jake's stash. They walked down the stairs together.

"Take care, man." Jake hugged Ian warmly before disappearing into the crowded street.

Ian floated back to his hotel room and spread out on one of the tiny cots. He rolled a joint with some of Jake's Annapurna bud, mixed with his own dubious purchase. A bottle of Coca-Cola and banana pancakes were already waiting for him on the rooftop patio. Ian wolfed down his food between drags of his funky cigarette. Finally sated, he drifted off to sleep, dreaming about forests of marijuana plants, brown-body toga parties, and hot showers. Momentarily afraid he had pee'd his pants while napping, Ian woke up disoriented to stinging hot rain pelting him from a low-lying summer cloud. The change in weather motivated him to return to his room for a proper nap, while his only set of clothes dried on the spare cot.

CHAPTER THREE

An enormous *sidis* tree squawked to life as kookaburras and green-tailed parrots cavorted in the morning sun. Vanilla-topped peaks shimmered in the distance. Staring across the vast city center before her, Zelda could hardly believe she was in Kathmandu, capital of the only Hindu kingdom in the world. Or at least the only one she'd heard about. She would have to ask somebody about that.

Despite the spectacular view from her rooftop terrace, Zelda was having trouble sitting still and finishing her breakfast. All she wanted to do was run downstairs and get lost in the mazelike streets of the inner city. She only had two days to herself before beginning her volunteer program, and she wanted to make the most of her newfound freedom.

Zelda let her eyelids close as she tried to remember the last time she'd done what she *wanted* to do, not what was expected of her. But she couldn't. Her life in Seattle had become one big boring routine. Every morning jumping in her car to join the same slow-motion race to the office, just to tweak some code and push a few pixels, then sit in another traffic jam to get home in time for dinner and Colbert. She felt like her life had become programmed, and she didn't know how to break the cycle.

When her boss offered her a full-time contract a few months ago, her parents had been so proud, talking enthusiastically about pension plans, stock options, and all the security a blue badge would bring. Zelda knew right then and there that she *had* to get the hell out of Seattle. She was only twenty-six years old, for God's sake. Did they really expect her to work eighty hours a week for the next forty-four years and be *happy* about it? There had to be more to life than sitting behind a computer all day. But she felt so trapped, so *stuck*, that she didn't know what those other options might be. Who knew whether coming to Nepal was the right choice, but at least it got her out of her Seattle doldrums.

Zelda wolfed down the rest of her muesli and yogurt, before skipping downstairs to pay her breakfast bill and find out more about the day's events. The hotelkeeper, a friendly older man quick to smile, filled her in.

"The Maoists are upset with the government again, so they have organized the strike today. There are many strikes in Kathmandu, it is not a problem. But be wary of large groups, especially if they are throwing stones at renegade taxi or tempo drivers trying to make money from lack of service," he said.

Zelda grinned broadly; there were some things she could figure out on her own. She decided to stick to her original plan and walk to Durbar Square, forgetting to ask who the Maoists were and what they wanted. Her friend Randy, a retired climbing guide, had warned her to watch out for "some dangerous guys from the West." But she was in central Nepal. She'd have to find an English-language newspaper before volunteering; best to have some idea of the major happenings in the country she would be residing in for the next few months, she thought.

Zelda had studied her guidebooks last night, carefully planning out a winding route along many of the inner city's larger temples. Friends had given her plenty of tips and reassured her that, even though the city center was huge, most of the must-sees were in Durbar Square, a short walk from her hotel. As she exited onto her hotel's wide steps, Zelda took out her tourist map, double-checking the name of her first turn. A moment later, the high-pitched sound of a flute pierced the air. Lowering her map, Zelda noticed two snake charmers only a few feet away, seducing their keep with reed flutes. She rubbed her eyes, sure she was dreaming. As she walked closer, she saw that the snakes were kind of dancing, swaying in time with the rhythm as they rose slowly out of their woven baskets. Entranced, she moved closer, mimicking the snake's motions. One of the men began shaking his hat at her, calling out for rupees. Zelda moved on.

Only three blocks separated her room from the tourist district. In that short distance, the tranquility of her tree-filled hotel block was replaced by a whirlwind of street vendors hawking jewelry, tiger balm, and hand-carved elephants to wide-eyed tourists. Crippled beggars dragged their shattered bodies through the muddy streets, alms cups jingling around their necks. Scrawny cows and mangy goats rooted around in rotting piles of garbage searching for a tasty meal. Rats – many the size of a small cat – scurried into homes and restaurants, flaunting health codes. Diesel exhaust, trapped by the tall buildings, hovered in a visible layer down most streets. Both sides of the streets burst full with restaurants, bars, and souvenir shops.

Zelda paused at the mouth of Jyatha Road, taking it in. Crunching her hands into fists, she forced herself to stay put and not turn tail and run back to the hotel. Everything she had seen, heard, and read about Nepal flashed through her head like a PowerPoint presentation, her friends' accounts of their own Asian adventures serving as a voice-over. The streets *did* look just like the pictures she had seen in all those travel magazines; however, their two-dimensionality had not prepared her for the overpowering noise and smells. Surely her friends had never said anything about the unbelievable filthiness of it all. Zelda hoped her vaccinations were working. Sucking up her courage, she hunched up her shoulders and launched herself into the heart of the tourist district.

By the time she had reached her first major turn, Zelda had stepped in too many piles of cow, goat, dog, and human shit to count. She rounded the corner, distractedly looking for something to wipe her shoes off with. A low guttural noise attracted her attention. She looked up to see a group of protesting strikers marching stridently towards her. It looked like a witch hunt, something out of the Middle Ages. Hundreds of men shouted in protest, most carrying large sticks set ablaze. Banners and signs bobbed violently above their heads. She stood there frozen, momentarily entranced by the dancing torches, before the men's angry cries brought her out of her daze.

Terror-stricken, she backed quickly up the street, ducking into a small side alley. Sweat streaming down her face, she willed herself to become part of the brick wall. Columns of angry young men marched past. She didn't know what to do – make a break for it or stand still until they were gone. There were so many of them. After a moment's hesitation, she turned and bolted in the opposite direction, running as fast as her legs would take her.

Zelda didn't know how many intersections she had crossed before finally stopping. Leaning against a parked tempo, she wheezed like mad as she tried to catch her breath. She strained to hear the protesters' cries, but they were gone. Willing herself to relax, Zelda took out her tourist map and tried to orient herself, but to no avail – the street names were scrawled in Nepali script, not with western letters. Her map was useless. Zelda let out a sigh of frustration. Well, she wasn't sure where she was or how to get back to Durbar Square, so she might as well try to enjoy whatever sites she did run into.

Looking around, Zelda saw a promising-looking shrine farther up the street. She was walking towards it when he found her. A well-dressed young man, not really a boy but further from manhood than his pencil-thin moustache suggested, stepped in front of her, blocking her way. His black-as-night hair and dazzling grin reminded her of a painfully thin Wayne Newton.

"Would you like a guide for the day? I am very helpful to you," he said, smiling widely.

"No, thank you, I just want to walk around by myself. I'm in no rush. Thanks," she said, striding away from him and towards a small stream of locals flowing in and out of a nearby courtyard. She quickly found herself staring at one of the most ornate temples she would see in Kathmandu. Silver and gold statues of dancing gods stared at her from above. Captivated by the delicate metal sculptures surrounding her, Zelda did not notice that the persistent young man had followed her into the courtyard. He whispered in her ear, "The Monkey Temple is more beautiful than this place."

She jumped a foot out of fright before landing in front of the unruffled man. "What do you want?"

"I am Khamel! I will take you to the Monkey Temple, not on the tourist way, but through the back of the city. It is very beautiful. I take foreigners this way all the time; they say it is very educational." Khamel spoke like the men in Hindu movies, straightforward statements delivered in an irresistible singsong. Still, Zelda sensed trouble. Sure he was small, but she had already seen that size didn't matter in a country where most children could easily kill her with their karate skills, and every man seemed to have a large metal blade attached to their belts. Besides, Zelda had spent hours studying her guidebook's list of the most important sites in Kathmandu, but she didn't remember any mention of a Monkey Temple. "Can you please go away, I don't want to go to the Monkey Temple, not today, not with you."

"But you must go to the Monkey Temple! It is the most important temple in all of Kathmandu, all of Nepal! I will show you the way. It is much better than this." Khamel looked around the courtyard, crowded with prostrating worshippers, with revulsion. Undeterred by her harsh words and reproachful gaze, the boy began listing off information to make his services known.

"That is Vishnu," he said, pointing to a handsomely effeminate god with long hair riding what looked like a winged bull, only it had a man's head and bird's beak. "And that is Shiva…"

Zelda wasn't sure what to do. She didn't need or want a guide. She loved the idea of getting lost in the city, imagining it to be the best way to see the inner workings of real Nepali culture. On the other hand, it would be great to know more about the various gods and goddesses governing their life. She *could* look each one up in her guidebook, but that would take forever. After a few more questions and explanations about the deities covering the building and surrounding structures, Zelda decided to make Khamel her day's companion.

She followed him along the "nontourist back way" to the Monkey Temple – as he repeatedly reminded her. Huge apartment buildings lined the banks of the Bagmati River, on the outskirts of Kathmandu. They crossed over the river on what Khamel quaintly referred to as a "cart trail." The thin metal bridge was clogged with ox-driven carts and mobile street vendors moving between the city center and suburbs. Zelda pushed her fear of heights aside, refusing to look straight down. Instead, she used their higher vantage point to look up the wide river. Its banks were filled with locals brushing their teeth, bathing, shaving, urinating, washing vegetables, doing laundry, and defecating, all within a few feet of each other. Islands of rotting garbage and decaying animal carcasses floated down the middle. Zelda blinked in amazement, slowing her pace as she tried to take it all in.

She still didn't really understand where they were headed but frankly no longer cared. This glimpse into daily city life was totally worth whatever she'd end up paying Khamel. She couldn't have ever *imagined* the type of poverty surrounding her. Zelda felt the spring returning to her step. If she could whistle, she would have. *This* was the Nepal she had hoped and expected to find. And besides, an important temple crawling with monkeys sounded like a perfect destination for her second day abroad.

Khamel, to ensure Zelda didn't forget his worth, prattled on about the impending temple and its religious attributes. "It has the most beautiful view of Kathmandu in all of Nepal. Holy men from Tibet congregate there. Lots of shrines to Shiva and scores of dreadlocked priests." Khamel created his own mantra, repeating between pauses, "It is very sacred," as if the holiness alone would stun Zelda beyond words.

They rounded a large bend in the road, and suddenly they were there: a small square filled with taxis, confused tourists, and screaming merchants. In the middle of the dusty clearing stood a fantastically decorated gate. It appeared to mark the beginning of a long path that wandered up the substantial hill before them.

"Swayambhunath! The Monkey Temple!" announced Khamel triumphantly.

After a moment of silence, Zelda asked, "Where exactly *is* the temple?" All she saw were weathered stone statues scattered alongside a series of tree-shaded staircases.

Khamel let out a frustrated sigh. "There," he said, pointing to the very top of the mini-mountain before them. "This staircase is the main entrance. They say if you can climb all three hundred and sixty steps, it brings you good luck." Khamel was already charging upwards.

Zelda followed slowly, drawn to the top by the chatter of birds and screeches of unseen primates.

She paid her entry fee and rushed through the last gate, anxious to get inside. An enormous eye stopped her in her tracks. It floated ominously above a half-dome the height of a five-story building, painted completely white.

"What is that?"

"It is a Tibetan stupa, a holy place for Buddhist peoples. The eye of Buddha reminds us he is always watching."

"And that one there?" Zelda pointed towards a large stone cylinder, covered in ornate carvings.

"That is an Indian stupa. Hindu people pray there."

"But they are right next to each other!"

"Yes?" Khamel looked at her quizzically before moving on.

Zelda wandered slowly through the statues and holy sites surrounding her. What she assumed would be one big temple was a complex filled with hundreds of mind-bogglingly beautiful shrines, stupas, temples and monasteries known collectively as Swayambhunath – all of which was squeezed onto a sliver of land sticking up in the middle of the Kathmandu Valley, "like a lotus flower blooming from Vishnu's belly," according to Khamel.

Zelda followed him obediently, listening attentively to his descriptions of the temples and deities surrounding them. They'd just reached the entrance of a large Hindu structure when Zelda imagined she heard someone calling out her name. Shaking her head slightly, Zelda refocused her attention on Khamel's explanation of the Hindu temple's attributes. A moment later she heard a distinct, "G'day, Zelda!" from behind. She turned to see the guy from the airport. *What is he doing here?*

"G'day, how ya going?" Ian called out as he approached.

"Hey, Ian! Fancy meeting you in a place like this," she exclaimed, misquoting the old *Casablanca* line.

"It's not really much of a surprise, now, is it? Swayambhunath is one of the top attractions in Kathmandu. And with the transportation strike today, I reckoned it was a good day to walk around and stretch me legs a bit."

"Did you finally buy a guidebook?"

He smirked at her. "No, I chatted up the hotel owner."

"Oh. Did you at least get your bags back?"

"No, not yet. They reckon they'll be in later this week."

"How will they contact you?"

"I was going to go back to the airport tomorrow and check," Ian said.

"Oh, what a pain. Maybe you can give them your hotel's telephone number?"

"Maybe. It doesn't really matter to me, so long as they find 'em. All my trekking gear's in those bags!"

Zelda noticed that Khamel was practically dancing with impatience. "Hey, how did you get up to the temple anyway? Have you been here long?" she asked.

Ian shrugged his shoulders. "I just walked. I've been here for a while; the monkeys are great."

"Well, this is Khamel, he's been showing me around," Zelda said, waving the suddenly shy boy over.

"G'day." He tried to shake the boy's hand, but Khamel turned away. Ian looked over at Zelda. "Good if I join ya?"

She glanced over at her guide, but the boy was avoiding her gaze as well. She shrugged her shoulders. "I guess not."

"Brilliant. I like your glasses, by the way. Very librarian-slash-dominatrix."

Zelda, to her great surprise, found herself blushing at his remark. "Oh, these? I've had them for years. I usually wear contacts, but there's so much crap floating around in the air…"

"They look good."

Her cheeks felt as if they were on fire. She dared not use her voice, only grinned at him in response. She hadn't taken a really good look at Ian at the airport, but now she couldn't help noticing how his muscles rippled across his legs as he charged up the stairs. Ian must work out a lot. He was pretty sexy in a wiry, grungy sort of way. A bit short and too tan for her tastes, but still.

They started up another winding staircase, elbows touching. Khamel followed closely behind, their unwilling chaperon. A strange noise began to drift down the tree-lined trail. Zelda thought at first it was birds, but the closer they got to the source, the more surreal it became. Almost guttural, but in a bizarre range of tones. As her group entered a large clearing, they were immediately confronted with a brightly painted building. Zelda recognized it as Tibetan from her guidebooks.

She ran noisily up to one of the massive metal-plated doors, pressing her ear to it so she could better decipher those incredible sounds. "It is a Buddhist lamastary," Khamel called after her. The door next to her swung open; an older monk in saffron robes poked his head out, looking for the source of the commotion. Zelda began to blush, looking down at her shoes, embarrassed for having made such a ruckus. With a laugh, the monk waved them all inside.

It took her eyes a moment to adjust to the dark interior. Hundreds of butter candles lit up the colorful walls. It seemed as if every available surface had been painted with delicate flowers, ferocious dragons, and fanciful birds. In the center of the room, around thirty monks of various ages were chanting in a range of volumes and tones. The devout men were clearly distracted by the outsiders' presence, some staring openly at Ian's wild blond hair, others at Zelda's long, uncovered legs.

"They are reciting their daily scriptures," Khamel whispered in Zelda's ear. She didn't want to believe him; the sound was too heavenly to be routine.

Zelda followed Ian and Khamel around the large hall, taking in the extensive collection of paintings and statues. *Thangkas* – stylized deities painted on cotton and silk by meditating monks – hung from every rafter. At the front of the building, six of the *thangkas* were covered by a colorful curtain of silk.

"Why are those gods covered up and not the others?" Zelda asked Khamel.

"They are sleeping now. If we come back later, perhaps they shall be awake," Khamel said.

Zelda wasn't sure whether he was being sarcastic or serious but let the topic drop and returned her attention to the holy beings who were still conscious.

Within twenty minutes of their arrival, the choir came to a ragged offbeat finish as each monk sang his final lines of prayer. As the last words were uttered into the now-still air, the head monk rang a bell. As if launched from a single gun, the previously sedentary holy men jumped up and shot out of the room. The tiny man who'd let them in came over and said, in halting English, "Lunchtime." With a sheepish grin, he followed his brothers' path and pace out the door.

The westerners went back outside, Khamel tagging closely behind. The three strangers walked leisurely around the brilliantly colored temples and gray stone statues dotted around Swayambhunath. On Zelda's right, a group of worshippers slowly circled a Tibetan stupa, turning prayer beads and wheels over and over in their hands. To her left stood a life-sized statue of Buddha, its golden hue reflected in the pool of water surrounding it. The serene statue seemed to attract both primates and *Homo sapiens* in large numbers.

As she watched tourists fight monkeys for granola bars and camera bags, Zelda couldn't help but wonder what her co-workers were doing right at that moment. Definitely writing a bit of code, worrying about compatibility issues, and fighting with her old manager about software updates. She thanked whichever gods were listening that she was here, far, far away from her office at Microsoft.

Zelda could feel Ian's eyes on her. When she looked up, he asked, "So why did you chose Nepal anyway? I thought Americans went to Hawaii or Mexico."

"Give me a break! Not every American swears by all-inclusive vacations." She kicked a pebble into the dense shrubbery surrounding them. A baby monkey chased after it, testing it for food. Zelda breathed through her nose, willing herself to calm down.

"Not too long ago, my friend Mary took six months out. Just like that – " Zelda snapped her fingers. "– she quit her job and backpacked around the world with her partner. After they got back, Mary couldn't stop talking about her travels, which, of course, did sound amazing." Zelda paused again, regarding Ian cautiously. He was still very much a stranger to her. Would he laugh at her like so many of her colleagues? But his face held no sign of disappointment or admonishment. She took a deep breath and continued in a rush, eager to get her story out.

"And so I asked to see her pictures, and we got to talking and, I don't know, I just asked her straight out, 'What was your favorite place?' And without a moment's hesitation, she responded 'Nepal.'" Zelda paused, thinking back to that magical moment in her basement apartment only a few short months ago.

"And I still don't know why, but that was it for me. As soon as she left, I started looking online for options. The next day, I bought a few travel books and read about the different volunteer programs they have in Nepal. It sounded so amazing – to help people so directly, I mean. It's totally different than writing out a check to some charity, you know? Besides, I haven't had a real vacation in five years and was getting pretty burned out. Volunteering sounded like a great way to see more of the world at the same time. After I found this program, everything kind of fell into place. And five months later, I'm sitting here with you, dodging monkeys and listening to real Buddhist monks sing."

"Good on ya, Zelda. What are you going to do anyway? Build some houses or dig a well?"

"Teach English," she replied, positively beaming. "I'm going to be one of those teaching-English-as-a-second-language people."

Ian stopped mid-walk, staring at Zelda, dumbfounded. *"You* are going to be a *teacher?"*

Zelda felt her face flushing red. "Yeah, but only for a few months. Teaching is, like, a noble thing. I mean, I don't really have much experience or anything, but I'm sure they will be giving us lessons next week. At least I think they will. And besides, volunteers can make a world of difference. How else can these kids *really* learn how to speak English? If no one like me was willing to take a few months out of their lives to come here and teach them, where would they be then? Okay, so I'm not backpacking around willy-nilly, but I'm still going to have plenty of time to see more of Nepal and Asia afterwards if I want to."

Ian held up his hands in mock defense. "Hey, that's great. I'm happy for ya."

Zelda swore she could see a smile forming on his lips. Her blood pressure began to rise. "What? What is it?" she demanded.

"Look, I know teaching is a noble profession – that's what I do for a living. I just can't quite believe that come next month, *you* will be standing before a classroom." Ian began to chuckle. "They are going to eat you alive!" he exclaimed, not trying to contain his belly laughs.

Zelda stared open-mouthed. She'd written Ian off as a loser, some sort of surfer dude whose great ambition in life was selling drinks on the beach between waves.

Ian smiled wryly. "Don't let the dreadlocks fool you, missy. These are new. My hair was already long. After my request for sabbatical got approved, I dreaded it and have been growing 'em out ever since, in preparation for this trip."

"Wow, I really didn't expect *you* of all people to be a teacher. I took you for beach bum." She twisted her hand into the hang-loose sign, unsuccessfully. "Sorry."

Zelda studied Ian critically, trying to rework her image of him. All her teachers had been stuffy and old – she couldn't imagine even one of them traveling around the world in their spare time, let alone growing dreadlocks. "Yeah, well, do you have any tips for me?"

It took Ian a minute or two to control his laughter. "Don't underestimate the little bastards. Kids are smart, much smarter than most adults give them credit for. Just watch your back."

Khamel had been hanging back, chatting with the other little guides hanging around Swayambhunath while keeping one eye on Zelda the whole time. But when the sun began slowly lowering itself behind the jagged peaks hemming in the Kathmandu Valley, he marched over to her and pointed to his watch. "We go back to the city now?" he asked.

Zelda looked over at Ian, asking for his approval by raising her eyebrows.

Ian shrugged. "Why not?"

They rose, following Khamel back towards the main entrance. They'd almost reached it when the cries of a large group of worshippers attracted Zelda's attention. She led her group over to the source of the sorrow. A Hindu priest was passionately chanting scriptures while throwing rice and flowers onto a shrine. Saried women offered endless bowls of meat, rice, and flowers to the small central statue, sprinkling red powder around the gods' feet.

"What's going on, Khamel?" Zelda asked.

Her guide gestured to a tiny boy lying motionless in his mother's protective arms. "He is sick. The priest is praying for him to feel better."

"Don't they have doctors here?" she exclaimed.

Khamel replied simply, "Of course. But why not ask for the gods' help too?"

CHAPTER FOUR

"One piña colada. There you go."

"Thanks, man." Tommy pushed aside the tiny umbrella and sucked hard on the straw. "Gosh, it really feels like you're in the tropics when you're sipping on one of these babies, know what I mean?"

The bartender grunted.

"If I was home right now, I'd probably be pulling back a Molson's. Funny, eh? A Molson's – can you imagine someone drinking one of those, here?"

The bartender jerked his thumb behind him, towards a case of Canada's finest.

"Who would be stupid enough to order one of those, *here*?"

The bartender glanced up at him, then began wiping down the bamboo-lined bar.

"You know, my friends are probably drinking Molson's right about now. Hosers. Probably wearing their woollies too. Crazy, eh?" The bartender hunched up his shoulders and disappeared into the stock room. Tommy called down the bar, "Crazy, eh, to think it's snowing in Canada right now – as we speak!"

Two fair-haired girls looked briefly over at him before moving to a table closer to the beach. Tommy followed them with his eyes. The palm trees lining the veranda were swaying gently in the wind, in time with the girls' hips. Tommy licked his lips slowly, pondering his chances. The bartender returned with a handful of lemons and began chopping them into thick slices.

"One of my friends is a bartender too. Sucker, pulling beers for rednecks."

The bartender shot him a dirty look before moving his cutting board farther down the bar.

Tommy yelled after him, "Yeah, and another friend is stuck answering phones for some pretentious law firm. How'd you like to have to say, 'Thank you for calling Bailey and Turner, how may I help you?' a thousand times a day?"

The bartender set his knife down and picked up a towel. He moved towards the sunlit terrace and began cleaning up the empty tables.

31

Tommy picked up his piña colada and followed him. "What an idiot, right? If you could choose between being stuck in a cubicle all day or being here – I mean, come on – here, right? Hands down. Right, man?" The bartender didn't seem to notice him, but Tommy kept talking anyway. "I should really treat them to a vacation. Chantal would love this place. The whole gang really. I should fly them out here, all of 'em!"

The bartender collected a few empty glasses and disappeared back behind the bar. Tommy took a seat at one of the tables, putting his drink down in front of him, and examined the pristine waters before him. Bizarre rock formations jutted out of the crystal blue sea. Long, thin fishing boats rocked in the bay, waiting on snorkeling tourists. Big-breasted bimbos frolicked in the frothy waves. Smiling in appreciation, Tommy suddenly realized he had never seen Chantal in a bikini.

Shrieks of laughter caught his attention. The two women from the bar were a few meters to his left, splashing each other in the horseshoe-shaped bay. Tommy wandered over and waded in, taking care not to cut his feet on shell fragments. He swam towards the girls, diving down to the bottom and resurfacing with a handful of sand. The women were already making their way back to their table. Tommy swam farther out into the open ocean and let the waves carry him to shore. He picked up his drink, walked over to join the two blondes, and stopped, blocking their sun.

"Great day for a swim, eh?"

The girls looked up. The one with smaller boobs giggled back, "Yeah."

"So how long are you ladies here for? I've been here for weeks; it's kind of my place, if you know what I mean."

The larger girl snickered again. "Yeah, right."

"I only winter here, really. Summers I'm back in Toronto. At my penthouse."

Now his target was rolling her eyes. Was she a double-D? He wasn't sure.

"I'm Tommy, by the way." Only the small-chested girl nodded. "Mind if I join you?"

The larger girl put a hand on her friend's shoulder, stopping her from speaking. "We're heading back to our room in a minute. Sorry."

"Oh, well." Tommy took a seat at their table anyway. "You sure I can't interest you two lovely ladies in another drink before you go?"

"No, thanks," the larger girl said, standing up quickly. Definitely a double-D. "Let's go, Jill," she said, pulling her friend towards a row of thatch-fringed villas facing the shoreline.

Jill shrugged her shoulders and obeyed, only turning back to briefly wave goodbye to Tommy. As they stumbled up the beach, he could hear Jill grumbling to her friend, "We could have gotten a free drink out of him! He wasn't *that* creepy."

Tommy fumed in his seat. "Lesbians," he muttered, grabbing his drink as he rose.

As he shuffled back to the bar, Tommy wondered again how Chantal would have looked in that little red bikini. He closed his eyes, seeing her big breasts waving back and forth once again. They did that when she screamed. Her voice echoed in his head: "You're never going to amount to anything! I've wasted enough of my time on you, you loser!" Tommy shook his head, smiling. "Just leave me the fuck alone" had been her exact last words. After all these months, it was no longer a painful memory but a reminder of everything he had recently accomplished. Chantal wouldn't be laughing at him now.

After returning his glass to the bar, Tommy grabbed his towel off the stool and wiped down his freckled skin and spiky red hair. Remounting his chair, he called out, "Cheers to Princess Beach," lifting his glass in expectation. Silence. Tommy drank up anyway. How he'd love to tell the old gang about this place and all these gorgeous women. He knew they would be jealous. Still he resisted emailing them. Eventually they would start asking how he managed it.

"Hey, can I get another one of these?" The bartender was chatting up a group of sorority girls and didn't seem to hear him. Tommy called out again, "Hey, man, one more piña colada down here." The bartender glanced over at him and then continued his conversation.

Tommy scowled at his slowly burning skin. A familiar wave of homesickness overtook him. It had been happening more often these past few weeks. Maybe he should go back home for Christmas and New Year's and look up some of his old buddies. After all these months, he'd have to surprise them with extravagant gifts, that's for sure. He might even get something nice for Chantal, just to show her there were no hard feelings. His friends would ask how he could afford the presents, of course. He'd just smile mysteriously and say that he had finally found his niche, in Thailand.

Tommy tilted his head back, momentarily lost in thought. He would have to score some big money if he was really going to impress his friends back home. His next appointment with The Greek was in just four weeks' time. Maybe he could ask him for an extra run, double his earnings before heading back. He sighed, twirling the straw in his empty glass. He didn't mind the risk so much; hell, he'd blown past so many customs officials without getting even a suspicious glance that he felt invisible. It was The Greek himself. Would he let him go back home to Toronto while Tommy was working for him? Did he trust him to be discreet?

CHAPTER FIVE

After a few hours of gaping in awe, the various gods and goddesses began mixing together in Zelda's head. The satisfied westerners led the way down to the front entrance of Swayambhunath, walking past monkeys, gods, and touts as if they'd been doing it for years. Zelda and Ian automatically began following the main road back to Kathmandu, walking in contemplative silence for most of the journey. Khamel, now silent, trailed close behind.

Zelda was on cloud nine. Everything about today – meeting her guide, the walk up, all the amazing temples, priests and pilgrims, even running into Ian – seemed so right. And Swayambhunath was more amazing than she could have imagined; certainly nothing like a visit to a church or synagogue. They could have easily spent another few hours walking around the complex and still not have seen every temple, shrine, stupa, and monastery crowded onto that tiny sliver of land. Zelda wondered whether all the holy sites in Nepal were as expansive as this one; if so, she was going to need more time to explore the country before flying home.

Ian opened his mouth to speak, then shook his head.

"Just spit it out, Ian."

He hesitated before saying, "You know your little guide's expecting money, right? These guys don't help pretty girls for fun. He's a young one too. Where did he pick you up?"

"That's it? We just spent the entire day in one of the holiest temples in all of Nepal, and that's all you have to say? I thought it would be something deep and meaningful," she snorted. "Yes, Ian, I know Khamel will want to get paid. Quite honestly I don't know how much he's expecting from me or how this is all supposed to work. We never really talked about it; he just started following me around, and anyway he's told me some really interesting stuff. I mean, he really seems to know a lot about the gods and statues…" Zelda babbled on, trying to justify herself.

"If he was an Ozzie, I'd say he's probably been bullshitting you the whole time. Why didn't you just consult one of your many books? You've been dragging them around all day anyway." He tried to look her in the eyes, but she was avoiding his baby blues. Ian shrugged his shoulders. "It was your choice. Anyway, I'm going to check my email, then head up to

Vishnu's Place for dinner and a smoke. Wanna meet up there later? Say eight o'clock?"

"Maybe, we'll see." Zelda charged up the street, head down, ready to be back in the comfort of her hotel room. But why? What else did she have to do tonight anyway? Her volunteer program didn't start for another two days – she had plenty of time to repack her bags before then. Besides, the idea of eating alone again didn't sound so appealing. Why shouldn't she join him for dinner? Despite his somewhat irritating behavior, Ian seemed harmless enough.

Zelda walked a few paces further before breaking the silence. "Yeah, okay. I mean, why not join you? I should probably email my family and friends again tonight anyway, let them know what's going on with me while I still can. Who knows how long it'll be before I come across an Internet cafe again, once I get placed with my first Nepali family," Zelda exclaimed, already dreaming of her new home, mud walls and all.

Silence resumed until her little party reached the outskirts of the city center. As they crossed back over the Bagmati River, Khamel burst out with, "Please. You are both welcome in my home for dinner. My mother is an excellent cook."

Zelda, hoping for the warmhearted experiences she'd seen in all those trekking documentaries, immediately jumped at the chance. This would be her first chance to see a real Nepali home from the inside, sort of like a sneak preview of her living situation for the coming months, she figured. Ian would surely understand. And besides, if he came with them, he might even learn a thing or two about Nepali culture. "Great! Thank you for the offer," she said.

"I already have plans in the city; I'm going to head back," Ian responded quickly.

"Please. It is an honor for our home. My mother always wants to meet the people I guide through the city so she can practice her English."

Ian turned his back to Khamel, saying loudly, "Zelda, I'm going back to check my email. Maybe I'll see you later? Vishnu's Place is on the main strip, above that Internet cafe I was talking about earlier." He added in a whisper, "Do you know what you're doing? I'd be careful if I was you."

Zelda didn't bother to whisper back. "What do you mean?"

"My mates back home warned me about these local 'guides'; they're all con artists. For all you know, he makes artwork that he's going to sucker you into buying, or his mother will drug your tea, and they'll take all your money. Or worse – he might just knife you once he gets you into his neighborhood and rob you. How much cash do you have on you?

36

Maybe you'd better give it to me. You can pick it up later, at the bar."

Zelda erupted. "What? Who do you think you are? We aren't traveling together. You can't tell me what to do and what not to do! And besides, how do I know you're not the con artist and you won't steal my money instead of him?"

Ian began sputtering a reaction, but instead threw up his hands in defeat. "Ya know, you're right. We aren't traveling together. Have a great time in Nepal, Zelda. Good luck to ya." He turned his back on her and continued walking up the main road, back towards Thamel.

How dare Ian try to boss me around like that! It was certainly a good thing they weren't traveling together, Zelda fumed. She turned to the boy and called out loud enough for Ian to hear, "I'm ready to go when you are."

Khamel's face lit up. He started walking towards a busy square filled with old men sipping tea in the late afternoon sun. As they weaved through the heavy pedestrian traffic, Zelda looked back, but Ian was already gone. "Good riddance," she muttered.

Khamel suddenly seemed much more relaxed, babbling about his brother's export business and his mother's fantastic curry. After a few minutes of walking, Zelda realized they had twisted and turned their way through so many neighborhoods and side streets that she would need Khamel's help to get back to her hotel. And it would be getting dark in a few hours. Zelda was now totally alone in Kathmandu with two hundred American dollars strapped to her waist and no real idea of where she was. She cursed to herself: *Damn, Ian might be right!*

They soon arrived at a tall apartment block in the middle of a densely populated neighborhood. Zelda looked up at the concrete structure in disappointment. It reminded her of the run-down inner-city apartments she'd seen in East St. Louis, the last time she visited her auntie and took the wrong exit. They trudged up five flights of crumbling steps before Khamel stooped to open five locks on a nondescript door. Zelda exhaled noisily, hoping with all her might that at least the interior would be authentically decorated.

She was ushered into the tiny living room, dominated by an overstuffed leather couch and twelve-inch Sony television set, complete with rabbit ears. A day-glow-green kite with the face of a Roswell alien painted on it hung proudly on one wall. Zelda was so repulsed she almost spit on the ground. What was going on here? She kicked herself for coming, not at all impressed by this shrine to Western culture.

Perched on the couch was a plump older woman, decorated in a glittering purple sari, extensive henna tattoos, and heaps of glittering gold. As soon as Zelda entered the room, she scurried into the kitchen, only to be replaced by Khamel's older and much larger brother. He emerged from a back room carrying a large stack of paintings.

Before Zelda could say anything, the nameless sibling began to rattle on about how these were painted by "real" monks, not like those *thangkas* sold in Thamel. "Here, look at this document," he exclaimed, handing her a photocopy of a document proclaiming the paintings were indeed authentic.

The older woman returned quickly with hot chai and a bowl of red curry, only enough for their guest. Zelda took two large bites and a gulp of tea before remembering Ian's warning. Realizing that up to now he had been right, she let the rest of her food and drink sit. As soon as Zelda put the cup down, Khamel's older brother threw two *thangkas* onto her lap.

"Please to look. I export these *thangkas* all over the world. Normally you must pay five hundred American dollars for each painting. But for you, only two hundred."

"What do you think, that I'm made of money?" she exclaimed, putting her hands on her hips as she tried to glare at him from the sofa. It was all happening so quickly, Zelda didn't know what to do or how to respond. She didn't even want to buy a *thangka*, and especially not at these prices. But she felt trapped. Would they let her out of here – unharmed – if she refused? Alone, in the middle of god-knows-where, she couldn't even get back to her hotel without Khamel's help. Only Ian knew where she was, and even he didn't know where Khamel lived. Zelda wondered whether that was even the kid's real name. And where the hell was he anyway? Her guide for the day had disappeared since his brother's arrival.

The mother said something low and urgent to the son. He snorted, folding his arms across his chest in response. The two glared at each other until Khamel's brother finally sighed in defeat. He turned to Zelda. "Okay, how much?"

All of a sudden, she felt like shopping. Zelda took her time searching through the thick pile of *thangkas* now lying next to her on the couch. She pulled out two of the smaller, more colorful ones and looked up at the brother expectantly. "I don't know, fifty for both?"

He looked like she'd slapped him. "These are authentic *thangkas*, made by real monks. Do you take me for a fool? One hundred dollars for each."

"One hundred for both."

The man began to speak, but his mother placed a hand on his arm, stopping him. They exchanged words again, both growing more animated as one argued their point to the other. Despite the man's bravado, his mother was definitely the boss.

Plainly against his will, Khamel's brother turned to Zelda, cleared his throat noisily, and mumbled, "My mother says you can have them both at that price."

Maybe it was all a routine, some sort of third-world scam, but Zelda was suddenly ecstatic. Two *thangkas* for only a hundred dollars. Of course she didn't know how much they were selling for in Thamel, but euphoria temporarily blocked that thought out of her mind. Her happiness was only surpassed by her desire to get the hell out of there before anything else happened. "Okay, I just need to use your bathroom," she said.

Khamel suddenly re-emerged and escorted her down the long hallway to the last door on the right. As she clicked the lock shut, Zelda stood still for a moment, listening. She wouldn't be surprised if her guide was waiting just outside, standing guard to make sure she didn't make a run for it.

Splashing water on her face, Zelda told her mirrored reflection to calm down, that everything was going fine, that she still had the situation under control. Khamel would surely walk her back to her hotel once she paid up. Nothing else was going to happen. She dug American dollars out of her money belt, folding two bills into her hand. Inhaling deeply once more, Zelda strode purposefully back to the living room, Khamel on her heels.

His brother had already placed the paintings into a carrying tube. Tempted to check the prints for a bait-and-switch, she looked at the man's well-formed upper torso and decided against it. She handed over two fifty-dollar bills without a word. The brother smiled for the first time since Zelda had arrived. Her elation evaporated. *Damn, I did get screwed*, she thought.

"Khamel will escort you home." Snapping for the boy's attention, the older brother dismissed her with "goodbye." Their mother had disappeared again.

Zelda could hardly wait to leave, beating her guide to the door and taking the flaky steps two at a time. She didn't catch her breath until she'd reached the bottom.

She waited for Khamel to ramble down the stairs and walk her back to her hotel, letting him babble about the uniqueness of her newly purchased *thangkas* the whole way.

CHAPTER SIX

Ian and Zelda rose with the morning sun, enjoying a leisurely breakfast in her rooftop garden. Fog rolled playfully along the muddy streets as the last rays of light poked up over the walls of the Kathmandu Valley. Trying hard to ignore Ian's already bouncy personality, Zelda sucked hard on her cigarette, attempting to forget about last night's turn of events and her pounding head.

Too freaked out to be alone, she had begrudgingly gone to the bar and made an uncharacteristic attempt at apologizing. Ian, freshly washed, heavily stoned, and a bit drunk, had accepted her words graciously. Somewhere between the third and fifth round of drinks, Zelda had decided that she needed to find out whether Ian's deep brown tan extended over his entire body. She took another drag, silently cursing the manufacturers of San Miguel again. At home she rarely ever drank beer, let alone half a dozen. Well, at least she'd gotten the casual sex portion of her trip out of the way, she thought. And early on too. She should be proud.

Zelda stubbed her cigarette out, closed her eyes and drifted back to sleep, a smile playing on her lips. Before she could enter the REM zone, the smell of burning cat piss filled her nose. She jerked her head up with a start. "What the hell do you think you're doing?"

"Huh? What's the problem?" Ian asked, through a white cloud of smoke.

"Look around you, man! If you haven't noticed, we can see into about a hundred apartments and hotel rooms pretty damn clearly from here. And therefore they can see exactly what we are doing out here. Haven't you noticed any of the 'Visit Us in Jail' posters hanging all over?"

Ian took a few purposefully big tokes of his joint before finally answering, "I didn't know that I was vacationing with my mother."

Zelda was already up and examining the flowers scattered all over the rooftop. She didn't know what to do. Sure, she smoked pot back home now and again; everybody did. However, she was not about to rot in some Nepali jail because of this guy; the sex was definitely not that great. On the other hand, she knew hundreds of tourists were doing the exact same thing as Ian right now and not getting into trouble.

"What did you say about jail now?" Ian called out.

"There are posters hanging all around Thamel featuring *hundreds* of names and photos of western tourists who've been caught with ridiculously small quantities of weed and hash, but were still sentenced to *years* in Nepalese prisons. I mean, I understand why anyone stupid enough to try to smuggle drugs, jewels, or even antiques out of the country would get such a harsh sentence – but for just a couple of joints?" Zelda shook her head in disbelief.

"I doubt they have a special jail for tourists, and I sure as shit don't ever want to see the inside of one of those places." Zelda walked back over to their table, eyeing Ian's drug paraphernalia lying scattered between their breakfast dishes as she calmly said, "Listen, I'm going to get moving. I've got a lot to do today to get ready for the volunteer thing. I'm not sure if you should be here if I'm not. Would you mind going back to your hotel now?"

"No worries. Now is good. I don't exactly have much to pack up." Ian winked.

Zelda walked him down the stairs, pecking him on the cheek as she opened the hotel's front door for him.

"Okay, so maybe I'll see you later then," Ian said.

"Maybe, I've got so many errands to run and stuff to do..." Zelda trailed off; her words sounded lame even to her. What did she really have to do today that was so incredibly important? Was Ian really so terrible she couldn't be bothered to meet up with him one more time? Still she held back from committing. After tomorrow she would be living with strangers 24-7; maybe an evening for herself wasn't such a bad idea.

"Sure. Well, I'll be at Vishnu's Place tonight, if you can find the time. Should be live music."

Zelda did her best to remain uninterested. "We'll see. Anyway, have a great time in Nepal, if I don't see you later tonight. Okay?"

Ian smirked. "Sure, Zelda. You too." He pecked her once on each cheek and left.

Zelda turned to run back upstairs, but the hotel owner popped out of his office and called to her. A well-washed portrait of Metallica dominated his chest. "Miss Richardson?"

"Yes?" Zelda asked, as she returned to the front desk.

"May I inquire...did you have a guest last night? In your room?" he asked.

"Ah, yeah. But don't worry; it won't be happening again, at least I doubt it. Is it a problem?"

"Not a problem, but there is an extra person fee."

Zelda's face turned bright red. "Of course there is! Ah, how much exactly is that?"

"Twenty rupees extra."

Zelda quickly put the money on the counter. "Okay, then…ah…thank you."

"My pleasure." The little man smiled broadly as he pocketed the money, then disappeared back into his office.

Zelda charged back up to her room, fuming. Ian should have paid to sleep with her, not the other way around. Maybe she'd ask for the money back tonight at Vishnu's Place. *Never mind*, she told herself, chalking it up to another part of her big adventure. Unforeseen expenses. Right now she had other things to worry about. Ganesh would be arriving at her hotel tomorrow early in the afternoon, and she wanted to be ready.

CHAPTER SEVEN

Zelda spent most of the day packing and repacking her bags, carefully weighing each item in her mind before deciding whether it would continue on her journey. She had already bought so many souvenirs that her once neatly packed luggage was bursting. And she'd only been here three days. Still she was having trouble believing that tomorrow, after months of careful planning, she would finally become a *teacher*, responsible for the development of young children's minds, or at least their English language skills. But instead of lifting her spirits, the whole idea brought her down.

Zelda sat back on her heels, rocking to and fro as she pondered her luggage and life. She didn't understand this unforeseen shift in attitude. She had been looking forward to this day for months now. *Snap out of it!* she chided herself. *This is your big chance to break out of your daily grind and really challenge yourself!* Zelda had felt so confident that everything was going to go great – up until today. But now, unsure of what lay ahead, she was beginning to get scared. Just the thought of standing in front of all those students filled her with dread.

She tried to remind herself why she had come – knowing perfectly well if she had stayed in Seattle and taken that full-time contract, the chance of figuring out what she really wanted to do with her life would have been severely limited. Despite her skill set, she knew she was not cut out for life as a computer geek. But then what was she supposed to do? What would give her a sense of fulfillment, or at least keep her interested for more than a few minutes? She still didn't have a clue.

Maybe she should have backpacked around for a few months, like her friends Mary and Don. But could she really have jumped on a plane and circled the world on her own? Zelda didn't think she had the guts to go through with such an undertaking. It had taken all of her courage just to book an open-ended ticket to Nepal. In theory she was giving herself the chance to see more of Asia after volunteering. Right now Zelda hoped she would make it through the next three months without giving up and flying back early.

Stop it, she screamed at herself. There was no use questioning her decisions now. Like it or not, tomorrow was her moment of truth, and it was far too late to back out.

Ten minutes after eight, Zelda found herself climbing the brightly colored stairs leading up to Vishnu's Place rooftop bar. A live rendition of *Sweet Home Alabama* drifted down the open stairwell. Orion and the Big Dipper twinkled high above. Gripping the railing, she told herself once more that she was only coming here to get tips from Ian about teaching and not to spend the night with him. She had too much on her mind to add him to the mix.

She crossed over the empty dance floor to the first of three thatch gazebos. "Knock, knock. Anybody home?"

"Hey, Zelda, you're just in time," Ian called out from the darkness, blowing out a giant puff of smoke in her face. Zelda slid into the round booth across from him. Ian signaled a tuxedoed waiter to bring them a round of San Miguel beers.

"How do you get away with smoking so openly here?" Zelda was already feeling a bit buzzed from the blast of secondhand smoke.

"Well, I order a lot of food and beers, and I tip really, really well. Plus I smoked out the waiters."

"You what?"

"I was the first person up here, and I just asked them straight out whether I could roll up a spliff. They said no problem and asked for one for themselves."

"Okay, whatever."

Zelda ordered fried *momos* before asking for the joint. Ian looked at her quizzically but handed it to her anyway.

"I thought this was above you, smoking so openly in the city. Want I should stand lookout, warn you if the coppers turn up?"

Zelda smirked at him through the blue smoke snorting out of her nose. "Look, I'm a little bit freaked out about starting this volunteer program tomorrow. I was hoping this would help, but..." She frowned at the joint, checking it for holes. "Maybe I just need to take another toke." She sucked as hard as she could, pinching her nose shut to prevent the smoke from escaping too quickly. Instead, Zelda exploded into a long series of coughing fits.

"Hey, are you okay? I thought you had smoked before."

"Sometimes," she choked out. "Apparently not enough."

"So what's the problem now, Zelda?"

She shot him a dirty look. "What are you talking about?"

44

"Something's got your panties in a twist. It's written all over your face."

"Thanks for caring." She took a long swig of her beer and let her lungs calm down before continuing. "I know it all seems so trivial to you, but I'm not sure I'm ready to start volunteering tomorrow. It's all kind of hitting home now, what exactly I'm supposed to be doing, and I'm kind of worried I'm going to be in way over my head."

'What do you mean?"

"I mean, I've only got two weeks to learn a language that makes absolutely no sense to me whatsoever. I'm about to go live with total strangers of whom I know nothing. And I'm already sick of the taste of iodine in my water, and I've only been here three days!" She grimaced as she spoke. "I don't know, this whole cultural volunteer program thing all sounded so cool when I was back home, safety tucked behind my computer. But now, it all begins *tomorrow*. I just hope I can do it, you know, stand in front of a classroom for two months and teach my students anything. Truth be told, I don't even know if I *like* kids." She finished in a whisper, surprised by her own words.

"Geez, Zelda. You seemed so keen yesterday. It certainly sounds like a challenge, but I've a feeling you'll manage to keep your head above water."

"I hope so." She tried to squeeze her tear ducts shut. It was time to change the subject – this was getting all too depressing. She nudged Ian's shoulder, attempting to slap it. "So what are you doing in Nepal, Ian? Come to hike Everest? Or are you trekking to Lasha?"

"I don't have any plans really, not yet anyway. I'm certainly not doing anything noble like you and giving up a few months of my life for a good cause," Ian said, popping a *momo* into his mouth, chewing noisily.

Zelda looked at him reproachfully, but his face remained sincere.

He shrugged. "I had the chance to take a few months off – with full pay – so I grabbed it. Simple as that."

"But you're just backpacking around, aimlessly going wherever you please?" Zelda asked.

"Well, ya. I mean, you could say I have a goal of sorts."

"What's that?"

Ian grinned. "To relive the hippie experience. To find peace, love and understanding. And if I stumble across my true soul mate while I'm at it, even better."

Zelda studied him skeptically. "Aren't you a bit late? Like thirty years, *man*."

45

Ian smirked. "I can't be the only one who's into having a good time. Take Jake, a bloke I met yesterday. So generous and kind, and totally into smoking out. He can't be the only one."

"I guess so. Well, good for you, for taking the chance." Zelda was awed by his bravery. She would never have dared to pick a flight and see what happened.

"Yeah, well, we'll see. It all depends on the money. I only have so much in my account. When that's up, so is my trip," Ian said.

"Oh, that must be kind of scary."

Ian grinned. "No, not really. I'm kind of used to it."

"Well, good luck to you then," Zelda said. She sipped at her beer, eyeing him carefully. Ian perplexed her; she'd never met anyone quite like him before. Even Mary and Don had carefully planned out their route and traveled together of course, at least for most of the trip. There were rumors the two didn't always get along, but then six months was a long time to be traveling with *anyone*, let alone your lover. "Anything – or any place – tickle your fancy yet?"

Ian's face lit up. "Well, I was thinking about heading to Pokhara to do some trekking. My bags arrived this afternoon, and I got a lead on a little slice of hippie heaven, from that Jake bloke I mentioned. All I have to do is buy a ticket and catch the bus on time."

"For how long will you be gone?" Zelda was surprised to feel a pang of sadness.

"About two weeks, I reckon. We'll see how it goes."

The joint must have been working its magic; his news really depressed her. She put a hand lightly over his wrist. "I'll miss you Ian."

He shook her arm off, chugging his drink. "Aw, I'll probably bump into you again when I get back to Kathmandu. Besides you're going to be busy teaching the world to read, right?"

Zelda ignored his sarcasm, focusing on the sadness of his impending departure. It wasn't that she was falling for the guy, but it was nice to see a familiar face in this most foreign of cities. And he was pretty damn cute in a scruffy sort of way. She rooted around in her purse, pulled out a business card and slid it over to him.

"Here's my email address, in case you want to drop me a line. Maybe we can hook up for a beer when you get back?"

Eyes wide, he picked up the card, examining both sides. "You made *business cards* before you came?"

"No silly, those are my old cards from work – the only thing still active is the personal email address. I thought it might be handy to have them, you know, for this sort of situation. Let me know when you're back and we can have a beer or something."

"Okay, sure. I'll let you know how it goes. Cheers, mate." Ian smiled, hoisting his glass. They met in midair. "To Nepal." In a flash, both polished off their third round.

The band broke out into a soulful rendition of "Layla." She loved that song, the way Clapton's voice cried out, the sliding guitar. The emotions of the moment, her fears about volunteering, feeling as if she would never see Ian again, overwhelmed her completely. She longed to be with him one more time. Okay, so she didn't particularly like him or necessarily love the sex, but these past three days had been so intense, it was as if she had known him all of her life, and now he was leaving her forever. She felt a tear running down her cheek. Zelda stared at the joint still clutched in her hand. "Damn, this is some good weed."

She rose unsteadily and took his hand, pulling him onto the dance floor. Ian kissed her neck, his hands softly stroking her hair to the rhythm of the slow guitar. She held him close, feeling his strong back through his dirty T-shirt. In a flustered whisper, he asked her back to his room for "a last night of romance." As soon as she breathed "yes," he ran off to pay their tab.

CHAPTER EIGHT

Zelda slipped out of Ian's place around two in the morning. She couldn't lie there silently on the cot next to him and pretend to be asleep, knowing in a few short hours, her big adventure would finally begin. Besides, from the sound of it, Ian wouldn't be in Kathmandu much longer anyway. It didn't really matter – soon she would make new friends, with her fellow volunteers.

Walking briskly through the cool morning air, Zelda hummed to herself, avoiding the gaze of a few drunken westerners staggering by. The streets were so still and silent it was surreal. Even the beggars seemed to have retired for the night.

Her gait felt light and springy once again. Almost all her reservations about learning the language, teaching children, and living with strangers had dissipated.

True, she had never volunteered for anything in her life, but people always talked about how they "found" themselves doing charity work. It seemed as if the bigger the challenge, the more they learned. And Zelda couldn't think of a bigger challenge for herself than to break away from the boring comfort of her urban life and come all the way to Nepal to volunteer.

She was filled with so many questions about the program and her family. Would her new home have mud walls? Running water? Would the family all sleep together in one big room? How about the animals? She read somewhere that livestock slept inside, to keep the family warm. Secretly she hoped it would be super-primitive; then she would be sure to find herself. At least she'd have a few new stories to tell, the kind that freaked people out at dinner parties and secretly made everyone in the room jealous.

And besides, she was part of a long-running cultural program that specialized in placing volunteer English teachers in Nepalese schools. Of course there wouldn't be any problems. Ganesh was used to transforming urban westerners into temporary teachers. He'd already prepared hundreds of volunteers before Zelda arrived. Surely two weeks was long enough to learn Nepali, or at least the basics. Zelda's new family would certainly practice speaking it with her.

Who knew, if things went well at the school, she could always join the Peace Corps instead of going back to the computer world. Maybe *that* was her true calling in life. Didn't the government pay you to learn a new language and live in a foreign country for two years? She would have to look into it.

A few hours later, she and the other volunteers waited with eager anticipation for their families to pick them up. Their trusty program coordinator, Ganesh, paced the lobby floor like an expectant father. Zelda felt naked without her box of donated books by her side, but Ganesh had insisted on taking it to his office for safekeeping. Just as well, Zelda thought, she didn't want her first family to feel slighted.

She studied her fellow students of the world, trying to remember their names. None were quite what she had expected. Christine, the one with long jet-black hair, was a student at Fresno State. The plump New Zealander was Sarah, a recently divorced forty-something homemaker who was constantly brushing dust and insects off her clothes and body, not all of them imaginary. She looked far too prim and proper to be here. Zelda wondered how long she would last. And finally there was the gray-haired lady, Doris, a chatty, retired schoolteacher who was looking for something to do with her time. Zelda repeated the names in her head in an attempt to distract herself from her growing anxiety.

As if cued from off-stage, all four families arrived within minutes of each other. Zelda's new brother, Nabim, a young man with a slight build and a subdued manner, shook her hand firmly. A flurry of suitcases, bags, taxis, and cries of "good luck" ensued, then Zelda was off – alone with Nabim – traveling at dangerous speeds through a ridiculously busy neighborhood. Meandering cows, tenacious bicyclers, and fearless pedestrians all fought their taxi for room on the narrow and windy road. Their cab slowed only once, in front of a huge temple ablaze with smoky incense as worshippers spilled onto the street in their religious fervor.

Eventually the taxi turned right, behind a row of fruit stands, and carefully maneuvered its way down a small alley. It stopped in front of a large gate. Between the rusty metal bars, Zelda could make out a modern three-story brick house. She blinked in surprise, puzzled by the structure before her. Did Nabim's family really live here? The house looked bigger than either of her parents' homes, the only difference being that Nabim's staircase wound its way along the outside of the building.

Nabim paid the driver and then helped Zelda carry her heavy luggage up the first flight of stairs to the front door. The veranda was lined with small red flowers Zelda had never seen before. Nabim unlocked six deadbolts and another gate.

"Please to follow me."

Tentatively Zelda entered the long hallway, covered in floral wallpaper. She could make out five doors, all closed. Nabim was dragging her bags into a large room on the left. She entered cautiously. Dominating the room was a trophy case filled with cactus-shaped salt-and-pepper shakers, a painted boomerang, a ceramic tile featuring a Dutch windmill, and a flamenco dancer doll. Zelda realized too late that she should have brought statues of the Space Needle or Starbucks coffee mugs as gifts. A couch and matching armchairs covered in yellow-brown tweed completed the room. Group portraits of Nabim's family, dressed in western-style suits and dresses, covered the walls. In some weird way, it reminded Zelda of her grandparents' living room. At least there was no discernable television in the room.

Nabim pointed towards a burgundy curtain in the far corner. "That is your room."

Zelda walked closer and saw that part of the living room had been partitioned off. Zelda pulled back the curtain, revealing a single bed and white dresser. A fake Tiffany lamp stood on the bedside table; a poster promoting skiing in the Swiss Alps was tacked onto the wall behind it.

"You like it? My mother decorated it herself," Nabim said, eyes twinkling.

Zelda did not know what to say. Where were the *thangkas*, photos of the Himalayas, Buddha statues, or even Tibetan prayer beads? Must she unpack her souvenirs and decorate the room herself?

"I have homework to do before my parents come home. Would you like something to drink?" Nabim asked, nodding his head as he talked. "Yes? Kreepa!"

Homework? Nabim's comment jolted her. She chided herself for assuming he would be working in the fields all day. Of course he was in school, she reasoned with herself, the women must do the farming.

"Where are your parents anyway?"

"At work. My father is a financial advisor for the Bank of Nepal, and my mother teaches classes in Nepali iconography at the University of Kathmandu."

Zelda fell onto the tweed couch, in total shock. Banker? Professor? His parents were better educated than most members of her own family. After all the stories and documentaries about typical families toiling in the fields all day just to make ends meet, nothing could have prepared Zelda for this.

Nabim was staring at her. "Are you okay?"

Zelda shook her head. "Yeah, I think I'm a bit tired, that's all."

A small girl appeared in the doorway, bowing her head slightly to Nabim. She was clearly trying, unsuccessfully, not to stare at the white person standing in their living room. Her "brother" snapped something in Nepali, and the girl practically ran from the room.

Nabim smiled once again at Zelda.

"Kreepa will bring you some tea in a moment, and my parents will be home very shortly. Perhaps you will rest?" He obviously had no interest in entertaining her. "Or you can go to the rooftop and enjoy our view of the valley?" Nabim was already backing out of the living room, smiling and nodding. "Yes? Okay. Bye-bye," was his sing-song farewell before disappearing into his bedroom.

Looking around the living room, all Zelda could do was shake her head in disgust. It wasn't their fault; it was just *so* not what she had imagined her house in Nepal would be like. Absolutely nothing like it in fact. Excluding the temple tops visible from the living room window, it was if she had been transported back to her grandma's place in rural Missouri, circa 1970.

Kreepa returned with a cup of hot milky tea and bowl of sugar, placing them gingerly on the coffee table. Tiny violets decorated the fragile porcelain.

"Jiminy Christmas, even the cups," Zelda muttered to herself. She looked up to see that the girl had backed away from the table but stood in the doorway, staring at her. Zelda still wasn't sure what or who Kreepa was; she guessed a younger sister or cousin. Nabim had been kind of rude towards her, but maybe it was a cultural thing.

She stirred sugar into her cup, hoping the girl would either say something or leave. When neither happened, Zelda looked up at her, stuck out her right hand, and said, quite slowly, "Hello, I am Zelda." She used her left hand to point to herself, overenunciating, "Zelda."

The girl doubled over with laughter, partially covering her mouth with her hand. She made brief eye contact with Zelda, but that brought another fit of giggles. Kreepa finally turned and stumbled out of the room, chortling.

Zelda watched her leave, more confused than ever. Had she offended the girl by offering her a hand? She sipped her tea contemplatively, trying to decide what to do next. Nabim had mentioned the views upstairs. No harm in checking that out before her new parents got home.

After chugging her drink, she exited out the front door again, this time continuing up the stairs to the second-floor landing. The only door was locked, and the curtains were drawn; Zelda's wandering eyes couldn't see a thing. She climbed another floor higher, only to find it closed off as well. A fragile-looking metal staircase wound its way up to the rooftop. She climbed it cautiously, surprised that the whole rooftop was one big terrace, half of which was filled with drying laundry.

As she made her way through wet saris and T-shirts towards the edge of the balcony, Zelda gasped in delight. Nabim was right; from up here, she had an uninterrupted view of the mountain range penning the city in. Fingers of green stretched over the valley's fertile floor. There was so much dust floating around that the air seemed to shimmer in the midday sun.

From up here, she could spy on her new neighbors' houses as well. Most seemed to be built like Nabim's, expansive brick structures with staircases running up the outside walls and ending in a rooftop terrace. Satellite dishes dotted the cityscape.

She ducked back under the longs folds of fabric fluttering in the wind, crossing over to the other side of the rooftop patio. Her eyes were drawn to a lengthy golden spire rising up from behind a high stone wall. She leaned far over the balcony's edge, straining to get a better look inside the complex but couldn't see anything through the thick foliage. *Must be some sort of temple*, Zelda thought. She would have to ask her new family about it later.

Zelda examined the rest of the rooftop; other than lots of hanging laundry, there was an odd collection of tools and machetes strewn about. She walked through the dancing strips of fabric to the other side of the terrace, stopping in surprise when she caught sight of a strange addition. Built into the far corner was what looked like a lean-to for midgets, closed off with a door of standard width, but only half the height.

She ducked down and pulled tentatively on the shiny brass handle, wondering what she would find on the other side. The door opened easily. A sweet but musty scent wafted out. Hundreds of small statues and framed pictures of colorful gods were propped inside the closet-sized space. In the center stood two large bronze representations of an elephant riding a rat and a man holding a trident. Zelda recognized them from her day out with Khamel as Ganesh and Vishnu. Incense cones, bells, mirrors, finger-cymbals, and offerings of food were scattered all around their feet.

Finally something authentic! She ran back downstairs to grab her camera and her new book, *Gods and Goddesses of Nepal,* so she could decipher the shrine's contents. While rummaging around in her room, she heard the outer door open and a strange voice sing out "Namaste!" Zelda peeked behind her bedroom curtain to see a round woman draped in a red sari and jangling gold jewelry entering the living room. She floated over to Zelda, grabbed her arms, and kissed her cheeks.

"Hello, hello! Welcome to my home," she giggled in a high girly voice. "I am Parwati."

Her enthusiasm was infectious. Zelda smiled warmly at the stranger, forgetting about the shrine upstairs. *This must be her new mother.* "Hello, so nice to finally meet you!" she exclaimed, kissing the woman back.

Kreepa was immediately summoned to bring them tea and biscuits. While they waited for the girl to return, Parwati turned to Zelda, studying her as if her long-lost daughter was home at last. She began talking in fantastic English, catching the younger woman up on all that was happening with her family during the busy festival season.

"*Dasian* is so very important. This is the most holy of times for us Brahmins, you know." Parwati placed a pudgy, ring-filled hand on her voluptuous chest, shining with pride. "As members of the highest Hindu caste, we cannot eat meat, tomatoes, onion, or garlic until the tenth day."

"Okay," Zelda said, nodding in incomprehension, making a mental note to look up this *Dasian* festival in her guidebook later. Ganesh had mentioned this morning that this was a particularly good time to be in Nepal because of all the celebrations, parades, and festivals. But she didn't remember him saying anything about food restrictions.

"Do you understand?" Parwati asked.

"Yes?" Zelda replied cautiously.

"Good, good. Now my son, Nabim. He has told you that he is a student at the university, yes? Electronics and industrial engineering. He is only seventeen but already in his second year," Parwati said, beaming with pride. "If he continues to get such good grades, we will send him to England for his master's program. His cousin is studying at Oxford; perhaps Nabim can join him there."

Oxford? Master's? Zelda only had a bachelor's degree, and she was the most educated person in her whole family, both sides. Zelda thought only royalty and oil sheiks could afford to send their children abroad. How could Parwati's son and nephew afford to study in a foreign country, and at Oxford no less?

"Otherwise Nabim will have to go to Stanford."

"*Stanford*?" Zelda couldn't stop herself from gasping.

"Yes, yes." Parwati sighed heavily. "My husband, Mahendra, it is his alma mater. Nabim can surely win a scholarship or some sort of award. He is very talented in math. But my son does not want to go there; he wants to study somewhere where the weather is cooler than Nepal. I am afraid California is too much like the Kathmandu Valley for him."

Zelda could not believe her ears. She would have given just about anything to have gone to Stanford, or Oxford for that matter. Her parents had laughed at her for days after she told them how much the tuition fees were at Ivy League schools. Maybe she should have studied abroad. She still could, Zelda reminded herself, if she ever figured out what she wanted to do with her life. She wasn't seventeen anymore, but she still had four years 'til she turned thirty. Life as she knew it wasn't over yet.

"Do you have any other children?" Zelda asked.

Parwati's smile broke slightly. "Yes, one daughter, Ranjana. She is in high school. After badminton practice, she will return home."

"And who is the girl who brought us tea? Kreepa?"

"She is our helper. She is the daughter of my sister's niece. They live in a small village far from Kathmandu. Kreepa stays here and helps our family, and we pay for her to go to school," Parwati said with a yawn, clearly uninterested. She suddenly grabbed Zelda's hands, shaking them violently, a big smile on her face. "Please tell me. My daughter, she loves the Big Apple. Perhaps you can help her to find a school in New York?"

Zelda was flabbergasted. She had never been to the East Coast before; how could she help Ranjana find a good school there? But for some reason, she was afraid to say no to her new mother, not wanting to disappoint her the first night. "I don't know. I guess I can try," Zelda said softly.

"Good, good." Parwati clapped her hands together in excitement, clearly pleased with Zelda. "There is so much more I must tell you," she said.

Parwati quickly turned the conversation back to the impending festivities. Zelda drifted off during her long-winded explanation about all the relatives who would be "stopping by" during the next two weeks. When Parwati began describing all the rituals surrounding *Dasian*, Zelda started to perk back up. There were special candles to light, meals to prepare, and animals to worship – in particular, the cow, from what she could gather. She had read about bovines being holy here in Nepal, but now that Parwati was telling her about all the rituals involved, it all seemed so ludicrous. It was a good thing the beasts seemed so docile, otherwise Zelda wasn't sure how they'd be able to get the red tika powder on the cows' foreheads and garlands of orange carnations around their necks.

Their conversation was rudely interrupted by a chaotic symphony of horns, cymbals, and fervent chants, seemingly triggered by the setting sun.

"What the heck...what is that?" Zelda exclaimed, her face contorting in panic.

The family was clearly trying hard not to laugh openly at her. "The noises?" asked Mahendra, her new Nepali father. He'd slipped quietly into the living room more than an hour ago and had not yet said a word, apparently afraid to interrupt his chatty wife. "That is the sound of the Hari Krishnas. It is their temple behind us."

"Hari Krishnas? Are you serious? They have a temple here?"

Mahendra looked puzzled. "Hari Krishnas are the highest order of Brahmin priests. They live devoutly, closed inside the walls of the temple next to us. It is an honor to live so close by."

Her father spoke so softly and reverently that Zelda had to lean in to hear him properly. "I apologize. I didn't mean to offend you. It's...well, the Hari Krishnas have a very different reputation in America." Images of bald, cymbal-playing airport beggars filled her head. "And not exactly a good one. It is just a bit of a shock."

CHAPTER NINE

It was sometime in the afternoon when Ian finally woke up. He rolled his tongue around his mouth and grimaced. Scratching at his head, he leaned over on one shoulder and flipped on the bedside lamp. Zelda must have left early; he didn't hear anyone else in the room, and her cot was empty. With a deep yawn, Ian made his way into the bathroom and took a soapless shower, brushing his teeth under the cool stream.

After donning a rumpled pair of shorts and a T-shirt, Ian grabbed his film canister to roll a joint. He shook it, frowning. Sod, he was already running low. He had been chain-smoking Jake's herb the past couple of days – not that anyone at his hotel seemed to care. Plus, there were so many kind pubs around; it was easy to smoke the day away. Bugger, he'd have to pick up some more weed before he took off, in case Pokhara turned out to be a bust. Ian grumbled at the thought of having to deal with another underage drug dealer, but figured he had little choice. None of the kind pubs he'd been in seemed to sell drugs.

Switching on the overhead light, Ian noticed a small piece of paper folded in half, resting on top of his backpack. On the front was his name in block letters. Amused, he opened it.

> *Dear Ian,*
> *Thanks for a nice evening. Maybe we can get*
> *together for a beer when you come back through*
> *Kathmandu? Just email me when and where.*
> *Take care of yourself, Zelda Marie Richardson*

The handwriting was very neat, a flowing cursive. He could just make out her name through all the swirls. Typical of her to leave a note behind. Why not drop her a line when and if he came back to Kathmandu, Ian thought. Zelda was definitely high maintenance, but it was good to see a friendly face now and again. He was just glad they weren't traveling together.

Ian decided to grab some lunch before scoring more drugs. Maybe he should try hash this time, see whether that was any better. Close to his hotel, he spotted a busy terrace overlooking a small square. He grabbed one of the last tables, stretching out in the wicker chair, enjoying the intense rays of the autumn sunshine. He couldn't be bothered to find another drug dealer right now, but so far there wasn't a whole lot else that interested him in Nepal. All of his mates had made Kathmandu out to be some sort of 24-7 drug-induced love fest – a hippie community reminiscent of San Francisco in the sixties, but transported to the rooftop of the world. His mates were constantly telling Ian stories about priests handing out chunks of hash to passersby, group smokeouts in different temple complexes, and even the occasional drug-induced orgy. But so far every westerner Ian had talked to was here to trek Everest, meditate at a Buddhist monastery, or volunteer – nobody seemed to want to just chill out. Except Jake; he'd been the first and only like-minded brother Ian had met so far. But even he'd been here to hike. Ian was beginning to feel as if he had been born thirty years too late. He wished now he'd paid more attention to the towns and temples his mates back home had mentioned. Or had they been pulling his leg the whole time?

The snake charmers and monkeys were pretty cool, as were the dreadlocked sadhus smoking big chillums in Durbar Square. But in general, Kathmandu seemed pretty damn overtouristed to him. You couldn't take two steps without being propositioned by someone pushing expensive tours, guided treks, cheap souvenirs, or black-market exchange rates. And exploring the city's many temples didn't interest him that much. He'd spent too much time in temples and pagodas when he was in China last year; this trip was about having fun, not getting cultural. Maybe in Pokhara he'd have better luck.

Pokhara; Ian could hardly wait. His mates might have been here five years ago, but Jake had harvested a healthy supply of superior-looking weed a few days ago. Ian felt a bit wonky just thinking about Jake's stash and all those fields of ripening buds. Kathmandu might not have lived up to his expectations, but Pokhara certainly had promise. His paradise must still exist somewhere.

Ian's stomach grumbled audibly. He turned to find the waiter when something in the crowded streets caught his eye. Just a few meters away, a dark-haired Nepali boy sporting a faded Jimi Hendrix T-shirt walked slowly through the sea of backpackers. Could it be? Ian jumped up and raced after him.

As he got closer, Ian could hear the boy muttering the now too-familiar pickup line: "Hashish? Marijuana?" It was definitely the same scrapper who'd sold him that horrible weed on his first day in Nepal.

The boy turned onto a smaller, less crowded street. Ian sprinted up to him and, placing one hand firmly on the boy's shoulder, rasped, "I got ya."

The boy bit Ian's hand and ran for it. Ian screamed in pain, blood rushing out of two pinprick wounds. Anger quickly replaced surprise. The boy shot down a narrow passage, Ian hard on his heels.

"Come here, you little bugger!"

The boy rounded another corner. A dead end. He turned on Ian, eyes wide with panic. Growling at the larger man, the kid bared his dirty teeth and raced towards Ian at full speed. Ian kicked out his right leg and tripped the boy as he tried to fly past, twisting his little dealer into a headlock as he fell. The kid's legs flailed briefly, and then went still. Ian shook him slightly. The boy glared up at him.

"You sure can bite," Ian said.

No response.

"That was some crappy weed you sold me, mate. Do you always try to pawn that stuff off on tourists?"

The boy shrugged.

Ian released his grip slightly. The kid didn't fight back. Ian turned him around so that they faced each other, keeping his hands high on the boy's neck to prevent more teeth marks. He backed the dealer up against the brick wall of the alleyway, just in case.

"So do you only sell shitty marijuana? Or do you have a better stash somewhere?"

The boy shrugged again.

Ian studied him curiously; the boy's defiance amused him. "Do ya have any hash?"

The kid bobbed his head up and down.

"In your pocket?"

Again a nod.

He let his arms fall away from the boy's neck. "Okay, pull out a sample and let me see it. No mucking about."

His dealer did as he was told. A moment later the boy's palm was filled with a block of hash the size of a golf ball, and as black as a moonless night.

Ian whistled long and low. "Damn, that looks a lot better than the last batch you sold me. How much for the lot?"

"One thousand rupees."

Ian tilted his head slightly, a bemused expression on his face. The boy's shoulders caved in. "For you – special deal – five hundred rupees. Today only!"

Ian worked the appropriate money out of his pocket with one hand, exchanging it for the hashish. Transaction complete, he stepped back, giving his dealer the room to run away again. But the boy didn't bolt. Instead, he stood his ground, eyeing Ian carefully. He wanted to laugh but was afraid the boy would take it the wrong way. There was something that he liked about him, almost admired. Here he was, a street kid in one of the poorest countries in the world, and he had enough grit to survive. Ian had dealt with plenty of defiant and difficult students in his day, and experience taught him they were usually the most interesting ones in the bunch.

"What's your name anyway?"

The kid looked away.

"Are you hungry?"

A slight movement of the head.

"Come on. I'll buy ya some lunch."

Ian climbed the stairs of the Sherpa Club. It was still early, only four in the afternoon, but he reckoned it would be open. Lunch had gone by quickly – the boy wolfed back two plates of daal bhat tarakari in record time, saying very little between bites. He'd taken off as soon as the last crumbs were consumed, without really answering any of Ian's questions about how he managed to scrape by or where he lived. He hoped there was at least a homeless shelter the boy could sleep at.

Ian didn't hear any noise inside the club but entered anyway. From what he'd seen so far, the Sherpa Club was always open. The door pushed open easily; the same man stood behind the bar. "Time for a safety break?" he asked. Ian's mouth began to water; the mantra had a Pavlovian effect on him.

"Hey man, how's it going?" Ian said.

"I am cool like ice, mister."

"Great. I'd fancy one of those mango lassi and vodka concoctions, if you please."

"Sure, partner, coming right up."

"Cheers, mate," Ian said, taking a seat at the bar. "You haven't seen Jake around, have you? The tall, skinny guy I came in with a few days ago?"

"They were in here last night. Jake said he and his friend were catching a bus to Mount Everest this morning."

"Ah, that's too bad." Ian took a big swig of his drink. Looking around the empty club conspiratorially, he lowered his voice to a whisper. "Do you mind if I smoke a joint? That hookah's a bit much for me right now."

The bartender smiled broadly, spreading his arms out wide. "Mi casa, su casa," he exclaimed, pulling a glass bong out from under the counter and lighting the bowl.

Ian took out his gear and began rolling. "Say, why do you say 'safety break' when you mean 'smoking out'?" he asked.

"A lot of trekking guides come in here. It is their code for smoking drugs when they are out in the field. Otherwise the tourists might smoke up all their supplies," the bartender said with a wink.

Ian laughed appropriately as he fumbled with his spliff, finally getting it lit. He took a few puffs, then threw back the rest of his lassi in one gulp. "Can I get another one of these?"

"Sure."

When he set Ian's drink down, the bartender's collar opened slightly. The jagged scar was still visible. From this intimate distance, Ian could see how red and pus-filled it was. Gesturing towards it, he asked, "Suppose you see a lot of bar brawls in here, eh?"

"You should see the other guy," the bartender said with pride, pulling open his shirt to show off the full length of his wound. The cut ran from his chin down to his third rib and had been stitched together badly. A grayish substance oozed out in a few places.

Ian wasn't sure whether he should laugh, offer medical advice, or be shitting himself. He chose to change the subject. "So do you know how long Jake's going to be hiking?"

"About five weeks."

"Too bad, I was hoping to ask him where exactly he went in Annapurna."

"It is one big loop. He did the whole thing."

"Do you know how many days it took?"

"About a month. Takes more if it is snowing," the bartender said.

"Oh." Ian was up for a hike, but not for such a long trek.

"But you can join the loop at different towns along the trail. Some people only hike for three or four days and then take the bus back to Pokhara. Or fly."

"Wait a second, a bus? A plane? What's the point of trekking up a bloody mountain if you can fly to the top of the thing anyway?"

The man laughed. "Not all of it is so accessible. And you see a lot more of the beautiful nature if you hike up. Besides, the local buses only run through the foothills where there are many villages. They cannot cross the mountain passes. Too dangerous."

"Are you a trekker?"

The man chuckled again, grabbing his midsection. "When I came to Nepal twenty years ago from Goa, I did many treks. I even worked as a guide for a short time. But now..." His big belly rumbled with laughter; gold chains danced in his graying chest hairs.

"So where do you reckon they grow the weed?" Ian asked.

The man looked at him with a twinkle in his eye. "In the lower regions, at either the beginning or end of the main trail."

"Thanks, man."

"No worries, matey."

Ian dragged himself through the strangely silent streets of Thamel, his pounding head slowing his progress. The sun was just breaking over the foothills when he arrived at the departure point, marked clearly by his travel agent on the map in his hand. An endless row of buses in a plethora of colors confronted his sleepy eyes. The sidewalks were overflowing with passengers and their squawking animals. He found his bus immediately, the fourth in line as promised. It was only half-past seven, still another fifteen minutes before takeoff, but passengers were already boarding.

Ian joined the queue, grabbing a seat next to the window. He stretched out in the airplane-style seat and closed his eyes. A few minutes later, the bus engine rumbled to life. A commotion up front jolted him out of his light doze. Four young Nepalese men were running down the aisles towards the few remaining empty seats. Ian grabbed his backpack out of the way, as a boy in an oversized biker jacket and fake Levis threw himself into the seat beside him and pretended to be asleep. The bus was already pulling out into slow lines of traffic as if nothing had happened. Too tired to care, Ian laid his head against the window and was asleep before the bus even reached the city limits.

Their bus was caught in a landslide. Ian was jolted awake, sure they were tumbling down into a ravine. He looked out the window and saw to his relief that they were traveling down a short road made of loose gravel and tar, apparently the entrance to a parking lot. No ravine, simply a bus with bad traction.

Their bus pulled up in front of a large modern structure, the Nepali equivalent of a truck stop. His seatmate was still pretending to be asleep. Ian squeezed around him, joining the rest of the passengers as they filed silently off the bus and marched into the large hall to receive their free lunch. He used a spoon, as opposed to most other travelers, who used their right hands to dip balls of rice and vegetables into their lentil soup, then pop them into their mouths.

A half-hour later, he followed the rest of the westerners back onto the bus. His seatmate put down his Playboy magazine and let Ian back into the window seat. He recognized the blonde on the cover from a few months back.

The boy smiled broadly at him. "Can I practice my English with you?"

"Sure, mate. Whatcha wanna talk about?"

"Why are you traveling to Pokhara?" came the staggered reply.

"Why do most people go? To do some trekking, most likely anyway. How about you? What brings you to Pokhara?" Ian asked, unsure how wise it would be to tell this stranger about his real motive.

"I am a trekking guide! My clients are waiting for me in Pokhara. I'm going to guide them for four days, through many of the holy sites in the Annapurnas."

"Brilliant. How big is the group? What route are you taking? Have you been a guide for a long time?" The kid looked at most sixteen, but so did most of the thirty-year-old men here.

The boy blushed before finally admitting it was his first gig. "But my cousin is very experienced. He has guided tourists many times. I have been his assistant on three trips before, but not in this part of Nepal. But this time, this time he is the cook, and I am the leader."

"Good on ya. Maybe this is the start of a new career for you?"

"Pray to the gods to make it possible. Besides, my cousin says the trail is very easy and well-marked. The tourists do not really need me to find their way around. But I will not tell them that."

Ian smirked, wondering how much these clients were paying for his unnecessary services. "Where are you going precisely?" he asked.

"First we fly to Jomsom. Normally it would take six or seven days to hike there from Pokhara. But my clients are very old; they do not want to walk that far. From Jomsom we trek to Muktinath and stay there two nights. Then we fly back to Pokhara."

"Bloody hell, that's action-packed. So you're flying up and down the mountain? You're not really hiking much, are you?"

"Indeed, it is quite simple. If you do not want to hike – like my clients – you only have to take the plane."

"How much is a plane ticket to Jomsom anyway?"

"Very expensive. But I do not pay. The family must provide me with a ticket. It is much cheaper to fly to Kathmandu from Pokhara, than to Jomsom."

"Cheers for the tip, mate, but expensive is out of my price range."

"Then might I suggest that you hike the entire twenty-eight-day route? I cannot wait to guide people over the whole trail. Perhaps you would wait for me? After we get back from Jomsom, I can take you through the Sanctuary Loop."

"Thanks, but I'm still not sure what I'm going to do yet," Ian said. Bloody hell! He wasn't even in Pokhara, and he was already getting propositioned. Besides if the trails were as well marked as the kid said, why should he pay extra for a guide? Ian started playing with his iPod when he remembered the boy's dramatic entrance. "Say, why did you race onto the bus at the last minute?"

"This is a tourist bus. It is forbidden for Nepalese people to ride it. But I know the bus driver, I do not have to pay." He smiled mischievously, then picked up his Playboy.

Ian admired the cover again before switching on the John Butler Trio, losing himself in the music as they entered Pokhara city limits.

CHAPTER TEN

Tommy had never really swum in the sea before coming to Asia. His mom used to tell him that Lake Erie was the ocean, and when he was little, he believed her. It was only when he was older and learned what "land-locked" meant that he realized how his mother had been making a fool of him all those years. Just like everyone he'd ever trusted – not that there had been many.

Tommy floated on his back, hands paddling lazily to keep him in place. A Chinese clipper, its massive red accordion sails stretched in the wind, rounded the point. He imagined himself on its bow, feeling the rush of the ocean under his feet as they cut across the water. Maybe he'd buy a yacht and sail around the world. Would Chantal like a boat? Would that make her happy?

Movement in the water attracted his attention. He scooped his hands around it, bringing it up the light. A tiny squid – no bigger than his thumb – swam furious circles in his palms, lightning flashes of color running through its body.

"What do you think Chantal would like? Hey!" He prodded the animal with his pinky, prompting a tiny spray of water and a blaze of red in response. "Not you, any-hoo!" Tommy sighed, releasing his prey back into the wild. He watched it swim quickly away, pulsing forward with strange umbrella movements.

After disappearing all those months ago, he couldn't show up on Chantal's doorstep empty-handed. But he didn't know what to get her. He never did; that was only one of their many problems. Clothes were out of the question. He didn't know her size. Besides, what good were beach wear and bikinis in Toronto?

He knew she loved chocolates and cakes. Who was he kidding, everybody could see that. But after twenty-plus hours in the air and all those X-ray checks, anything edible probably wouldn't taste so good. Besides, what kind of message would candy send? "Hey, I'm doing great, wildly successful in fact, and I'd really like you back in my life." No, he didn't think so.

Tommy smacked at the water in frustration, launching tiny rockets of salt water into his eyes. "Ooww!" He rubbed at them furiously, overtly mashing the salt deeper into his eyeballs.

He tried to walk back along the shallow bay's sandy bottom, but tripped over a half-buried rock, falling face-first into the water. He punched his fists into the sea bottom, cutting his knuckles on pieces of dead coral. "Aaahhh!" Tommy screamed, writhing in pain. Blood trickled out of the wounds, slowly mixing with the salty sea. He tried to turn over onto his back but something was pulling him to his feet. He thrashed instinctively for a moment before going limp.

"Hey, man, are you okay?"

Tommy looked up through tear-stained eyes at his savior: a blue-eyed boy with sandy-brown hair and a rippling torso. His own flabby stomach turned in revulsion. Probably Californian, he thought.

"Get your hands off of me! Stupid jock!" Tommy jerked his shoulders violently, breaking the man's hold on him and promptly fell back into the water.

"Dude, just chill. I was trying to help, you know, a brother in need?" The good Samaritan was backing away.

Tommy struggled to his feet, trickles of blood dripping off his hands. "I don't need your help, thank you very much," he huffed, crossing his arms over his chest, and inadvertently covering himself in thin trails of blood.

"Whatever, man. But you should, like, put a Band-Aid on that before you go back in the water. Sharks, you know. See ya!" The blond jock was already swimming away.

Tommy glanced down at his chest; it looked like a drunken Zorro had tried to carve him up. He started to heave in reaction to seeing all that blood – his blood – but stopped himself just in time. Taking great care to keep his hands above the surface, he lowered his body back into the water.

Relatively blood-free, he lurched back to the bar, carefully holding his arms out in front of him like some ultra-skinny Frankenstein. After wrapping a few napkins around his wounds, he ordered a Sea Breeze with extra fruit.

"Oh you poor thing. Did you cut yourself diving?" a soft voice cooed.

Tommy almost blurted out, "No, you stupid cow!" but stopped himself in time. The girl standing next to him wasn't too bad looking. "Yeah, but it's no big deal, you know? Just grazed my knuckles on some coral when I was surfacing. Luckily I got back into the boat before the sharks smelled the blood."

"Oh, sharks! That must have been really scary." The girl wobbled as she talked – clearly she'd already had a lot to drink. Her hands were covered in rings of gold and silver, their stones sparkling in the strong midday sun. A memory of Chantal, the last time they saw each other, flashed into his mind. Or, rather, her hand and the imprint her slap had left on his face. If she hadn't been wearing so much jewelry, it probably wouldn't have hurt so badly.

Chantal loved to wear rings. It wasn't like he could have gotten her a classy ring before; he was always scraping by. But now...the sudden irony sent Tommy into a laughing fit.

"Can I get you and your friends another drink?" he asked, trying to control his giggles. The girl didn't seem to notice, but then she was pretty tipsy.

"Sure, thanks. We're sitting over there." She pointed to a group of ten, mostly girls. "Come and join us." She looked up at him, smiling, eyes a bit glazed over.

Tommy didn't mind that she was drunk; he couldn't remember the last time he'd gotten laid. Not since he'd arrived in Thailand, that's for sure. You couldn't be too careful with the local girls, and, well, most of the tourists he'd met weren't his type. He looked the girl up and down again, smiling. She was a bit short and too skinny, but she'd do. It was high time to enjoy himself.

"Great, I'll be right over," he said.

He grinned in anticipation as he watched her carefully weave her way back to her table. He'd just paid for all eleven drinks when a hand clamped down on his shoulder. Tommy winced in pain, glaring at the source. His savior had returned from the sea.

"You doing alright, buddy?"

"Sure, yeah," Tommy mumbled, willing the man to leave him alone.

"You can't be too careful, you know. The ocean can be a killer. Rip tides and shit. You'd better take care of yourself, man. Stay close to the shore."

"Yeah, okay."

"Cool, well, see ya!"

The guy walked away; Tommy sighed in relief. He stuffed a few baht back into his wallet, looking forward to chatting up his new girlfriend, when a shriek of laughter erupted from the terrace behind him. He heard the good Samaritan shouting, "He said what? No way, man, he wasn't diving."

Tommy turned to see the jock with his arm thrown casually over his new girlfriend's neck. Of all the girls swarming around this place, it had to be her! They were all laughing and looking over at him. He froze in his tracks. All of his life, people had laughed at him. Well, fuck them and fuck her. He'd show them all what he was capable of.

Tommy scooped up his Sea Breeze and stormed out of the bar.

CHAPTER ELEVEN

Notebook, check. Pens, check. Water bottle, check. Zelda couldn't think of anything else that she might need. After shoving all of her school items into a daypack, she slipped on a shapeless blue dress she'd picked up in Thamel. She hoped the – to her eyes – authentic design would allow her to blend in better with her new neighbors. The fact she was at least a foot taller than almost everyone around her did not help. She swished the dress to and fro and few times, admiring herself in the mirror. Zelda never wore dresses at home; the feel of the fabric brushing against her skin felt nice, but her legs felt strangely naked.

After making her bed, she waited in the living room for the other family members to rise, but no one came to see her off. She wasn't entirely sure anyone was home; the rest of the family slept a floor above her. With a shrug, she set off for class. According to her map, it was a straight shot to the volunteer organization's main offices, where her language courses were held.

Her new family lived behind a large open-air market that was already in full swing. Everywhere she looked there were pleading, screaming women fighting over vegetables and animal parts. The air was ripe with the smell of frying samosas and *roti*. Taxis and tempos beep-beeped their way through the shopping crowds, showing little regard for human or animal life.

Zelda could barely walk through the market without bumping into edgy women on the lookout for pickpockets. She contemplated jumping into a cab, but Ganesh had repeatedly reassured her that her new home was only a short distance to the office and easily walkable. He obviously had never been here on market day, she thought.

Her panic reached a crescendo when she arrived at the only major intersection she'd have to cross in order to reach her classroom. A large Hindu temple stood on one corner of the busy artery, and a collection of popular shops on the other. In both directions, cars and people whizzed by.

She didn't dare to cross over the street until the traffic lightened, but the longer she stood there waiting, the worse it seemed to get. She looked around desperately for a crosswalk or pedestrian bridge, but there didn't seem to be any way across the street. As she stood there paralyzed, an elderly man hobbled up to the intersection and stood next to her for a moment, before starting his death march across the four-lane highway. She watched in admiration as the man crossed safely into the second lane, wondering whether she should join him. Before she could react, the old man bounced off the hood of a car coming up behind him, sending his cane flying. Zelda gasped in shock. She wanted to run out and help him but didn't dare. Cars beeped their irritation as the man slowly righted himself and calmly collected his walking stick, continuing across the road without obvious injuries. Zelda was not yet willing to take such a chance.

She ran a block farther up the street, hoping she could find a lull in the traffic. No such luck. Fuming at the cars, refusing to be hindered by them any longer, she looked around for another person crossing over, hoping to tag along this time despite the possible consequences. She had to get to class; Ganesh and the others were waiting for her. Though no people were waiting to cross, two cows and a goat were happily chewing on a rotting pile of garbage next to her. Zelda wondered how holy these cows really were.

Approaching the beast standing closest to the road, she spoke softly to it as she held her hands out before her. "Here cow, good cow, come here, cowwyy..."

Zelda had never stood so close to a real-life heifer before and could not get over how big they were. Or that repugnant smell they seemed to exude. She began pushing on its side, gently at first, trying to usher it into the street. Its girth would stop any renegade vehicles, she figured. The animal didn't move a muscle.

She shoved against its side a few times, increasingly harder, but to no avail. Okay, if force wasn't working, she'd try bribery. With disgust, she picked up a piece of garbage with two fingers, holding it out in front of the beast's nose. The cow only stared off into the distance, rhythmically chewing its cud.

Cursing its stupidity, all of her fears and frustrations about the coming three months came pouring out as volleys onto the animal's flanks. "Come on, you stupid cow, would you just help me out and get across the goddamn street!" she screamed, not daring to consider what this might look like to other passersby.

Nothing. She stopped for a moment to catch her breath, telling herself not to cry. There had to be a way across this godforsaken street. As if out of sympathy, the skinny beast moved a few steps into the street, sending cars screeching to a halt. Zelda watched in amazement as the cow lumbered into the first of four lanes, oblivious to the problems it was causing. She quickly ran to its side. Together, they meandered over to a pile of potato peelings melting in the morning sun, on the other side of the road. She patted the animal's side in thanks and then ran full speed towards her coordinator's office.

At 9:04 a.m., Zelda pushed open the appropriate gate and entered a dusty courtyard. Inside the high stone walls of the compound was a five-story concrete structure. A hand-painted sign decorated with peeling lotus blossoms proclaimed it to be the Laxmi Office Complex. She sighed. It wasn't even worth taking a picture of. She knew she shouldn't be disappointed by these nondescript buildings anymore; she'd seen enough to know they dominated the city's landscape.

Climbing an open-air staircase running up the middle of the building, she looked for anything indicating the exact location of Rajesh's office. On the fourth floor she finally spotted a small red and white Nepal Cultural Programme sign tacked onto one of the doors. She knocked softly. No answer. She began pounding on the thin wood, just as Ganesh opened a door farther up the hallway.

"Hello, my friend. I am very glad to see you today! The others are already in the classroom. Please to follow me."

"I am so sorry I'm so late, and especially on our first day, it's just traffic was so *crazy* and –"

"Yes, yes. It is not a problem. We have not yet started. Please to sit down."

Zelda followed him into the windowless classroom. The rest of the volunteers grinned and waved at her as she entered. Sarah and Doris sat side by side in the front row. Christine, the youngest of the group, patted the stool next to her. Zelda smiled at her in gratitude, joining her in the back of the small room. The concrete walls were decorated with memory cards for learning the Nepali alphabet. She remembered using them as a kid: *A* is for apple; *B* is for boy. She took a seat under *S* is for sari and unpacked her bag as silently as possible.

"Thank you all for coming to Nepal and being part of this program," Ganesh said, beaming. "This is an exciting time for us all. Together we will learn more about this beautiful kingdom and its many cultures through lessons here in this classroom and day trips to cities close to Kathmandu. And of course we can all look forward to our week-long trip to Chitwan National Park at the end of your two-month teaching assignments; a well-earned reward, I am certain."

Ganesh turned and picked up a pile of paperwork, handing several sheets to each of the women. The paper was so thin it was almost transparent. Zelda could hardly believe it had been printed on without falling apart. She told herself to not write too hard, lest it rip.

"During the next two weeks, learning the Nepali language – Nepali – will be your most important task. But before we begin, it is important to understand more about the Nepali culture. As you have already noticed, Nepali culture is very different from your own," Ganesh said, chuckling. The women responded with the appropriate giggles.

"There are many differences between the ways in which westerners and Nepali are expected to behave. Some things that you do in your country – like kiss your boyfriend in public, come home after dark, or walk around in a bikini top – are strictly forbidden here in Nepal. It is good for you to read this list –" He held up the first sheet of paper. "– and try to remember these rules when interacting with your families and neighbors."

Ganesh gave them a few minutes to review his handiwork before clapping his hands together, throwing them a pearly grin. "But let us now talk of health matters." His manner became quite serious. "There are many wonderful things about Nepal," he said, smiling at them warmly before his face reverted to its somber mode, "but also some hidden dangers you must be aware of. Count yourself exceptionally blessed by all the Nepalese gods if you do not get diarrhea during your visit with us. Many visitors and locals are stricken by this disease."

Ganesh proceeded to detail the four different types one could get and how, before spending an equal amount of time describing the various cures. "But," as their trusty program coordinator reassured them, "with due respect and the right combination of treatments, getting diarrhea would be no reason to cut your trip short."

The women exchanged grim glances. If shitting uncontrollably for days with a high fever and tendency to release rotten-egg belches was not enough reason to go home early, what would be? Sure, Zelda had read about these diseases in her guidebooks before coming, but the reality of drinking only iodine-filled water for months on end was suddenly far less romantic than it seemed a short time ago.

In the course of the next few hours, she learned more about infectious and viral diseases than she ever wanted to know in a lifetime. She was immensely relieved when Ganesh clapped his hands once again, dismissing them for an hour.

"After lunch we will begin learning Nepali," he said.

"Ganesh? When are we going to learn how to teach?" Zelda asked. To her dismay, Doris and Sarah snickered.

Ganesh studied her carefully, clearly bewildered. "A thousand pardons. I do not understand the question."

"When are we going to learn more about *how* to teach our classes? Do we have to create lesson plans or teach out of a specific book? Should we talk to our students in English, or should we be able to translate everything for them? That's what I mean. We only have two weeks to prepare, and it would be nice to know what you expect from us."

Ganesh smiled broadly. "Yes, yes. I understand." He sat on the edge of his desk, hands folded over one knee. "I am here to teach you about Nepal, the land, its customs, and some of its language. Indeed, when you are at your school, you will be working as a teacher and treated like the rest of the staff. At most schools, you are expected to make the lesson plans yourself. Sometimes the headmaster will have prepared them for you. Whether you speak to your students in Nepali or English will depend on their level. Please to talk to your headmaster about these matters, or the other teachers."

Zelda could not believe her ears. This was not what she'd signed up for. She had no idea how to teach a class of children anything, let alone English. Ganesh was supposed to teach them *how* to teach, that was part of the deal. Wasn't it?

"It is good to use your creativity to help engage the students," Ganesh continued, addressing all of them. "You do not always have to have so strict a lesson plan. You can teach them songs or play simple games with them, ones from your own childhood. I am sure the headmaster of your school can assist you. And as for the books –" Ganesh looked down at Zelda, chuckling in a fatherly fashion. "– Nepal is not like your America; here we do not all learn from the same textbooks. But the headmaster will have sample lesson materials for you, created by previous volunteers at your schools. It is not a problem!"

She could feel her blood pressure rising and her eyes boiling over. She was so mad she could spit. Her anger rushed out in words before she could stop herself. "Yes, it *is* a problem, Ganesh. How can you be so nonchalant about this? I mean, we all came here to teach, right? So how are we supposed to succeed if you don't help us out?"

Ganesh's smile remained stiffly planted on his lips. "Tell me, Zelda, did you not see on the application form that the staff of the Nepal Cultural Programme recommends that all volunteers have previous experience teaching?"

She froze in her seat.

"Did you also not see on our website that we are a *cultural* organization, who helps to arrange volunteer placements, but we are not teachers ourselves?"

Her cheeks were ready to burst into flames. How could she have been so stupid as to bring this up in front of the other volunteers? "I know. But with my work schedule, it was impossible to pick up a teaching certificate on such short notice. Because teaching experience is only recommended, I assumed you would be providing us with more specific information or examples of how to teach these children the English language. Besides, I wrote on my application form that I didn't have any formal training. Why did you take my money when you knew I couldn't teach?"

"Miss Zelda, please to calm down! It is not a problem, I assure you. You can teach our children many things, even without the proper credentials. We are very happy to have you here, all of you. If you are so concerned, I can give you some books on teaching and old lesson plans. Perhaps they will help you to feel more confident?"

She nodded yes. Damn it! As if she didn't have enough to worry about already. And now more homework on top of homework. Why hadn't she just kept her big mouth shut? It probably would have been smarter to ask the other volunteers for advice instead.

"Now it is time for lunch. Yes, yes, it is a very busy day indeed."

By five o'clock, Zelda's head was swimming. Nepali was nothing like high school French, not that she'd ever really mastered that language either. She looked around the room, noticing the other three volunteers appeared to be as exhausted as she felt. When Ganesh finally dismissed them for the day, all four women trudged wearily down the stairs to the gated courtyard.

"Is anyone up for a drink?" she asked.

Doris responded first. "Maybe another day, I'm beat. Besides, my family is expecting me back home right after class. They like to eat dinner early, I guess." She stifled a yawn. "Thanks for the offer, though."

The other two nodded in agreement.

"When my family heard that I recently became single –" Sarah spat the last word out. "– they decided to make it their mission to find me a good husband. Tonight the first candidate is coming round to meet me." She laughed as if it was the stupidest idea she'd ever heard, but Zelda could see the desperation in her eyes. Was she really hoping to meet a man here? Zelda couldn't fathom the thought.

"Yeah, and my sister is going to show me how to sort rice tonight!" Christine chimed in. How could she be excited about that, Zelda wondered. She was bursting to ask them all about their families, houses, and neighborhoods, but clearly the others weren't in the mood. Another day then. Still, Zelda did feel a bit left out. She didn't even know when her family would be getting home, let alone eat dinner. And they certainly hadn't offered to teach her anything.

"Okay, good night, ladies!" She waved them off, her smile dropping as soon as they were out of sight. She was not quite ready to go to her house despite her exhaustion. She was still ticked off at her program coordinator and feeling more unsure by the minute that she would be able to learn Nepali, let alone stand before a classroom for two months. Why didn't Ganesh make teaching experience mandatory if he wasn't going to help them more?

But what could she do about it now? Quitting was not an option. She'd made far too big a deal about how amazing this experience was going to be just to show up back in Seattle a month later. No, she was going to have to go through with the whole volunteer thing, despite her program coordinator's deceit.

Zelda ducked into one of the many bars on her route home and ordered a beer, hoping it would help her relax. The other customers – all male – eyed her as if she was a whore. Too late she remembered that proper Nepali women didn't go into bars, let alone unaccompanied. Downing her beer in three gulps, she left a generous tip behind.

The dreaded intersection was serenely quiet, now dominated by the chants of Hindu worshippers from the corner temple, not the horns of diesel trucks or daytime shoppers. She knew she should get home before dark, but it was so nice to walk in the warm autumn air through these peaceful streets. Back in Seattle it would be cold and rainy, not eighty degrees and sunny. Who was she kidding – even when the weather was nice, she never took the time to just walk around. She was always too busy, rushing around in her car, scurrying between work and home. It felt so good to have nothing to do for a change.

Reveling in her newfound freedom, she ambled down the quiet avenue, examining the painted doors of the market stalls, taking in the advertisements for Bollywood movies, all the while avoiding the staring locals, obviously intrigued as to why a white woman was wandering around this suburb all alone. She walked aimlessly down side alleyways and through open squares, soaking up the sights, before realizing it was getting dark fast and she had absolutely no clue as to where she was.

Zelda started to double back but realized, as soon as she turned around, that none of the streets looked remotely familiar to her in the twilight. She pulled out her English-language map of Kathmandu, turning it this way and that, trying to orient herself. But it was useless in this suburban neighborhood. Most of the shops were closed or closing, and streetlights were few and far between. The roads, which minutes before had been so inviting, now seemed foreboding and sinister. She saw danger in every darkened alleyway. She picked up her speed, but after a few panic-filled minutes, she finally realized there was no way she would recognize her family's tiny side street in the enveloping darkness. Finding Ganesh's office would be a long shot too.

Shit! She stopped under a streetlight to contemplate her options. Suddenly she remembered Nabim writing down her new family's phone number in her school notebook the night before. "In case of emergencies," he'd said. Zelda had felt like a two-year-old at the time, but was now extremely grateful. All she had to do was find a phone. She hadn't seen any public pay telephones anywhere during her wandering and didn't dare knock on a stranger's door. She had to find a shop; they would certainly let her use their phone if she bought something.

As she attempted to retrace her steps, a flickering light coming from a small side street caught her attention. Peering cautiously around the corner, she saw a lone shopkeeper selling vegetables to a few women. Five candles lit up his wares; Zelda barely recognized them as beans and tomatoes. Her approach was noticed. Before she could decide whether this was a good idea, the shopkeeper and his clients called out to her, waving her over. Encouraged by their enthusiasm, she skipped over to the group, notebook in hand. But they were all talking so fast Zelda couldn't understand what they were saying.

She told herself to breathe; everything was going to be fine; she couldn't be that far away from home. Putting on her most dazzling grin, she pointed to the numbers Nabim had written down a few hours ago. "Telephone?" she asked, hoped someone in the group could speak English.

They all looked at her quizzically.

She sputtered out "ring ring," while pantomiming picking up a telephone receiver and talking into it. The shopkeeper's face lit up, and he ran to the back of the store, quickly returning with a heavy black phone. Zelda picked up the receiver and dialed her family's number.

After five rings, she heard, "Namaste, Nabim Naga."

"Hello, Nabim, it's Zelda. I am so sorry, but I don't know where I am or how to get home!" She could feel the tears welling up.

"Zelda? We were wondering where you were. Bless the gods that you are not hurt. Where are you? What do you recognize?"

"Nothing. I don't recognize anything; it's too dark," she said, sniffling. She didn't know how much longer she could hold off the impending flood.

"Whose phone are you using?"

"I don't know his name. Just some guy selling vegetables. He let me use his phone."

"Please to let me speak with the man."

She shoved the receiver into the shopkeeper's ear. Nabim must have asked for directions because after a few moments of silence, the man said something in Nepali before handing the phone back, smiling.

"Hello, Zelda? I am coming to find you," Nabim said. "Please to stay by the shopkeeper. Thank you." And then he was gone.

Zelda was so grateful she bought a sack full of beans and a few pathetic-looking tomatoes from the man, figuring they would make a good offering to Parwati for making her new family worry. Five minutes later, Nabim came around the corner whistling, his broad grin in force.

"Hello! My my, what have you been doing today?" Nabim asked, laughing.

Zelda could feel tears of relief dripping down her cheeks. She wiped them quickly aside. Her brother approached the shopkeeper, embracing him warmly before handing him a fifty-rupee note. Nabim then turned back to his lost western sister.

"Come, let us to return home."

Nabim's cheery silence was replaced by Parwati's motherly concern as soon as she entered the family threshold.

"Where were you? Why did you not come home after school like the other girls do?" Parwati demanded, while dabbing at her tear-stained cheeks.

Zelda's offering of vegetables did nothing to curb Parwati's obvious disappointment. She was glad that neither of her "parents" had recognized the smell of alcohol on her breath; then she really would have been in for it. Parwati sent her to bed without dinner, sternly warning her not to come home late again, without asking her permission *first*.

"Respectable women do not wander around the streets of Kathmandu unescorted – especially at night! Ganesh must have told you that much at least?" Parwati implored, frowning in anger.

Zelda retreated to her room a woman chastised. Or, rather, a girl chastised. She had never been treated like this before, not even by her own mother, let alone a substitute one. Her anger – *how dare Parwati talk to me like that!* – was quickly replaced by the realization that she would have to play their cultural games for the next few months if she was going to fit in. She punched her pillow in frustration. She was here to teach *them*, not the other way around! With a heavy heart and an empty stomach, Zelda lay awake fuming and fussing, until she finally drifted off into a restless sleep.

CHAPTER TWELVE

Ian tried his best not to cut his penis on the beer can's sharp edge. The rocking of the boat made it virtually impossible. *Damn!* A stream of blood mingled with his urine. He zipped back up – carefully – and dumped his pee over the side. The empty can he threw into the bow.

Taking another long drag off his chillum, Ian blew out perfect smoke rings while enjoying the view. The Annapurnas looked so soft and round from here, like big puffy pillows he could roll around in. So different from the angular peaks of the Himalayas.

Leaning back onto his daypack, Ian rubbed his forehead, trying to recall all he had heard about possible trekking routes in the past three days. There was certainly no shortage of available guides in Pokhara. It seemed as if everyone he'd met since getting off the bus had offered to lead him through the mountains, even this morning's waiter. Several claimed to know where the best marijuana was growing this time of year, though they refused to tell him exactly where until he paid up. Their eagerness to please – and get his money – made him a bit suspicious. And anyway, all the trekking routes were longer than he had hoped for. A few days were alright, but more than a week didn't sound like his cup of tea. He really wasn't into cold-weather climbing; give him a sandy beach any day. He *could* splurge and fly to Jomsom, but what would be the point? Marijuana didn't grow in the mountain passes; that much he'd learned already.

And then there was the troubling news of the Germans. Two tourists killed for a bit of cash. Ian didn't especially want to be knifed, robbed, and thrown off a trail, left for dead. Besides, his mother would wring his neck if she ever found out he was planning on hiking alone. He didn't remember his mates ever mentioning any dead trekkers. From their stories, he'd been expecting holy men with burning chillums to be waiting for him at the airport, ready to envelop him into another, more spiritual realm. But in reality, money seemed to be the most worshiped object in Nepal, so far as he could tell.

Absent-mindedly he picked up a pebble from the bottom of the boat, turning it over in his fingers before chucking it across the water. He watched idly as it skimmed the surface – once, twice, three times – before finally disappearing into the murky black lake.

Ian knew he didn't have to hike alone; there were plenty of other options, but they all seemed less than ideal. The group treks seemed almost suffocating, they were so well organized. He *could* put up a sign in one of the many gear shops in Pokhara or respond to one of the other notices he'd seen, placed by other single trekkers looking for hiking companions. But he couldn't be bothered to go to all that trouble. Besides, hiking in pairs hadn't seemed to have helped the Germans much. Ian took another hit of his pipe, letting the smoke out slowly while considering his options.

A few minutes later, he tapped the ash out of his chillum, picked up the oars, and headed back to shore. After a few hours on the water, it felt as if the earth was swaying; he couldn't seem to find his balance. Stumbling back up the hill towards his hotel, he passed an Internet cafe. A few of the terminals were free. Thinking of his mother again, Ian went inside to let her know he was having a brilliant time and, most importantly, that he was very safe. What she didn't know wouldn't hurt her.

It took him a while to get connected, but the emails home went pretty quickly. His typing skills had improved dramatically during his university days. After paying a few rupees for the service, Ian resumed his journey back to his hotel. Just outside the Internet cafe, he spotted a local holy man hobbling along the main road, his dreadlocks dragging behind him along the ground. Attached via a leash to the man's crutches was a monkey dressed in a pink sweater. Ian watched in fascination as the pair shuffled up the hillside. He jumped slightly when someone put a hand on his shoulder. He turned and saw Arjun behind him, his seatmate from the bus ride over.

"Hey, how's it going, mate?"

"Good, good. Thank you." With his leather jacket thrown over his shoulder, the boy looked like a Nepalese James Dean. *Rebel without a Clue.*

"Why aren't you trekking? Or did you just get back?" Ian asked.

"Oh, it is very sad. The old lady started to feel sick in Kathmandu, before the family even came to Pokhara. She is sick already five days. The doctors here cannot find a problem. Yesterday we met to discuss the trip and the entire family decided to cancel. They all go back to Kathmandu today, on the airplane. The old lady must go to the hospital there." The boy's shoulders were slouched over in rejection.

"That's some bad luck."

"Yes, yes. It is very sad. I was looking forward to being a guide. Please to tell me, what are you doing now?"

"I was going to go back to my hotel to chill out. I've been on one of those rental boats all morning."

"Ah yes. Lake Phewa is very beautiful. Tell me, did you visit the temple on the island? It is very holy."

"Naw, just paddled around a bit."

Arjun looked puzzled. "Oh. Well, I am walking to meet my cousin at our aunt's house. You are most welcome to join us for lunch, if you wish?"

"Sure; thanks, mate. I'll follow you."

They made their way along the main drag of base camp Pokhara. Souvenir shops, trekking outfitters, restaurants, guide companies, Internet cafes, and bars lined both sides of the wide street.

Looking curiously at Ian's dreadlocks, the boy pointed to a small, nondescript club at the end of the tourist strip. "Perhaps you would like to go there later. Many tourists with hair like yours go there."

"Oh yeah? Why's that?"

"They have a marijuana tree that is so old it is two stories tall. The club is built around it."

Ian's jaw dropped, drool automatically spilling out. He couldn't tell whether the kid was putting him on or not, but figured it was worth checking out.

"But it is only open in the evenings. Perhaps we can go there later, with my cousin?" the boy continued.

Ian nodded his head vigorously. "Oh ya, we should definitely check it out. Do you smoke grass too?"

"No, no. But my cousin does."

Arjun turned onto a small road leading away from the city center. Ten minutes later, they entered a rural neighborhood. Ian about shit himself when he saw a few marijuana plants growing wild in the pastures along the side of the road. *Jake and his mates were right!* Without thinking, he climbed through the barbed-wire fence and ran towards his latest find. Upon closer inspection though, he saw the plants were still way too small to produce any buds. *Damn!* Ian kicked himself for not asking Jake more questions about exactly where he had gone hiking – or rather harvesting – when he'd had the chance. He pricked his thigh on the barbed wire as he jumped back over the fence to rejoin his friend.

"Here we are," said the boy, stopping in front of a tin-roof shack. A squat Nepalese woman stirred an industrial-sized pot, using both hands to move the huge spatula. Lentil soup splashed onto her colorful apron.

Ian smirked; *dhal bhat* for lunch again. The boy walked up to the woman and spoke warmly to her, placing his hands on her shoulders. After they exchanged greetings, the woman disappeared inside.

"Please to sit here," Arjun said, pointing at a picnic bench set up next to the cooking area. "My cousin will arrive shortly."

The woman returned with glasses of water and freshly brewed tea. She spoke in Nepali to Ian, often covering up her quick smile with the back of her hand. He grinned back at her, nodding.

"What is she saying?" Ian asked his friend.

"It is an honor to have a westerner in her home. Tourists do not come to this place. And she has never seen someone with a white face and hair like yours, from so close by."

It was Ian's turn to blush. "Tell her it is also an honor for me. And that I could use another glass of water."

"It is not a problem. Would you also like a beer?"

"Brilliant; two of each, please. I guess it was all that rowing, but I'm dying of thirst."

A few minutes after their second round of drinks arrived, Ian heard a deep voice call out behind him, "Hello, Arjun; *namaste,* man!" A man in his early thirties, with a small goatee and gold stud in his right ear, hugged his younger cousin heartily, kissing him on the cheeks. "This is a surprise, one of your clients?" The man turned to Ian, smiling warmly and offering him his hand. "Hello, I am Rajesh. It is good to meet you."

While they ate, Rajesh shared story after story of drama and intrigue on the surrounding mountaintops, in near-perfect English. Ian was captivated. Rajesh sounded like the kind of bloke who'd be a perfect guide for him. And he would surely know where the best crops were; Ian could smell freshly burned weed on Rajesh's T-shirt.

Only when their aunt came to refill their water glasses did Rajesh's mood change. He shouted at his younger cousin, then aunt, in Nepali. Both looked sheepishly over at Ian.

"May a thousand gods pardon my cousin and auntie. Tourists never come here, so she did not know. And my cousin, well, he is very young and still has much to learn. Our most deepest excuses for your troubles," Rajesh said.

"Sorry? I don't follow."

"They forgot westerners have to have iodine in their water, or it has to be boiled first."

"Or?"

"Your stomachs are not used to the bacteria in Nepali water. We were

81

born here and have drank it since birth, so our bodies are immune to the germs. But you westerners..." He shook his head sadly. "Your bodies cannot handle them. A thousand pardons. Let me get you some Imodium and iodine to take with you. You aren't staying in a hostel, I hope? Or a shared room?"

Ian could feel his face draining of color. "No, why?"

"It depends on how much water you drank. Either diarrhea or a high fever. If either one lasts for more than a few days, you will need to go to a doctor. How many glasses did you have?"

Ian tried to remember, but his mind blanked. Diarrhea or high fever – for a few days? What the heck was in the water anyway? "Dunno. Three, maybe four glasses?"

Rajesh was quite still for a moment. "Okay. I will write down the address of the hospital in Kathmandu for you." He rose and walked into the shack.

Brilliant, there goes my trekking plans, Ian thought. He turned to his younger companion. "Hey, Arjun, when your cousin gets back, can you take me to that bar we saw on the way over?"

"It is not a problem."

Chapter Thirteen

"*Piunu.*" Zelda furrowed her brow in concentration, repeating the word to herself. "To eat?" She flipped the card over. To drink. "Damn it, I'm never going to remember all these words!" she screamed into her pillow. She'd made the stupid notecards in hopes of learning Nepali faster, but they didn't seem to be helping one bit.

If only her family would converse with her in Nepali, then she would be sure to remember more. The Nagas were nice people and all, but they were clearly more interested in practicing their English with her than putting up with her halting Nepali. It was Parwati's doing, Zelda suspected. With her children's final exams coming up soon, they could certainly use the practice. But didn't Parwati understand that she only had two weeks to learn basic Nepali? Otherwise how was she going to teach those cute little kiddies English if they couldn't understand her? Zelda sighed deeply, staring at the flashcards on her nightstand. *Just once more, come on, you can do it*, she told herself, forcing her hand to pick up the thick pile and begin flipping through the verbs once more.

When the letters began to blur together, she flung the cards across her bed and trudged upstairs. The Nagas were huddled around the television, curtains drawn. Only the father sat apart, leafing through an English language magazine, a stock market ticker tape featured prominently on the cover. Their big-screen television blasted out the high-pitched Hindi music so popular in Nepal. Only the lead singer and her video love interest were wearing traditional costumes. The background singers were dressed in western clothes: pink tube tops, black leather microskirts, fishnet stockings, and silver platform heels. Zelda was amazed they could perform the intricate dances without falling over. Parwati sat perched on the edge of the couch, peeking at the screen through finger slits.

"What's wrong, Parwati?" Zelda asked.

"The clothes! Those girls must be so cold."

Zelda started to laugh, but one look at Parwati's face stopped her in her tracks.

Her mother continued, "It is shameful that they dress so. I do not like it. These women are a bad influence on my daughter and nieces. And my son will think all women are whores! How can he not, if women dress and act like this?" she sniffled, clearly on the verge of tears.

Zelda looked up at Parwati's daughter, dressed in dark trousers and a pink cotton blouse. Her son's skin-tight T-shirt was tucked into his knock-off Levis. Parwati herself wore a sari every day, but her children looked as if they dressed at the Gap. Even her husband fancied western-style three-piece suits. Since she'd entered their home, Zelda had made a point of wearing a traditional *kurthaa*, a long, shapeless tunic that covered loose-fitting trousers. Although it felt as if she was walking around in pajamas all day long, she did it out of respect for the family. But taking a closer look at her siblings dancing and prancing around the living room floor, she wondered why she bothered.

A sudden commotion in the front yard sent the family racing to the window. Her father, Mahendra, threw back the thick curtains. The bright afternoon sun was blinding, and it took Zelda's eyes a few seconds to readjust. She could just make out an old man and a goat standing in the front courtyard. The man was waving at them. Mahendra clapped his hands in delight and ran downstairs, the rest of the family hot on his heels.

"What is it?" she asked. Their excitement was palpable.

Already halfway down the stairs, Nabim called back, "My father's birthday present has arrived!"

"Present?" Zelda knew it was Mahendra's birthday today. The whole family had been in the temple most of the morning getting blessed. Because Zelda wasn't Hindu, she wasn't allowed to join them. She figured she'd missed out on some amazing ritual, but apparently there was more to the birthday celebration than prayer. She sprinted down the last flight of stairs into the courtyard, excited to finally be a part of a traditional Nepali rite.

A fat, brown-haired goat was chomping on the family's hedge. Zelda expected Parwati to start scolding the animal or push it away, but her mother didn't seem to notice. She and Mahendra were engaged in a furiously fast-paced conversation with the old man, negotiations clearly underway. Zelda held back, trying to work out what was happening.

The old man was wrapped in an enormous white linen cloth that covered his legs like a diaper, then wrapped around his torso. A worn-out red jacket was thrown over it. His wrinkled body and the swaddling of his clothes reminded her of a creepy baby Jesus. A huge *kukhuri* – a curved knife, its blade easily a foot long and eight inches wide – hung loosely from his waist on a thick leather belt. Zelda could hardly believe the man could stand with it on, let alone lift the thing.

After a few minutes of heated exchanges, they'd apparently come to some sort of agreement. Mahendra clasped the old man on the shoulders and called for tea. The creepy baby Jesus took a flat stone from his jacket pocket and sat on the ground, cross-legged. He drew his impressive knife and began sliding the stone across the blade's edge, sharpening it.

"Nabim, what's going on?" Zelda asked.

The boy's eyes gleamed with anticipation. "You'll see. It is a surprise!"

She squatted on the ground next to him, sipping her drink, waiting.

After a while, the man rose and resheathed his knife. Slowly he approached the goat – now chewing up Parwati's hibiscus plant – singing to it. He caressed its head, massaging its neck. Zelda was entranced. The goat stopped chewing, letting the man lead it into the middle of the courtyard.

Mahendra whispered something into Nabim's ear. The boy sprung up and ran back inside, returning moments later with the biggest cooking pan in the house. The family watched intently as the old man calmly walked around to one side of the animal, continually massaging the animal's neck as he moved.

The man began singing harder, louder. The rhythm was mesmerizing, his broken voice transfixing. Zelda felt her body swaying in time and her eyelids growing heavy. Before her eyes closed completely, the goat let out a last bleat, then WHAP! In one smooth motion, the old man unsheathed his knife and brought it down hard, precisely in the middle of the goat's neck. He raised and lowered it again quickly, severing the last vertebrae. The goat's head fell with a thump onto the ground, blood spouting profusely out of its neck.

As her family began cheering, Zelda felt faint, grabbing at the grass for support. Her brain refused to acknowledge her retinas' last transmission. Yet there were specks of red on her green tunic. Zelda started to wipe them off, but stopped short of touching the fresh blood. Her stomach was doing summersaults. *Do not puke, do not puke* became her mantra. The rest of the family was still clapping and singing, her father beaming with pride. Nabim ran towards the goat's flailing body as soon as the head touched the ground, holding the pan under its severed neck until the animal's knees gave way.

Zelda felt as if walls were closing in on her; she *had* to get away from this gruesome scene. She tried to stand, but her legs weren't cooperating.

Her sister, Ranjana, laughed heartily, poking her in the ribs. "Are you hungry, Zelda?"

She could feel herself turning green as realization sunk in. "Oh my God!" Zelda screamed as she tore upstairs, reaching the family's western-style toilet just in time.

"Zelda? Are you in there?"

Zelda lay on her bed with a cold cloth over her forehead. She had never seen a real, live animal killed before, and certainly not for food. It was far more gruesome and disturbing than she could have imagined. Less than an hour ago, that cute goat had been in her courtyard, eating her mother's flowers, and now it was being hacked into bits on her rooftop patio. The whole house shook with every swipe of the blade. How in God's name was she supposed to eat that poor animal tonight? The thought made her want to become a vegetarian.

"Yeah, I'm in here," she called out wearily.

Nabim and Ranjana held back the curtain to her room. "We want to show you the surprise. But maybe now is not a good time, if you are not feeling well?"

Another surprise? Good Lord, what next? "Okay. I guess now is fine." Zelda laid the wet cloth on the bedside table and sat up.

"It's my father's birthday cake!" Nabim announced joyously. He lifted the curtain to reveal Kreepa the servant girl, holding a pan. The same pan Nabim ran to get when they killed that poor defenseless goat. But now the pan was filled with blood: thick, dark, and congealing.

Zelda could feel the vomit rising. "That is DISGUSTING!" she shrieked, covering her mouth in horror.

Her siblings looked crestfallen. "But this is a very rare delicacy. My father is most pleased with his present."

"But I thought the goat was the present! Oh right. Oh God." She wanted to burst into tears but was too shocked to even do that. A rare delicacy? They were kidding, right? She studied Nabim and Ranjana's faces for glimpses of mischievousness. They sure seemed to be serious. Zelda gulped. She had promised herself before coming to Nepal that she would eat and drink whatever was put in front of her. If it was good enough for the locals, then it was good enough for her. But there had to be limits.

Behind the curtain, she could hear her mother gasping in shock. "What are you doing?" Parwati yelled.

Finally, Zelda thought, *we'll get to the bottom of this practical joke.*

Parwati whipped back the thin curtain, her face a mask of pure rage.

"Put that back in the kitchen at once! Your father will *kill* you if you spill even a single drop. Go upstairs and help with the goat, now!" She turned to Zelda, her expression softening slightly, shaking her head. "Children."

Zelda's face fell. Her brother and sister weren't kidding around. She gulped hard, returned the cloth to her forehead and lay back onto the bed, trying desperately to think her way out of eating goat's blood cake for dessert.

CHAPTER FOURTEEN

Tommy glanced over the selection of rings and pendants again. Nothing. He moved on to the next blanket, picked up a thin gold band, and twirled it in the sunlight. Smirking in disgust, he threw the ring back down. It all looked so cheap. He walked farther down the market, towards the shops at the end. Hopefully they'd have a better selection. If he was going to bother getting Chantal a ring, it had better be a diamond one. And it had to be real.

He walked slowly along the shop windows, studying their wares carefully. Tommy wasn't that experienced at buying jewelry, but he knew quality when he saw it. A diamond set in a gold band caught his eye. Finally, something that looked like it had been made with a touch of care. He walked inside, carefully examining their wares.

"Hello, mister. You wanna look at something?"

"Yeah, I'd like to look at this ring."

"Certainly."

It was simple but elegant: two thin bands of gold woven together, a diamond perched in the middle. The stone was the diameter of a BB pellet, but as thin as a cornflake. He'd seen bigger. "Yeah, it's for my fiancée. She's at home, you know, working. The poor girl. But I'm sure she'd love something like this." He thrust it into the light, tiny rainbows dancing inside the stone. "How much?"

"Thirty thousand baht."

"How much is that in Canadian?"

"Sir?"

Tommy grabbed the calculator off the counter, mumbling to himself, "Twelve hundred dollars. What?" Those were Toronto prices. He was still in Bangkok, for God's sake. But he figured these shops were used to bargaining.

"Yeah, Chantal loves diamonds. She's got a whole collection. That I bought for her, of course. She doesn't need anybody else since she's got me, no sir."

Tommy turned the ring over in his hand, considering the purchase. He'd saved up a bunch of baht already; one more big run and he'd be set for a year at least. Sure, he could afford this flimsy ring, but he didn't want to blow too much of his cash in one go. Besides, he already had plans for his savings. He was going to rent himself a five-star hotel room right downtown; that, he had already decided. He would even offer to get a room for his hick friends, if they'd bother to drive in to see him. New Year's Eve, the finest champagne and lobster for dinner. Maybe Chantal would join him. Maybe she would be wearing this ring.

"Can you try it on? Chantal's got bigger fingers than you but…" he asked. It fit the woman like a glove. "Damn."

"Do you know what size of finger your fiancée has? Maybe bigger than this? Yes?"

Tommy glared at the woman. "If I knew what her ring size was, I would have told you by now, wouldn't I?"

The clerk remained unruffled. She pulled out another tray and grabbed a similar design, but with a wider band. She slipped it on her finger; it slid right off. "Better for you, yes?"

"I don't know. It's so hard to tell just by looking at it. Do any other girls work here? A plumper one, maybe?"

The clerk shook her head.

Tommy grabbed the ring and jammed it onto his thumb. It fit. He knew Chantal's fingers were bigger than his own. Sighing in frustration, he pointed to the largest ring in the display case, not wanting to risk buying one that was too small. He could always get the band enlarged in Toronto, he supposed, but it would be probably be expensive. And he wasn't going to waste any more money on Chantal than necessary. Besides, he wasn't even sure where she was living right now, and if that bitch mother of hers wouldn't tell him where Chantal was staying, he'd be stuck with this thing.

Tommy snatched the third ring from the sales clerk's hand. This one hung loosely on his thumb. Now they were talking. "I'll take that one for thirty thousand baht."

The clerk's eye's popped open. "Sir, that ring costs *one hundred* thousand baht, not thirty thousand."

"That's ridiculous! Why it is so much more expensive?"

She held the two rings next to each other. She was right; the wider design was misleading. The third stone was the size of an overripe pea. Tommy had seen bigger.

"These are real diamonds, mister. Not fake crystals, like on the blankets," she said, spinning the ring in the light, letting it sparkle. Tommy hesitated. These diamond rings were so much more expensive than he could have imagined. He figured a few hundred – not a few thousand – dollars would have gotten him a huge rock. Maybe not in Toronto, but definitely here in Bangkok.

"If you love your fiancée, this one is better," the sales clerk said.

Tommy's head snapped up in surprise. He didn't love Chantal. "Well, I'll think about it. Can I have your business card?"

The woman clicked her tongue in irritation. She put one of their cards on the counter, turning away from him to replace the jewelry. He picked the card up: Chang's Jewelry Import/Export. Something clicked in his sun-stroked brain.

He studied the jewelry cases with a new eye, inspecting their contents more closely. When he finally found a pendant with a diamond the size of his pinky-top, he asked, "Excuse me, how much is this one?"

The clerk looked up at him, cocking her head to one side.

"I was just thinking, maybe I should get her a necklace instead. As I don't know how big her fingers are."

"That one, very expensive." She was shaking her head slowly.

"Okay, but you can tell me how much it costs, right?"

The clerk looked uneasy. "Five hundred thousand baht."

Tommy grabbed the calculator off the counter. Twenty thousand Canadian dollars. A sickly sweet smile spread across his face. The Greek *had* been holding out on him. Well, he'd show Harim not to try to pull one over on old Thomas Braintree.

With newfound purpose, Tommy headed for the door. "*Swadee ka.*"

CHAPTER FIFTEEN

Ian had never experienced so much pain in his life. Each hour, on the hour, a wave of diarrhea flooded through his body, quickly followed by a stream of vomit. Rotten-egg belches rose continually from his throat. Arjun's cousin had been right: It was a good thing he had the bathroom to himself; it was going to take him hours to clean up this mess once he felt better. If he ever felt better. His stomach cramped up again.

He wiped off his mouth and pulled up his skivvies. Someone was pounding on the door. Or was that just his head throbbing? Not ready to face a healthy human in his condition, Ian called weakly through the room, "Ya?"

"Please, it is Arjun. I have more medicines for you."

"Cheers, just leave them outside." Ian was grateful for all the medicines and frequent – too frequent – visits. But he wished the kid would leave him alone for a few hours so he could try to get some proper sleep. He knew Arjun wanted to apologize face to face, but Ian couldn't work up the strength to dress himself.

"Please to tell me, are you feeling better now?"

"No, mate; not really. Maybe tomorrow. Least I hope so."

"Okay." There was a long pause, but Ian didn't hear any footsteps. "I will come back soon with more foods and medicines. Bye-bye," Arjun said.

"Ya, bye." He knew from previous visits that there was no use arguing; the boy was determined. Arjun would keep coming back until Ian let him in or could walk out the door on his own two feet.

After the footsteps receded, he tucked a towel around his waist and cracked open the door, revealing a large pile of electrolytes, iodine, Imodium, vitamins, crackers, and more fruit. He picked up the plastic sack of goodies, adding it to the pile of pills and tablets on his bedside table that Arjun had brought him over the course of the past three days.

He dumped another sack of electrolytes into some lemonade and chugged it back. Its bitter taste was only partially masked by the sweetened juice. Eyeing the name of the hospital in Kathmandu once more, Ian wondered when it would be time to bite the bullet and seek medical attention. He'd tried eating a banana and a candy bar a few hours earlier but had no luck keeping them down.

Naw, he was sure the medicines were doing the trick; he just needed to give them a bit more time to do the job, that's all. Lying back down on the bed, sweating profusely, Ian prayed silently for relief as the next wave of nausea hit, sending him racing to the bathroom.

Ian slapped his own face, trying to stay awake. The airport's speaker system crackled to life. "Flight 72A to Kathmandu, now boarding at Gate 1." He shuffled towards the gate, his backpack still strapped on. After what happened the last time, he'd refused to check his luggage.

A group of stewardesses ushered him and eight other western tourists outside, onto the open tarmac. The smell of diesel fuel and oil hung in the air. Their plane stood at the ready; Ian could see the pilots already in the cockpit, headsets on. It was one of those old transport planes with propellers. He was relieved to see it was big enough to hold forty or so passengers; he was looking forward to stretching out and sleeping on this hour-long flight. Ian could barely stand, he was so weak; only pride prevented him from leaning on a fellow passenger or stealing one of their walking sticks.

A mobile staircase had already been rolled up to the open door. Still, the stewardess held them back from boarding. Ian looked to the terminal, expecting to see more tourists making their way towards them. Instead, sirens suddenly pierced the morning stillness. Two police wagons raced across the tarmac and screeched to a halt, directly in front of Ian and the other waiting westerners. Policemen sprung out of their vehicles, threw back the doors, and dragged ten grubby prisoners out onto the black asphalt. The condemned men were shaggy and unshaven, shackled at the wrists and ankles. The boys in blue pulled out their batons and beat the prisoners' legs and arms while screaming at them in Nepali until they formed a line. The officers then dragged them, one by one, onto the waiting plane.

Ian could feel his bowels moving. He was about to ask the stewardess to take him back to the departure hall when the policemen jumped back into their wagons and sped off, lights ablaze. The stunned westerners were immediately pushed towards the rollaway staircase. Ian saw that an older American couple was refusing to board. A stewardess tried to reassure them by saying the men were convicted smugglers, not murderers. But still the Americans were both shaking their heads violently and clutching their bags close to their bodies. Ian didn't blame them, but he didn't have the luxury of choice. Despite all of Arjun's pep talks and pills, this bug wasn't going away. He'd been sick for a week already; he *needed* to get to Bir Hospital.

With apprehension, Ian stepped inside. The prisoners had been placed in the seats farthest back. *Great*, Ian thought, *right next to the toilet*. He'd have to suck it up for the hour-long trip. A taxi could surely take him to the emergency room once they'd landed. The westerners filled the seats closest to the cockpit. Despite the emptiness of the three rows behind him, Ian didn't dare move. One of the stewardesses handed him two cotton balls and a lollipop. Ian watched the other passengers stuffing the cotton into their ears and the candy into their mouths; he followed suit.

The engines roared to life. Ian clapped his hands over his ears in pain. He'd never heard such an atrociously loud noise in all his days. Stuffing the cotton balls deeper into his ears, Ian tightened his seat belt as their plane broke free of gravity and rose effortlessly into the clear autumn skies. Soon they were passing over the twisted and cracked spine of the world. Ian could almost see the tectonic plates pushing the earth upwards. Supremely beautiful.

The next morning, Ian woke to the screams of the dying. Red-brown stains covered the walls and sheets of his hospital bed. He glanced at the IV tube dripping nourishment back into his veins, sighing in frustration. His bladder was about to explode, but Ian couldn't bear the thought of entering that bloody toilet room again. The smell alone could kill a person.

One more day of this and he should be good to go. He had to get out of here, out of Nepal. It was time to move on to the next stop on the backpacker trail, heading east. Relaxing on a warm beach and sipping margaritas would surely help him recover more quickly than lying here in this stinking hospital. Dabbing the sweat off his forehead, he wondered briefly how Zelda was faring, hoping she was doing better than him.

CHAPTER SIXTEEN

Zelda knocked on Christine's door at precisely 10:47 a.m., two minutes later than planned. A young girl answered. The scent of fresh orchids wafted outside as she opened it, so delightfully different from the constant smell of feces and rotting garbage hanging around most of Kathmandu. Stacked neatly next to the door were Christine's two small day packs and a camera bag. Zelda's cheeks flushed at the thought of her own backpacks, each easily twice the size of her companion's total load. And that wasn't counting her box of donated books, still safely tucked away in Ganesh's office.

Zelda followed the servant girl through the inner courtyard filled with the fragrant plants and trees that gave Christine's home its sweet fragrance. She took in the expensive *thangkas* and impressive golden statues dotted amongst the elegantly carved wooden furniture – in authentic Tibetan style, Zelda noticed, bitter with envy. Christine's house exhibited none of the Nagas' distinctly westernized tastes. Why couldn't she have been placed somewhere like this too?

As they entered the expansive living room, she saw Christine embracing her Nepalese mother. More like squeezing her to death, Zelda thought. Her father, five brothers, and three sisters formed a loose circle around the two weeping women. Embarrassed to disturb this emotional farewell, she looked away as the servant girl announced her arrival. The family and Christine turned to look in her direction, tear-stained faces all.

"Oh, Zelda, you're here already," Christine said.

"Actually I'm a few minutes late, with traffic and everything," she muttered.

Christine looked at her wristwatch. Her arms were covered with thin red metal bracelets, usually worn by married women. They must be presents from her family, Zelda figured.

"Of course, it's almost 11 a.m.!" Christine wiped the back of her hand across her cheeks, clearly having difficultly composing herself. In rapid-fire Nepali, Christine bade her mother a warm goodbye, kissing her on both cheeks. Zelda was amazed by her companion's fluency; their own conversations never went beyond "Where is the toilet?" and "Can I get another round?"

"If you need more time, I can send the taxi away. It's just I should let him know; my bags are in the backseat," Zelda said.

"No, no. It's okay. It's time to go." Christine hugged and kissed each member of her temporary family, murmuring reassurances of future dinners and long visits – very soon, very soon. Finally she turned to Zelda, red-eyed and puffy. "Shall we?"

Zelda tried to give Christine a reassuring smile, patting her awkwardly on the shoulder. She always got weirded out by intimate contact with strangers and vague acquaintances but figured this was a good time to make an exception. They walked out to the awaiting cab, followed by the weeping clan. Christine didn't stop waving – bracelets jangling – until their cab finally turned off the family's private road.

Zelda couldn't help but think of her own sendoff earlier that morning. The Nagas had been very polite, sure. First her Nepalese mother had given her some bananas, decorated with a thin red ribbon. Then her brother, sister, father, and several visiting cousins shook her hand and wished her well, thanking her for honoring their family with her presence. In comparison with what she'd just witnessed, it was a bit of a letdown. It wasn't that Zelda particularly *wanted* her family to shower her with gifts when she left; it was just that, well, Christine's whole family was weeping as if they would never see their only daughter again. Even the servant girl. Zelda doubted she'd hear from the Nagas again, let alone drop by for dinner.

"I'm glad you were up for coming, Christine. I mean, it must have been tough for you to leave so soon," she said.

Christine brushed off a single tear, thrusting her chin up into the air. "Yeah, it's okay. I didn't realize it was going to be so hard to leave them either, otherwise..." She looked out the window, seemingly entranced by a man welding on the side of the road. A group of curious locals surrounded him, despite the sparks flying all around. "Ah, I had to leave sometime, and tomorrow would have been just as hard. Besides, it'll be good to see Bhaktapur before we start teaching. And as my village is like, two or three hours from Kathmandu, I doubt I'll have the chance to see much more of the valley any time soon."

Zelda could feel herself growing red. Was Christine baiting her again? It had been a bone of contention within the group that their upcoming teaching assignments were so wildly different. On the volunteer application form, each volunteer was supposed to indicate their preference for an urban, suburban, or remote teaching post. All four women claimed to have requested a remote assignment, in a rural village.

Ganesh *did* tell them on the first day of classes that nothing had been decided – their placements depended on which families were willing to take the women in. Yet after watching them for two weeks, Ganesh had decided only Christine was sufficiently prepared to live so far away from the country's capital. Sarah, Doris, and Zelda had all been assigned to schools in the Kathmandu Valley, the most urban part of Nepal.

Zelda's new village was only a half-hour bus ride away from the city center. She was pretty pissed off at first – after all, she'd come here to live with a real Nepalese family and have that whole cultural experience, not stay with someone who could swap home decorating tips with her grandmother. But after hearing more about Christine's village, how it was only a few mud houses on a single street with a bus that came around every three days and no one had a telephone or Internet connection, Zelda had to admit that maybe Ganesh was right. She didn't think she could handle living in such an isolated place and being out of touch with her American family and friends for so long. Still, there was no point in Christine rubbing her nose in it.

"Yeah, that's going to be pretty wild. But aren't you a bit scared, living *so* remotely?" she asked.

Christine looked bewildered. "Scared? Why should I be?"

"No, it's just, I mean, you'll be so far away from everything and everyone. And you'll be all by yourself if something goes wrong." Secretly Zelda was quite glad their trusty program coordinator was only a few minutes away by motorbike from her own school.

"People do *live* there. It is a village."

"Yeah, I know, it's just –"

"Zelda," said Christine with attitude, cutting her off, "I *asked* for the most remote village possible. It's all part of my plan to get into UCLA's anthropology program next fall. I figure if I put together a kick-ass travel journal, or write some amazing article about my experiences here, the admissions committee won't be able to say no."

"What do you mean?"

"Just what I said. I want to attend the University of California in Los Angeles. They have, like, one of the best anthro programs on the West Coast! So I figure this is a good way to up my chances of getting in."

"Wow! What a great idea. I never would have thought of that," Zelda responded. Suddenly it didn't seem so unfair that only Christine was assigned to such a remote post. Ganesh must have known what she was up to. Still, her companion didn't have to be such a jerk about it.

"Yeah, well, it was my boyfriend, Chad, who got me thinking about coming to Nepal. He was in Kathmandu two years ago, you know, as part of his master's. He had a budget for six months and all the camera gear he needed to make a documentary about street kids in Thamel. The footage he did get was amazing, really inspirational. But after two months, he had to leave."

"Why?"

Christine sighed heavily and rolled her eyes, as if she was bored with having to repeat the story, yet again. "He befriended a bunch of these homeless children – street kids – and bought them meals and even some clothes, you know, to win their trust so he could film them. A few of the locals got angry – they accused Chad of trying to pimp a couple of the kids out to rich foreigners and even of misusing them himself. They kind of ran Chad out of Nepal."

"That's insane! Does that kind of thing happen here all the time?"

Christine snorted. "How am I supposed to know? It happened to Chad, that's for sure. Man, I've never seen him so scared as when I picked him up from the airport."

"But I don't get it. Why did you want to volunteer here, after everything that happened to your friend?"

"Lots of NGOs are active in Nepal," Christine said with a shrug. "Doing volunteer work here is a great way to build up my contacts. Because of what happened to Chad, I figured if I was going to come to Nepal, it would be better to be associated with a cultural organization right from the start. So nobody gets any funny ideas."

Zelda tried to keep her face from pinching up in disbelief. During their first week of classes, Ganesh had talked a lot about the various nongovernmental organizations working here, many of them American and British in origin. "Sure, I can see that." She was still having trouble believing Christine would want to come here to do research and networking after what had happened to her boyfriend.

Their taxi driver laid on the horn as he tried to move through the beggars and animals blocking the entrance to their hotel's small courtyard. Zelda looked up at the freshly painted, colonial-style hotel she'd checked out of two weeks earlier. She could hardly believe so little time had passed since her arrival in Nepal – their classes had been so intense that it felt like months, not weeks. "Home sweet home," she said.

The women checked back in quickly, dropping their bags on their respective beds before heading back outside. As soon as they were on the hotel's steps, Christine had her map out, orienting herself. She began walking slowly – head down – towards the main road, Zelda tagging along behind. She wished she'd brought a hat; the midday sun was brutal. As she started to automatically turn right, following the normal route to the large central city bus stop just outside Thamel, Christine called her back.

"No, take a left here. The other left! We're going to the *southern* bus depot; see here on the map? That's the X Ganesh made. Hey! Look out for the tempo." Christine grabbed Zelda's tank top, pulling her back from the road just in time. The little car's diesel fumes blackened her face as it sped by.

"Thanks," Zelda mumbled, resolving to get it together. She'd felt like a fumbling idiot ever since she'd picked her fellow volunteer up. At first she'd been pleased when Christine had unexpectedly said she wanted to join her on this day trip. Though she was glad for the company, Zelda was beginning to have second thoughts. Only on the cab ride over did she realize that despite spending two weeks in a classroom with her, she barely knew Christine, or any of the other volunteers for that matter. During their language lessons, there had been no time to really talk. All of their families expected the volunteers to come home right after school, and lunch was usually a rush of sandwiches and feeble attempts to practice their Nepali with each other.

"You okay now? Ready to go?" Christine asked.

"Yeah, sure. I'm right behind you, Chris," she said, wiping the soot off her face and glasses.

"It's *Christine*," the younger woman said, over enunciating her own name.

Zelda could feel herself blushing. Why had she invited this little brat along again? "Sure, *Christine*," she said, waving the imperious girl forward.

The women carefully picked their way through the honking traffic and grazing cattle to the tiny side street marked on Christine's map. A minibus was quickly filling with passengers.

"Is that it?" Zelda asked.

"I guess so, but there's only one way to find out, isn't there?" Christine flashed Zelda a large smile, bowing to let her pass.

She bit her lip, forcing herself to grin back through clenched teeth. She entered the bus first, politely asking the driver in garbled Nepali whether this was the bus to Bhaktapur. He looked at her puzzled, glancing back to his assistant driver for help.

Christine stepped forward, fluently asking the same question, to which the driver immediately responded yes, then smiled warmly and waved them on. Christine paid for the ride, and the pair settled onto the last free bench.

Humiliated, Zelda slid in next to the window. She tried pulling it open, but the handle wouldn't move. The bus seemed pretty full, and she was glad they didn't have to wait around for the next one in the punishing sun. Wiping the sweat off her forehead and neck, she looked over at Christine to see how she was faring, but could see no perspiration whatsoever. Figures, Zelda thought, sweat would be too good for her.

Notebook out, Christine was already scribbling furiously, her long black hair cascading over her bent head. It seemed like the dark-haired vixen was constantly taking notes on everything she saw – and asking a ton of questions – with no sign of shame or embarrassment. She would have loved that salty blood birthday cake, Zelda thought. Still she didn't say anything for fear that Christine might laugh at her. It had taken all of her willpower not to barf over the table when the Nagas served that red jellied mess to her. She didn't want to relive the sensation just for the sake of Christine's submissions packet.

In Zelda's mind, the bus had been full when they got on, but still the driver continued to take on passengers. She glanced around impatiently. Her guidebooks said Bhaktapur attracted far fewer tourists than Kathmandu; by the looks of her fellow passengers and their farm animals, this was true. They had been waiting – no, cooped up – for at least ten minutes in the humid midday sun, and she was starting to worry that she might faint. The combination of hot air and defecating animals was proving to be a lethal combination.

"Do you think the driver's going to leave anytime soon, or is he waiting to fill the roof too?" Zelda chuckled, almost poking Christine in the ribs to get her attention. She stopped herself just in time.

Christine, without taking her eyes off the notebook, whispered back conspiratorially, "Give me a minute, will you? I want to document their styles of clothing and jewelry before the bus starts moving." She smiled slightly and continued sketching. Zelda snuck a peek at her notebook and rolled her eyes. The drawing was as detailed as a photograph. Was there anything Christine wasn't good at?

Zelda looked around with disdain; the aisles *must* be filled to capacity now, she thought. Her view of the door was blocked by a group of Tibetan women with baskets of potatoes strapped to their backs. But still the bus did not move. She couldn't understand what the holdup was. Zelda willed the engines to start. She tugged again at the tiny window next to her, but it still refused to budge. Her long legs were already cramping up, squished into the narrow bench. Christine's feet didn't touch the floor.

Finally, the last three passengers and two more chickens joined the sweaty group. The tiny engine roared to life, and they were off in a stinky flourish. Zelda leaned her head against the window, watching the world drift by. Her seat allowed fantastic views of the rolling fields covering the valley floor, carved up by irrigation troughs and winding footpaths. Colorfully dressed women hacked and pounded on the fertile soil. Frequent stops brought more passengers traveling with livestock aboard. At the height of the journey, Zelda counted forty-six humans, seventeen chickens, and one fidgety goat riding in the Japanese minibus built for twenty. Unfortunately, animal nature got the best of the situation, and too soon the goat tried to eat another traveler's sari. The woman's indignant reaction brought the bus to a halt, ejecting the goat and his angry master.

Zelda giggled at the absurdity of it all, reveling in her regained freedom. After two weeks of carefully planned days, where every minute seemed to be accounted for, she was glad to have some unstructured time for herself and finally have the chance to reflect on all she'd learned, seen, and done.

So far, this bus ride had been one of the most authentic experiences of her trip. Sighing deeply, Zelda finally admitted to herself that this volunteer thing wasn't turning out to be what she'd hoped for. It wasn't that Ganesh or her Nepalese family were cruel to her; in fact they were all really nice, kind people. There was no denying there were many, many differences between Seattle and Kathmandu. But there were so many more similarities to America than she could have imagined.

Everyone in her Nepalese family watched CNN and the BBC and liked to discuss the latest soccer game scores – football here – gains in the stock market, improvements in technologies, and the price of oil. Her mother complained about her husband working late too often, and that her kids watched too much MTV and liked to dress in skimpy clothes. The kids complained their mother was too old-fashioned, wearing western-style clothing around the house to irritate her, then changing into traditional garments before going outside. Her husband said almost nothing, spending most of his time reading his newspapers and popping indigestion tablets.

It felt too familiar, too much like home. Zelda groaned in frustration. She had traveled how many thousands of miles only to find that – despite a few obvious cultural differences and language – people in the suburbs of Kathmandu pretty much had the same worries and fears as people in

Seattle and probably the rest of the world too.

"There. Done for now," Christine announced triumphantly, returning her notebook to her daypack. "See those girls up there? No...in the front row." She pointed without shame.

Zelda whispered, "Yes; now sit down."

"They remind me so much of my little Nepalese sisters. Look at their haircuts – just adorable." Christine stared off into the distance, obviously trying to hold back a flash flood of tears. "I'm sure the next family's going to be great too. It's just, I feel as if I made a connection with them, and I can't imagine any family being nicer to me."

"Yeah, you seemed pretty smitten with each other."

Christine ignored Zelda's sarcasm, rubbing at her eyes. "Right, and yours? Were you happy with the Nagas?"

"Yeah, they were pretty cool. Maybe not as 'hands-on' as your family, but then they were busy with their jobs and all the festivals."

Christine's face shone with happiness. "Ah, the festivals. I must have taken a thousand pictures in the past two weeks. My mother was really good about explaining everything to me. She knows I'm an anthropologist."

"Studying to be one."

"Yeah, well, I've almost got my bachelor's. Anyway, the whole family took the time to explain the intricate details of all the rituals to me. In Nepali, of course. I mean, it's all for my research. I even got to help make some of the pickled vegetables and smear colored yak-poop on the house."

Zelda's blood boiled. Christine's experience sounded like everything she'd hoped for. Why Christine and not her? Zelda had enjoyed staying with the Nagas, and participating – peripherally – in their celebrations, even though her presence was pretty much ignored. Not that she was ungrateful. Granted, most of the time she'd been there, the Nagas' house had been full of cousins, aunts, and grandparents who regarded her as little more than a temporary curiosity. Nobody took the time to explain what was happening during the various festivals and ceremonies, nor did they show much interest in learning more about her or the West. And their English was perfect, even the youngest girls'. Zelda had very little to teach them.

She kept reminding herself that she was going to be placed outside of the city in a small village; there she would certainly find some children to help. And the festival season was long from over. So what if her teaching post wasn't as remote as Christine's? Her next family was bound to be more traditional. Maybe she should pretend to be an anthropologist, like Christine. Ganesh wouldn't have to know.

Their bus was slowing down. Looking out the window, Zelda saw that the mud huts and fields were giving way to multistory buildings. They must be entering Bhaktapur. A few minutes later, their bus stopped at an unmarked corner of an enormous parking lot. She made a mental note of the location and followed her companion outside.

"Crazy bus ride, eh?" Zelda said, flashing her traveling companion a wide grin.

"Yeah, sure." Christine was already pulling out a map, all business. "Look, if we follow this road –" She gestured towards a small hill in front of them. "– we should come out at the main city gate." She started up the cobblestone street before Zelda could respond.

A few minutes later, they were paying their way into the historic city center. After entering through an ornately decorated gate, the women stood in awe, silenced by the delicate beauty of the buildings surrounding them. Zelda's guidebooks hadn't lied to her; Bhaktapur was indeed a wild departure from Patan and Kathmandu. Fanciful spires, grand statues, and new mythology surrounded them. There were hardly any other people walking around, and no screaming touts or pushy blanket merchants in sight.

"Which way should we go?" Zelda whispered, letting Christine take the lead.

"That white pillar-looking temple – the one with the staircase – looks pretty cool. Let's check it out."

The women climbed five flights of steps to the top of a three-tiered temple. It was built out of a hard white stone she didn't recognize. They leaned on the railing of a small walled-in terrace, enjoying the commanding view. The Ganesh Himalaya range loomed just above the city skyline, the snow-capped peaks shimmering like a desert mirage. She closed her eyes and breathed in deeply, letting her lungs fill with the smog-free air.

Suddenly the shrieks of an angry mob roared up from the staircase behind them. Zelda searched for an escape route, but – too late – they were quickly engulfed by thirty screaming teenage girls dressed in identical blue-and-white uniforms. Camera flashes came from all sides, blinding the disoriented westerners.

Two smiling, well-dressed men fought through the mass of girls until they reached Zelda and Christine. In broken English, they explained they were on a school-sponsored cultural excursion to Nepal. They were

Indians, living just across the border, and the men were the girls' teachers. Could they take a photo please? The two volunteers were rapidly surrounded by a wall of smiling faces. The teachers took picture after picture, until all of the girls got a photo of themselves with the foreigners. Between snaps they would ask, "Where is your father?" "Where is your brother?" They couldn't understand why these women were walking around in public without a male escort.

As the last flash triggered, the giggling schoolgirls waved once again and screamed in chorus, "Bye, bye," disappearing as quickly as they'd come. Zelda and Christine sat in silence for a full minute before realizing that neither woman had gotten a picture of the schoolchildren for themselves.

"Wow. I wonder whether our kids will be anything like them."

"I hope not. They all seemed to speak English pretty well," Zelda grumbled.

"Did you read any of those books on teaching yet?" Christine asked.

"Most of them," Zelda snapped back. The books Ganesh had lent her were very theoretical and of little help, yet she was not about to tell Christine the truth. She was getting tired of feeling belittled by her fellow volunteer, especially one who was at least three years younger than her. "I've gotten some good tips out of them," she lied.

She wanted nothing more than to spill her guts, tell Christine how petrified she was by the thought of standing in front of a group of schoolchildren. But she couldn't. Truth be told, she was kind of afraid of Christine; she always seemed so at ease with herself and everything happening around her. Zelda wished she could be as confident and self-assured as her younger companion. But these were traits she clearly lacked, and being with Christine only reminded her of all of her shortcomings.

Hoping to change the subject, Zelda asked, "Do you want to get something to eat at that cafe?" She pointed to her left, towards a large collection of tables.

"Sure."

The two Americans headed back down the steep staircase.

Their post-lunch ramblings around Bhaktapur brought Christine and Zelda through a plethora of mazelike squares and mysterious compounds. Everywhere she looked, worshippers were streaming in and out of religious complexes, many with offerings of rice, tika powder, and palm fronds.

Zelda darted this way and that, snaking through the cobblestoned streets and small alleyways of the inner city. Rounding a darkened corner, she almost trampled a foot-tall clay water jug. After stopping to regain her balance and letting her eyes adjust to the difference in light, she made out thousands of similar pots drying in an enormous courtyard.

From behind her, Christine squealed in delight. "Fantastic! I was hoping to get a shot of the potters square. Zelda, stand next to that jug on your right, so I can get some perspective on it."

Zelda did as she was told, careful not to touch the drying earthenware. She'd never seen anything quite like it. Seemingly thousands of pots, jugs and canisters made of clay were drying in the blazing sun. A few lone Nepalese men sat hunched over in the middle of the long rows of pottery, presumably to stop thieves or ne'er-do-wells.

Christine amused herself by taking photo after photo of the clay-filled square, before engaging their creators. Zelda priced a few pots but decided against buying such a delicate and impractical memento. Instead, she popped into a music store and bought a few recordings of local singers. Back outside, she saw that Christine was still absorbed with the pottery. Zelda ambled over to her on sore feet, worn out from walking around all day.

"Hey, Christine? I'm thinking about heading back to Kathmandu. I'd really like to take a shower before we go out to eat later."

"Okay, sure. Tell you what, I want to talk with these guys some more about their throwing technique. I'll meet you back at the hotel later, then we can go and eat." Christine dismissed Zelda with a wave, turning back to the potters before she could answer.

Zelda was mortified. How could Christine do that to her? They had come together, hadn't they? Her companion's total ease with her foreign surroundings only amplified Zelda's feelings of inadequacy. She didn't want to go back to Kathmandu on her own, but she didn't want to hang out with a bunch of old men she couldn't understand, either. "Sure, no problem. I mean, I invited you along for the day, right? Fine. I'll see you later then, enjoy your chat," she said, already walking away.

Christine called after her, "You know how to get back to the bus stop from here, right?"

"Of course I do. See you back at the hotel in a couple of hours." Zelda's cheeks were burning; she didn't bother to turn around. In point of fact, she had no idea where she was, or how to get back to the bus stop. Because Christine had been so keen to lead the way, she had not paid attention to where they were heading. Feeling sorry for herself, Zelda wound her way back through the vast touristic center of Bhaktapur towards the main gate. After a few frustrating wrong turns, she finally spotted the large parking lot where their bus had dropped them off.

She was almost at the bus stop when she heard the sobs. A girl with red ringlets was sitting cross-legged on the ground, crying as if the world had ended. Only a few weeks ago, Zelda would have turned tail and run at the sound of those tears; she couldn't deal with overly emotional people. But these weeks of freedom had softened her heart – a smidgen anyway. She did her best to help. "What's wrong with you?" she asked.

"It's all gone!" the girl cried, mascara streaks running down her cheeks. She couldn't have been more than eighteen years old.

"Did you lose your wallet or something?"

The redhead shook her head no.

"Did you get robbed?" Zelda asked.

The intensity of the wailing increased dramatically as the girl nodded her head and held up her backpack. An enormous slit on one side exposed the now empty inner pockets.

"Oh, no. What did they take?"

"EVERYTHING! My wallet, my camera, even my postcards! Now I can't even get back to Kathmandu!"

"Hang on." Zelda dug a few hundred rupees out of her wallet. "Here."

"Oh my God, thank you! Thanks so much!" the redhead sobbed, ringlets shaking. Before Zelda could react, the girl was up off the ground, hugging her.

She stood still stiffly as the girl embraced her. After the younger woman finally released her, Zelda mumbled, "Come on, it's not that much. Just relax. Is anything else missing?"

The girl straightened up and began rummaging through her few remaining possessions. "Let's see. My passport, all my cash, my daddy's credit cards, driver's license…oh no! My lucky pen! Can you believe they got my lucky pen too?"

"Well, I guess it wasn't so lucky." The girl shot her a dirty look before Zelda continued, "Look, you can go to the embassy tomorrow and get a new passport. I take it you left some money in your hotel room?"

"Some traveler's checks."

"See? There. You'll be fine. The passport might take a few days, but everything's going to be all right. Just relax."

"But my daddy's going to kill me!"

"Make sure to tell him that they used a really big knife to cut into your backpack and he'll be thrilled you're alive."

"Oh yeah." The girl's snuffling subsided dramatically. An awkward silence took its place.

"I'm Zelda," she said, squatting down and sticking out her hand to the younger girl.

"Julie."

"So how long have you been in Nepal, Julie?"

"Three months now."

"Wow, that's a long time. Have you been trekking the whole time… or?" Zelda wasn't sure what the "or" could be. Julie sure didn't strike her as the type who would have stayed in Nepal for so long. More like someone who'd brag about going to Fort Lauderdale for spring break.

"Oh, I haven't done much trekking. I've been volunteering as a teacher in a village on the outskirts of Kathmandu for the past two months."

Zelda's jaw dropped. She could not believe her ears. *This* blathering girl had been a volunteer teacher! Zelda snorted. If Julie could do it, so could she. A wave of confidence flowed over her; Zelda felt herself relaxing for the first time in weeks. She had so many questions about teaching, daily life in Nepal, the families and customs – what luck it was to run into this girl. "Me too! I mean, I just finished my Nepali classes yesterday. I haven't been to my school yet. I move there tomorrow. Wow, what a coincidence. What was your family like? Did you speak Nepali with them or English? Did your school's director give you lesson plans, or did you have to make your own?" Before she could get the interrogation underway, the girl broke down again.

"I was supposed to be leaving in a week!" Julie wailed, throwing her now-empty backpack onto the ground. "I was just doing some sightseeing before I went back. I've been so busy with the volunteer program, I didn't have time to see Bhaktapur earlier. Damn it! The embassy better be able to get me a passport! Do you think they can get me one this week?"

Zelda patted her knee awkwardly. "I have no idea, but I'm sure they can arrange something for you."

Unfortunately Julie – despite Zelda's cautious questioning – did not seem to be in the mood to elaborate on her recent experiences. She sat sniffling loudly, dabbing at her nose until the bus arrived a few minutes later. Afraid to provoke another bout of tears, Zelda didn't push.

After the bus's passengers disembarked, the thirty-odd persons now waiting to board converged on the small door *en masse*, along with Zelda and Julie. The westerners pushed their way into the roomier back and braced for the bumpy ride. Zelda wondered whether her underarm deodorant was still working but realized that even if it was, it definitely could not freshen up the poop-scented air.

They were just beginning to hit twenty miles an hour – cruising speed in Nepal – when the screech of rusty brakes brought the bus to a halt, throwing them all forward. The mother goddess Laxmi – disguised as a dirty Brahmin cow – had wandered onto the highway, the only road connecting Bhaktapur with Kathmandu. And it was not getting off. Oblivious to the many auto and truck horns bleating their disapproval, the cow sat down directly in the middle of the two-lane road and calmly began chewing its cud.

When no one sprang into action, Zelda asked in too-loud English, "Why doesn't someone push it off the highway?" She assumed wrongly no one but Julie would understand her.

"No one wants to hurt it or even be suspected of hurting it," Julie responded.

"What do you mean?"

"Twenty years!" called out a Nepalese teenager from the front of the bus. "Twenty years for the death of a cow! It is only fifteen for a man!" he cried.

Zelda went white as she remembered herself pounding on the side of one a few weeks ago. She knew they were holy, but jeez. Wiping the sweat off her forehead, she looked back down the narrow highway and saw that cars, buses, and trucks were now backed up for several villages. The honking and the heat finally tried even the patience of the Nepalese. A makeshift road crew of locals took it upon themselves to direct traffic around the sedentary dairy factory, allowing their bus to slowly resume its journey home.

She gazed out the window with new interest. Meeting Julie had revitalized her spirits and alleviated some of her worries, at least temporarily. If that whiny cheerleader could survive as a teacher for two months, so could she. No problem. She relaxed into her seat, a smile of satisfaction crossing her face. For the first time in weeks, Zelda was looking forward to tomorrow, the day she would become a real volunteer.

CHAPTER SEVENTEEN

Tommy hit refresh. The page was taking forever to load. "Don't you have a faster connection available? Another computer somewhere maybe?"

The clerk shook his head and returned to his newspaper. Tommy dabbed at his forehead; whoo-hee, was he sweating buckets. He cursed the ceiling fan's inability to circulate the thick humid air, then the Internet cafe's lousy servers.

Throwing a few baht on the counter, he slunk back outside. The slight breeze made the sun bearable. He pushed a few lost-looking tourists out of the way and walked farther down Khao San Road. It was a madhouse here – nothing at all like his villa in Krabi. Every centimeter of the street was covered in market stalls and food carts, with seemingly millions of smelly, sweaty hippies stumbling between. The smell of frying curries and white men's body odor was overwhelming. He needed a shower – just walking through the sticky crowd made him want to scream.

He wished he knew someone he could talk to about this stuff. None of his hick friends back home would have the first clue. And the people he knew here, well, he couldn't discuss his plans with them, now, could he? Fingering the business card in his pocket calmed him slightly. That jewelry shop had been a sign; of that, Tommy was sure. He may just have found a way to earn enough to retire early, if he played his cards right.

He frowned, slowing his pace as he pondered how much money he would need to get himself set up somewhere new. He had to find out more about the diamonds' worth before he dared consider the next step. It would have to be the score of a lifetime to make it worth looking over his shoulders for the rest of his days. Tommy knew Harim was one of the most powerful and well-connected smugglers in the Golden Triangle, with friends in every backwater village and town, no matter how far from civilization they might seem to be. He also knew Harim had a way of making problems disappear, permanently.

Tommy forced himself to look carefully at everything that was on offer, searching for a faster Internet connection. A large yellow sign blinking neon promises caught his eye. *Finally*. He rushed inside.

"High-speed Internet my ass," he muttered a few minutes later. But at least the pages were loading. He'd had Harim's stones in his hands so many times he could compare them to the online examples with an expert eye. He scrolled through several sites explaining how diamonds were categorized and appraised, depending on the quality, size, and cut. What caught his eye were the commission rates; they were shocking. That is, it was as if they were stealing from him. Tommy chuckled at the notion. Taking all of those fees incurred at legit shops into account, maybe he would be smarter to sell a few stones here in Bangkok, before flying on to destinations unknown. Thai jewelers were bound to be more flexible than western ones, he reckoned. Tommy tapped his chin, considering. Either way, from what he was seeing online, netting one hundred thousand for the whole lot wouldn't be a stretch. And it wasn't as if he'd actually paid anything for them.

Tommy leaned back in the chair and suppressed the urge to chuckle out loud. One hundred thousand would be more than enough to set up a new life somewhere cheap and close to a beach. As various exotic destinations popped into his head, Tommy's grin disappeared. He still had to work out how he was going to slip past The Greek. It would have to be the perfect getaway. Harim was smart, really smart. One of those clever guys who seemed to just *get* things. Tommy usually steered clear of guys like him; they were always making fun of him behind his back. But not Harim, up until now anyway. The Greek had handled him with more respect than anyone else in his life. At least that's what Tommy had thought, up until yesterday.

He would have to cover his tracks. But how? Say he was robbed on the way to the airport, or in his hotel room? But how could he *prove* to The Greek that the jewels had been stolen? He couldn't file a police report, now, could he? He'd have to find a way to make Harim believe him. He could get into a bar fight, get himself punched in the face, all black and blue, then say he interrupted the burglar as he was fleeing. The Greek would *have* to believe him then, at least at first. But Harim wasn't known for his empathy; would he take out his anger on Tommy anyway?

No, better yet, he could say the stones were confiscated by a greedy Nepalese border guard at the Kathmandu airport. He'd call Harim all panicky and scared out of his mind. The Greek would have no choice but to trust him. If Tommy pulled that trick in Bangkok, Harim would be sure to find out right away that he was lying. He would have to fly to Kathmandu as expected and then get the first chicken bus to India he could find. From New Delhi he could fly just about anywhere. Harim couldn't have connections all over the world ready to act at a moment's notice. Or could he? It was a risk Tommy would have to take. He just needed a few hours' head start, that's all. After that, he'd be free and clear.

His course of action decided, it was as if a weight had been lifted from his shoulders. Tommy knew he should be scared; he *was* in way over his head, but it all seemed so fucking James Bond, it actually gave him a hard-on. Tommy smiled, leaning back in his stool, and folded his arms behind his head. With the money he'd already saved, plus this score, he'd be set for *years*. But if he did this, if he went through with it, he could never come back to Thailand or anywhere in Southeast Asia. Never ever again. So where should he go? He'd heard a lot about Costa Rica and Belize. Both countries sounded like pretty big tourist traps, nice and cheap. Tommy could blend in there; he was sure of it.

Chapter Eighteen

Zelda winced as she fastened the last of forty hooks and eyes holding her tight-fitting bodice in place. Slipping on a handful of thin metal bracelets, she rechecked her sari in the floor-length mirror, smiling in satisfaction. Having spent the past two days practicing how to get the damn thing on, she was pleased to see her efforts had paid off. All that was missing were the henna tattoos and nose piercing, and then she could pass for one of those women in Bollywood films.

Her costume was just an undersized tube top fastened around her modest breasts, with a two-meter-long strip of fabric wrapped intricately around her waist. Luckily it came with a petticoat, in case the material came loose. The exposed midriff made her so self-conscious it had taken her a week to work up the courage to try the thing on. Normally she would never wear something so skimpy and revealing, but here it was totally normal and even expected. Not that she would ever be confused for a real Nepalese person, of course. But she wanted to at least try to look the part.

With her sari finally in place, there was nothing left to do but go downstairs and begin her first day as a teacher. She was so nervous she could hardly sit still, yet her legs refused to move towards the door. She'd been visualizing herself standing in front of her first class for so long, she could hardly believe the moment was finally upon her.

Her mind was abuzz with questions: What if her students ignored her? Or, worse, couldn't understand her? She had no real experience in dealing with kids, the closest being a yearly visit to her now five-year-old nephew in San Francisco. None of her friends or immediate colleagues had babies, at least not that she knew of.

Sure, she had given plenty of in-house training seminars and workshops before, but those had been to her peers. Her closest brush with teaching strangers had been leading a half-day seminar for senior citizens on how to use the Internet, part of her company's "make a difference" day. And that had gone horribly wrong. If she had no patience with old people, how in the hell was she going to be tolerant and loving towards *children*?

Zelda sat cross-legged on her bed, extended her arms, and touched her thumbs and forefingers together, while whispering "ohm, ohm, ohm, ohm" over and over again until her breathing subsided. Only last week, as a special surprise, Ganesh had treated all the volunteers to a meditation session at a yoga center in the city. Despite the fact their teacher was from upstate New York and *not* Nepalese, it had been pretty educational. She continued the breathing exercises, circling the air through her nostrils as she tried to remember why she was here in Nepal – to discover her true self while helping others develop and grow. It was either teaching English or building houses, and God knows she couldn't drive a nail without taking her thumb off.

Wiping the perspiration off her upper lip, Zelda told herself if she didn't get down to the courtyard, Headmaster Padel would drag her downstairs, kicking and screaming, if necessary. Not wishing to cause a scene, she finally turned the door handle and exited the room, accepting her immediate fate. *After all,* Zelda's subconscious reminded her, *you wanted to do this.*

She flip-flopped her way down the short flight of stairs to the muddy courtyard below. Children were lined up in long rows, openly staring at the newest arrival and whispering amongst themselves. They were all dressed in crimson sweaters and blue slacks or skirts.

The rest of the staff was standing to one side of the courtyard, gathered around the headmaster. With their bowed heads and intense expressions, Zelda was momentarily reminded of an American football team, huddling together before the final play. The headmaster, tall for Nepal, towered over the others. She straightened her back and made a beeline towards him. They'd met briefly yesterday, and it had not gone well. Mr. Padel made it painfully clear to both Zelda and the school's owner that he was not pleased to receive yet another volunteer who would only be around for a short while. She bristled with indignation when she heard this – she was giving up two months of her life to teach these children English. The least he could do was act as if he was grateful.

She cleared her throat loudly to announce her arrival, hoping Mr. Padel would acknowledge her. No chance. She knew she should speak Nepali with him, but her mind went blank as soon as she caught sight of his sneering expression. She sputtered out a few random phrases before finally reverting to English. "Good morning, Mr. Padel. How are you doing today?" she asked.

A few of the other teachers clapped their hands under their chins and bowed at her, calling out, *"Namaste."* Headmaster Padel finally turned to face her, cutting her off from the others with his large frame. He looked down at Zelda with pure, unbridled contempt. "Good day. Today you will start by teaching group three," he hissed.

Before she could ask where group three met or what exactly she was supposed to teach them today, he marched away from her, towards the center of the courtyard. He clapped his hands together loudly three times, signaling to the children that it was time to begin. Immediately a hush fell over the small courtyard. Mr. Padel spoke clearly and succinctly. Zelda thought she understood him to say, "My dear students. It is a delight that you are returning to us after the Tikhar holidays. We will soon start our classes, but first let us welcome a new teacher to our school, Miss Zelda Richardson." He turned towards her, smiling radiantly.

Zelda was a bit confused; in front of his students, the man's expression and attitude softened considerably. He seemed glad to have her here. At hearing her name, she waved eagerly to the students lined up before her, unsure whether she should try to say something or not. She got out a pretty decent "*namaste*" before Mr. Padel clapped his hands two times, dismissing them all. She tried not to look offended.

The children dispersed immediately, filing into their respective classrooms. Their teachers trailed behind. A series of mud-brick rooms covered by tin sheets were built around the courtyard. Two large openings were cut into one side of each room. In Zelda's mind, doors and windows should have filled the gaps in the walls, though she didn't see any hinges or other signs that the builders were even intending on finishing the openings off. Despite the sweltering heat of the October sun, she shivered, trying to imagine how it was going to be teaching here in the middle of December, wrapped in a bedsheet and exposed to the elements.

Crammed inside were twenty desks and a blackboard mounted to the wall next to the entrance. The gaps in the walls let in enough light so they didn't need electric lamps to see, not that Zelda saw any light bulbs or switches. Though most of the houses in her new village were wired for electricity, it was anything but reliable. In most rooms hung both oil and electric lamps.

Zelda had been in her new village for two days now, yet she still wasn't entirely sure what she should do or say once she found her classroom. Last night, in a moment of desperation, she'd tried to ask her new family what was expected of her as a teacher. After all, her new "father," Mr. Rana, did own the school. But their English and her Nepali didn't allow an extensive briefing. She tried not to dwell on the Ranas too long; she needed more time to get to know her new family better, and wanted to remain as open-minded as possible before passing judgment. They seemed like lovely people, a big family "blessed with" six girls and three boys, according to her new father. Their house was gigantic, even by American standards: ten bedrooms, four bathrooms, and huge terraces spread amongst four levels. The kitchen and shower area took up the top floor.

In their courtyard was the school. Her Nepalese father had founded it years ago but now spent most of his time in the city, generating new business contacts and applying for subsidies. At least that's what he told the family. Zelda swore she smelled whiskey on his breath when he came home last night, although drinking alcohol was strictly forbidden by their religion.

If only she could speak Nepali better. Why didn't her first family talk in their own language with her more often? They knew she only had two weeks to learn a whole new way of thinking, speaking, and even writing. How could they have done that to her, knowing she was here to help?

She'd only been with the Ranas for forty-eight hours now, but she could already tell that her language skills – or lack thereof – were going to cause problems in her new household. Only the father and oldest daughter spoke a decent amount of English, but they were hardly around or available. Mr. Rana went to the city every day, seven days a week, and only came home for dinner. And his oldest daughter, Reecha, was busy planning her wedding, meaning she and her mother spent most of their time bantering around scraps of paper and fabric, making lists and arguing. *For some things, you don't need a translator*, Zelda thought.

The rest of the family's English was almost nonexistent, save the odd phrase or word, and they were clearly not pleased that Zelda wasn't able to communicate better. Her new brothers and sisters chatted to her the first night, waiting expectantly for a reaction, only to shake their heads in disappointment when it didn't come. She did try her best to talk with them, but her Nepali was so basic and halting it was a big waste of time for everybody.

Zelda cringed at the thought of living here for the next two months, not being able to hold a real conversation with anyone. The other volunteers were placed too far away to meet up, not that she'd be allowed to leave the house unescorted anyway. She sighed in frustration. Teaching would at least give her something to do, other than dwell on her shortcomings. Today *had* to go well; it was the only way she could prove to her new family and Headmaster Padel that she did have some worth. She would redeem herself in front of the classroom and tonight surprise her family by giving them the gifts she'd brought from America. Surely the presents would help make everything okay again. Hopefully it would loosen Headmaster Padel up too; after all, one of the gifts was textbooks for the school. Ganesh had brought her precious box over on his motorcycle yesterday. Who knew? Maybe her new father and Mr. Padel would be so grateful they would name the school library after her.

Zelda spotted Headmaster Padel walking across the empty courtyard towards his office. The rest of the teachers and students were already in their classrooms. She ran up to his side and placed her hand lightly on his upper arm, immediately regretting it. Mr. Padel stopped in his tracks and threw his shoulder forward, releasing her grip. Zelda could feel herself going crimson. This was *not* how she wanted to begin.

"Sorry. I just wondered which class was mine?" she asked.

"Oh? Did you not understand my instructions?" He smiled sweetly down at her.

Anger welled up inside. She so wanted to slap that malicious grin off his face, but Zelda pushed her indignation down, resolving to stay calm. Her eight weeks of teaching were just beginning; now was not the time to pick a fight with her new boss.

Zelda tried to laugh off his comment. "Yes, well, my Nepali is obviously not that great – yet. Would you mind telling me in English what it is that you'd like me to do today?" she asked politely, silently resolving to spend more time studying her Nepali workbooks.

Headmaster Padel pointed towards the third room on his right. "There. You will teach them – group three – English today. Each day you will teach a different group. Tomorrow it will be group five, and the next day group four. Yes?" He practically spat the words at her, before striding off towards his office.

She started to follow – *how dare he talk to her like that!* – but forced herself to veer off towards her classroom.

"Okay, great," she yelled after him, as he slammed his office door shut. *It would be nice if you could at least show me where the lesson books were,* she wanted to add. Or how long the classes were. Or what exactly she was supposed to do. Her eagerness to save the world one child at a time evaporated in that instant. Why wasn't he the slightest bit thankful to have some extra help for a few months? He couldn't really expect her to stay here forever, teaching for free. Ever so briefly, she considered leaving – walking back to Kathmandu and catching the next plane home. But after all these months of preparations and boastful speeches, she couldn't give up now, even if she really wanted to. She could never face her family and friends again. No, she would have to grin and bear it. *It's only two months,* she reminded herself, *and if Julie could do it, so can you!*

Taking a deep breath, Zelda stepped gingerly into her first class. Eleven wide-eyed children stared back at her. She was shocked to see they were still very little, or at least smaller than she expected eight-year-olds to be. She opened her mouth to speak, but no sound came out. She looked around the room anxiously, finally fixating on a broken piece of chalk. Picking it up, Zelda bounced it in her hand a few times, hoping her actions would give her the allure of authority. She wrote her name in block letters across the top of the blackboard before twirling to face her students, grinning like an idiot.

"Hello, class. My name is Zelda." She spoke slowly and concisely, pointing towards the blackboard with the chalk. "Z – E – L – D – A." She smiled at her name, then at the children. "Why don't we start today by writing our names on the chalkboard?"

Excited murmurs escaped from the children.

"Okay, who wants to begin?"

Silence. The children were looking at their desks, the ceiling, or each other, anywhere but towards the front of the classroom.

"Okay, you there." She pointed to a little boy in the front row. Smiling kindly at him, Zelda softened her voice. "Why don't you begin?" she asked.

He stared at his new teacher blankly.

She wondered whether they could even understand her. Since she'd entered the room, none of the children had uttered a word. Zelda wanted to pull the boy out of his chair and escort him to the chalkboard, but after this morning's incident with Mr. Padel, she was afraid to touch the child. Instead, she mimed the boy rising and writing his name on the board. "You can write your name in Nepali if you want," she added, performing the pantomime once more.

The boy rose slowly, clearly an unwilling victim. She wondered whether this was just a show for the others or whether kids always acted like this. The other children began giggling. Zelda shushed them, refocusing her attention on the boy. She gave him a piece of chalk. "Just your first name. You can do it," she whispered, urging him on.

With slow and careful movements, the boy wrote his name on the board in the beautiful Nepali script that Zelda still could not read properly.

"Okay, great! That's fantastic!" She stared at his name, trying to decipher it, but to no avail. After a moment's silence, she asked, "Can you

116

say your name out loud for me?"

"Barun," muttered the boy, staring at the dusty tip of his black shoe.

"Okay, B – A – A – R – U – N. Like that?" She sounded it out, writing in block letters on the board next to the Nepali script.

The boy studied her handiwork for a moment before crossing out the second *A*. "Barun," said the boy, in a clear strong voice.

Zelda felt an enormous swell of pride rush through her. She'd done it. She had told this boy to write his name on the board, and he had understood her. She wanted to run up to the rooftop terrace and scream across the valley, "I can do this! I can teach!" She started to hug Barun, but he recoiled too quickly, slipping out of her embrace and running back to his seat. Zelda didn't care; she *knew* she had made a breakthrough, had somehow reached this child. Her student. Now she just had to repeat the same gesture with the other ten. Trying to hide her excitement, she thanked Barun and asked the next pupil to step up to the blackboard.

Slowly – very slowly – Zelda began to get a better idea of her students and their names. Their body language and theatrics gave clues as to who the class clowns were, and who took the lesson seriously. After she'd written out the eleventh name in English, she stepped back and looked at the blackboard with enormous satisfaction, positively beaming. She quickly wrote the names of her pupils down in her own notebook, her hand shaking with excitement.

She glanced at her watch, assuming they had been at this for hours. She tapped on the glass, puzzled. The hands were still moving. Only twenty minutes had gone by. And she still had no idea how long her class was supposed to last, or what the lesson plan for the day should have been. She looked around the room for clues, realizing for the first time that none of her students had textbooks; at least none were out on their desks.

Going to Headmaster Padel was not an option. Considering his reaction this morning, she'd have to get friendly with a few of the other teachers. But for now, she would have to do some improvising. Should she teach them to sing a song or play a game, like Ganesh suggested? She didn't need a book for that. Zelda tried desperately to recall the exact words to a few campfire songs she'd learned as a child, but the rhymes escaped her. And teaching them to hum the melodies was pointless. What games could they play? Hangman or tic-tac-toe would be pretty difficult with eleven kids. She racked her brain for a few more minutes, but the pressure was too great. Her mind remained blank.

With little other choice, Zelda turned to her pupils, "Okay, kids – I mean, students – what should we do now?"

CHAPTER NINETEEN

"Hey, it's The Greek!" Tommy yelled automatically, immediately regretting his choice of words. Luckily the singular guest on the hibiscus-lined terrace – a deeply tanned man wearing a silk shirt and shorts – only flinched slightly, but otherwise showed no sign of recognition. He seemed to be engrossed in a local newspaper, designer sunglasses holding back his long, dark wavy hair.

As Tommy weaved through the tables, he called out again, "Hey Harim! How are you doing?"

The man's chiseled jaw contracted slightly as Tommy approached his table. He glanced again at the front page, smiling as he closed up the newspaper and folded it in half, carefully placing it on the edge of the table. Tommy gulped when he saw the headline on the front page. Another dead tourist found in a container ship that had departed from Bangkok Port only two weeks ago. Was that why Harim was smiling? He had once hinted how he took care of those who dared cheat him, but Tommy was still not sure whether Harim had been boasting or making empty threats. He never wanted to find out.

"I'm doing fine, and yourself?" Harim said. His deep voice still held traces of a faint Mediterranean accent.

"Good, man. Great, actually. You know me, right?" Tommy replied, careful to keep his carefree attitude in place and not think about what Harim would do to him if he ever found out what he was planning.

Harim chuckled.

Tommy grinned broadly. "Mind if I join you?"

The older man pointed at the chair across from him. "Please, sit."

"So how are you doing? Just chilling in your penthouse? Or do you, like, go on vacation now and then?"

"I enjoy myself, don't you worry. The more important question is, how are you doing? Are you still enjoying being in sunny Thailand instead of shivering your balls off in Toronto?"

"You betcha. This beats a Canadian winter any day. My friends would be really jealous if they could see me now!"

"Didn't you say a few of your friends were coming to visit, last time we talked?"

"Sure, of course. The whole gang's been out to see me," Tommy lied without blinking an eye. Since he'd fled Canada, none of his so-called friends or family had bothered to email or call, let alone visit. "I meant the last place. Man, that villa on Princess Beach was the bomb! Gorgeous girls everywhere, I tell you what."

"Excellent." Harim grinned broadly, exposing model-perfect teeth. "Glad to hear you're still enjoying the good life." The smile dropped as the crackle of branches disturbed their conversation. Something or someone was rustling around in the shrubbery behind them. Harim tensed up, twisting automatically towards the source of the noise. Two broad men in Hawaiian shirts appeared from behind the bushes, drinks in hand. Harim's left eyebrow shot up.

One of the men called out, "Dropped my sunglasses in the hedge."

Harim relaxed visibly and turned back to Tommy, as if nothing had happened. "Are you going back to Krabi, after your next run?"

"Naw. I mean, it *was* going great until these sorority bitches showed up. Rich daddies, I guess. Anyway, they kind of spoiled the authentic sphere, know what I mean?"

Harim smiled; Tommy could see he understood. "So I'm kind of between pads at the moment. I was thinking about checking out some of the islands on the east coast when I get back. Maybe Ko Tao or Ko Samui. The place I got in Bangkok is a dive, but who cares, right? I'm not planning on being there long any-hoo." He winked conspiratorially. He had to make sure Harim thought he was coming back to Thailand right after his next delivery, just as he'd done the past nine times.

"I'm glad to hear things are going well for you." Harim motioned towards his newspaper. "I just read that the weather conditions in Nepal are perfect for trekking right now. I've booked you an open-ended return ticket, so you can stay as long as you want. You leave in three days. Come back when you are ready. You know how to reach me." In one fluid motion, Harim inched the newspaper closer to Tommy and raised his iced coffee to his lips.

Tommy could only watch in awe and admiration; maybe one day he would be so smooth. "Okay, sure. Thanks, man," he answered as enthusiastically as he could manage. Hiking? Please. He'd rather spend his time on a warm beach, surrounded by big-breasted women and drinking Sea Breezes. During his past runs to Kathmandu, Tommy had shut himself up in his hotel room and smoked endless chillums of hash until he caught the next plane back. Good. It didn't matter what kind of ticket Harim booked for him; he wouldn't be using it anyway.

Harim grinned, clearly pleased. "See you in three days?"

"Definitely," Tommy said, winking with his whole face. He stood up quickly, resisted the urge to call the older man by his nickname. After Harim had taken the time to explain to him how offensive it was to call a Turkish man "The Greek," Tommy didn't want to make that mistake again.

He took two steps away from the table before doubling back to grab the newspaper. His airline tickets and five-hundred-dollar advance would be taped to the sports section. Tommy could see Harim shaking his head slightly as he walked back towards Khao San Road.

CHAPTER TWENTY

Surfacing quickly, Ian pulled off his mask and snorkel, sucking in the salty ocean air. Kicking with his fins, he surveyed the rocky bay surrounding him. It was so peaceful here. The ocean was like a warm bathtub, the sky above a soft field of blue. The only sounds – sea birds and waves crashing on the barnacle-covered rocks.

Even though he was only a few meters from the shoreline, no other swimmers were in sight. From his vantage point, he could see a few of the many beachfront terraces, most filled with pancake-eating tourists. The rugged shoreline was covered with giant ferns and hibiscus bushes competing for light under the dense palm groves. The trees bent and turned every which way, their roots held in place by soil the color of drying blood.

Ian chuckled with delight, confident he had made the right decision in leaving Nepal. He knew it as soon as he stepped off the plane. The clear skies, palm trees, and loads of gorgeous women in bikini tops and too-short skirts made him feel right at home. It had taken a few days to recover completely from his bout with Nepalese diarrhea, but Khao San Road had been good to him. And this protected bay on Ko Tao was heavenly.

He let himself float with the waves for a while, before finally replacing his mask and flipping over onto his belly. Pushing softly against the receding water, he slowly kicked his way back to shore. The sea floor was a rainbow of coral, with silly-looking fish darting to and fro. A few kissed at his legs, sucking the salt off. Sea anemones in shades of red and green waved their fat tentacles at him as he passed overhead, their fist-sized mouths frozen in a surprised O. When his fingers felt sand, Ian stood. The water just reached his thighs.

He shook his dreadlocks out, water spraying everywhere. Giggles erupted from behind him. Two long-legged blondes, definitely not bleached, were wiping beads of saltwater from their faces. Ian walked over to them and threw his springy locks over his head, showering them like a naughty dog just in from a rainstorm. The spray only increased their laughter; the girls were clearly enjoying his attention.

"Oh thank you! It's so nice to cool off," said the one closest to him.

"Glad to be of help." He smiled broadly, offering her his hand. "Name's Ian. Goodtameetcha."

Grinning, the girl took his hand, squeezing lightly. "My name is Veny. And this is Sigrid." Her eyes never left his.

"Could I get you ladies a drink? I'm dying of thirst," he said.

They both laughed again, breasts bouncing softly in their tight bikini tops.

"That would be nice." Veny said. She turned to Sigrid, speaking in a language he didn't recognize. But they both kept slyly looking over at him as they whispered. Ian took it as a good sign.

Letting them chat, Ian casually checked Veny out. She had high cheekbones and legs that seemed to go on forever. Even from here, her hazel eyes sparkled. He forced himself not to stare. Girls like that didn't stay single by choice; her boyfriend must be out for a swim. Pulling off his flippers, he brushed the sand from his ankles.

"We will join you," Veny finally said in English. The girls stood and began gathering up their things. When they were ready, Veny turned to Ian. "We go now?"

He nodded and, before he could react, Veny put her arm through his and began guiding him towards a nearby terrace. Ian felt his spine lengthening and his stomach flattening out. Sneaking a peek at his lovely companion – still chatting to her girlfriend – he wanted to pinch himself. How had he gotten so lucky? They sauntered up the cobblestone path, lined with bright pink flowers and blooming cacti. A pair of white-tailed parrots squawked at them from a nearby tree; Ian squawked back.

When they reached the thatch-covered patio, Ian saw a large group had taken over most of the tables. They were chatting happily to each other, passing around spliffs and laughing. Veny and Sigrid kept walking, waving as they approached.

"Hey, Veny! Come, join us!" called out a man with short curly hair. His English was heavily accented; Ian could barely understand him.

Veny introduced him to the other nine. They seemed like a really relaxed bunch, a good mix of single girls with a few couples thrown in, all longtime friends from the University of Oslo in Norway. Ian and Veny pulled up chairs. Someone passed him a joint. Sigrid went off to buy them beers.

Veny laid her hand on Ian's knee, stroking it gently, saying, "Tomorrow we are all going on a snorkeling trip. We already rented a boat to take us around the island. You should come with us. It will be fun." She smiled at him seductively, blinking her long lashes slowly. Her hand was making soft circles around his kneecap, gradually working its way up his thigh.

Ian grinned from ear to ear. His mates back in Darwin were *never* going to believe this. "Sure, sounds like fun," he said, trying to stay casual. Taking a long puff on the joint, he relaxed into the wicker chair, in total bliss.

He'd finally found his hippie paradise.

CHAPTER TWENTY-ONE

Tommy sat on the corner of his pathetic excuse for a bed, tapping his foot impatiently. Insects scurried inside the thin walls. A piece of flowered wallpaper – out of place in this otherwise dingy gray cell – peeled off the ceiling, almost reaching the bed's headboard. These sorts of backpacker hostels revolted him. But it seemed the appropriate meeting place for what was about to happen.

He glared at his wristwatch; the thin grin forming on his face soured. *Where is that idiot?* He'd been waiting for more than an hour now and was beginning to think he'd gotten screwed. Making sure to keep his face behind the curtain, he gazed out the window again, scoping the street below. Nothing but the same Thai guys pushing fake IDs and illegal CDs on dim-witted tourists.

Pulling the thin curtains shut, Tommy screamed out in frustration. He should have known it was too good to be true. That asshole had offered him almost twice as much as the going rate. Maybe if he hadn't gotten greedy, he could have sold them by now and be on his way to the train station. If this jerkoff didn't show in a half-hour, he would have to try his luck in Kuala Lampur. Maybe it'd be even easier to hock a few of the gems there. He had a fifteen-hour layover until his flight to Mexico City departed; plenty of time to try. Even if there were unseen delays, he'd still be out of Asia before the week's end. Tommy smiled, pleased with himself. He'd thought of everything.

Pacing around his tiny chambers, he wondered whether it was time to pack up. He'd waited long enough. Two short raps, followed by three long knocks on his hotel room door stopped him in his tracks. *Finally!*

Tommy practically ripped the door from its frame, yelling, "Siam, my man, what took you so long?"

It was not the slightly built, soft-spoken jeweler he had been expecting, but instead two much larger, broader figures dressed in Hawaiian shirts.

"What the?" Tommy was being lifted off the ground and thrown against the far wall of his room. Fear instantly replaced anger. As if he were a ragdoll, the two men scooped him up and threw him onto the bed, face down.

Shoe soles echoed off the concrete floor as a third figure entered the room. Tommy couldn't see who it was – he couldn't turn his head because one of the henchmen was pushing his face into the bed – but he had a sneaking suspicion who it would be.

"So Tommy, having such a good time in Thailand that you decided to stick around a bit longer?" The all too familiar voice made Tommy attempt to rise and beg Harim for mercy, but four forceful hands held him down, crushing his face further and further into the mattress. He struggled to breathe. The smell of stale piss and semen filled his nose. His voice box didn't seem to be working; only a strange gurgling noise escaped his lips.

But Tommy's mind was racing. Who in the hell ratted him out? Nobody knew what he was doing or where he was staying, except that fucking jeweler!

"What's the matter? Didn't expect to see me again? I'm rather insulted." Harim picked up a hotel chair and placed it next to the bed. He leaned over Tommy's face and stared into his left eye. Tommy felt as if Harim's dark eyes were piercing his soul.

"Twenty thousand American dollars for one diamond, eh?" Harim said, whistling long and low. "That's more than I was expecting to make. I could really learn something from a businessman like you!" Harim punched him hard on the shoulder. Tommy screamed into the mattress.

"What's wrong? Cat got your tongue?"

Tommy writhed around on the bed, trying to roll over. No dice. Harim's thugs still had ahold of his arms and weren't letting up. He couldn't believe his crappy luck. Of all the jewelers in Bangkok, Tommy had to pick one who was working for Harim. He could kill that son of a bitch. Tommy howled again, but this time out of rage.

Harim laughed callously. "I told you once before, this is *my* town. Can you imagine his surprise when you came into his shop and tried to sell him one of his own diamonds? In contrast to you, he is loyal."

Out of the corner of his eye, Tommy saw Harim nod. The goons pulled him up off the bed and onto his feet. Harim exploded, rising so fast the chair spun out around his feet. His upper right caught Tommy totally unaware; the Canadian's head whipped back hard into the thin wall. Shards of plaster flew in all directions.

"What did I say to you, right from the start? Do not fuck with me or my business. You try, and you will wish you were dead. And what did you do, Tommy? Huh? You fucked with me *and* my business!" Tommy's face drained of blood as Harim's tone and body punches became more and more vicious. "Now you are going to have to live with the consequences." The Turkish man's laughter crescendoed in a high-pitched cackle. "Maybe I used 'live' too lightly."

Tommy could feel his bowels draining as his legs went limp. Harim's sidekicks pulled him back up, wrenching his shoulder blades.

"Better be careful, Tommy, nobody would think twice about yet another stoner hitting his head against a wall or, better yet, falling out of his five-story hotel room after smoking illegal drugs. You really think the Bangkok police are going to waste their time on your sorry ass?" Harim's left hook emerged out of nowhere, slamming into Tommy's stomach.

Tommy spit up bile. He tried to find the words to beg for his life, to make his boss take pity on him and let him live. If only Harim would stop hitting him, maybe he could catch his breath and explain it all. The diamonds, the money, the traveling, none of it mattered anymore. He just wanted to live. He *had* to see his mother one more time. And to make peace with Chantal. He had no right to kill her cat, let alone string it up like that. Tommy was only twenty-five, much too young to die. He still had so much to do, to see, to experience. How could he make Harim understand?

"Where are my diamonds?" his captor roared.

Fear robbed Tommy of speech. Only air bubbles and groans escaped his lips. The Greek slammed a chair into the wall above Tommy's head. Shattered wood rained down.

"Backpack. Upper left pocket," he shrieked.

"Damn, Tommy, in your *backpack*? Glad to see you at least chose the pocket with the zipper!" Shaking his head in admonishment, Harim slowly pulled a small black velvet satchel out of the zippered pocket, and then dumped its contents onto the bed. Twenty perfect diamonds, all roughly the size of large pearls, sparkled back up at him. Harim nodded again, and his henchmen tightened their grip on Tommy's arms.

"I fed you, sheltered you, even put clothes on your back. Yet after all I'd done for you, you betrayed me. How can I trust you to walk the streets, knowing all you know?" His voice was full of disappointment, not rage, making Tommy even more fearful for his life.

This was his moment to redeem himself, lay it all out there, and beg for mercy. "I really don't know what happened, I was —" Tommy blubbered.

"Oh, bullshit. Save your lies. You thought you could screw me over. Abuse my trust and make a profit for yourself. End of story. You're nothing but a pathetic thief whose life is now worthless."

127

One of Harim's goons threw a thick hand over Tommy's mouth; three more hands pulled him onto the bed, this time face up. Harim hovered over him. Without a word, he started rummaging through all of Tommy's pockets, throwing his meager possessions into Tommy's green backpack.

With a twisted smile, Harim shoved his left hand down Tommy's pants, pulling up his money belt. A snap of the wrist revealed a small knife. Harim's face filled with sick glee as he slowly moved the blade down Tommy's torso. Tommy sucked in his breath, trying to control his whimpering. Harim slid the knife across Tommy's hip and, with a flick, freed the belt's cord from his waist.

"Please! I don't want to die!" he shouted through the henchmen's fingers, tears streaming down his face.

Harim looked down on him with contempt. "I'm not going to kill you straight away, but you will wish I had."

Tommy tried to choke back his tears as he contemplated the Turkish man's words.

His captor diligently searched through the bathroom and chest of drawers. Once he was finished collecting all traces of Tommy from the room, Harim threw the Canadian's backpack over his shoulder and headed for the door.

Tommy's heart skipped a beat. Harim was leaving. He'd gotten what he came for, and now he was going to let him go. Tommy prayed it to be true.

Hand on the doorknob, Harim turned once again, smiling sickly at his prisoner. "You really didn't think you were just going to walk out of here, did you?"

Tommy felt a sharp pain on the back of his neck, then there was only darkness.

CHAPTER TWENTY-TWO

Zelda puffed hard on her cigarette, blowing the smoke out her bedroom window. She knew it was seriously frowned upon – by her family, the students, and Ganesh – but she couldn't seem to stop. It wasn't like she was the only smoker in the village; far from it. Most adults smoked nasty filterless cigarettes from India, but apparently only men were allowed to do so publicly without causing offence. At Ganesh's request, she'd pretty much quit before starting the volunteer program, but after her first day of teaching, she'd snuck out to the closest shop to buy a pack and had been sneaking them in when she could. She wasn't back to her Seattle norm of a pack a day, simply because she was almost never alone and dared not smoke in front of any Nepalese. But still, she couldn't stop herself from lighting up whenever she got a moment alone.

She opened her bedroom window a bit further and waved her journal back and forth, ushering the wisps of smoke outside. Three minutes to seven, according to her travel clock. Her mother would be expecting her upstairs for dinner right about now, and she didn't want to get caught. She pinched her nose in frustration, not really in the mood for dinner with the Ranas tonight. They would surely want to hear more about how she was faring. Considering she had stumbled through her first week as a teacher, Zelda had little to be proud of.

Teaching a class full of kids was a hell of a lot more difficult than she ever could have imagined, sitting in her basement apartment only a few months ago. When her Seattle friends had laughed at her, told her there was no way she had the patience to be a teacher, she swore right then and there that she would prove them wrong. She was Zelda Marie Richardson. She could do anything she set her mind to; she just had to want it badly enough, that's all.

But persistence couldn't replace knowledge or experience, and Zelda possessed neither. Stabbing her cigarette into the ashtray, she cursed Mr. Padel for not giving her a lesson plan, textbook, or any guidance whatsoever. She cursed Ganesh for not preparing her better. Most of all, she cursed herself for not trying harder to learn Nepali.

Glancing at the pile of presents by the door, Zelda decided to let them sit there a little longer. It would be better to give them to the family after dinner anyway. She'd planned on giving them their gifts on her first night. But so far, every meal had been a blur as all nine members of the household ate quickly before dispersing to finish their homework, plan Reecha's wedding, or watch the evening news. But seeing as it was Friday night and the kids presumably had the evening free, she figured tonight she'd have the best chance of getting them all in the same room together.

She rubbed rose-scented lotion onto her hands in the hopes of masking the odor of burnt tobacco. Not that she could smell it herself – since arriving in Nepal her nose had been perpetually clogged by the enormous amount of dust in the air. She'd never been able to *see* air before. The wind carried the topsoil from the open fields, unpaved roads, and endless construction sites with it, across the valley floor. Her Nepalese mother was locked in a never-ending struggle with nature, constantly sweeping the house with her whisk broom. But within a few hours, the pale-red stone floor would be dark brown again, no matter how hard she tried.

Her travel alarm clock beeped softly seven times. There was no getting around it; she had to go upstairs and eat with the family. What should she say about her first week, Zelda wondered as she clambered up to the rooftop. The truth or a rose-colored version thereof? During the course of the week, she'd stood before every class of students and had failed miserably, consistently. Probably because she still had no real idea of what she was supposed to be teaching them.

Her many brothers and sisters were already seated on mats spread around the kitchen floor. The younger ones flicked beans and bits of potato at each other until their mother's gaze prompted them to stop playing and take small bites of their dinner. The older ones shoveled food in as fast as they could, avoiding eye contact or conversation. Their father sat at the only table, dipping *roti* – flat bread – into his thick stew with the evening paper spread out before him.

Zelda accepted her serving gratefully, sitting cross-legged next to her oldest sister. She looked into her bowl, trying to discern the contents in the dim lighting. It seemed to be a concoction of unfamiliar vegetables, beans, and potatoes. Zelda wished she knew what the ingredients were but still couldn't find the right translations. Her dictionary contained only the most basic of words and was clearly geared towards the trekking crowd. Yet another item on her list of questions to ask Ganesh.

She asked in halting Nepali what they were eating. The mother fired off her answer too fast for Zelda to understand, leaving her feeling helpless and stupid again. No one else even looked up.

They ate the rest of the meal in silence until everyone appeared to be sated. Except for the mother, Zelda noticed. Only after everyone else had been offered a second portion did the older woman pour the dregs of the stew pot into her own bowl.

The father pushed his plate away and picked up his newspaper, signaling to the children that dinner was over and it was time to clear the dishes, whether they were finished or not. Only their mother's plate was spared. The younger children collected the dishes and took them out to the open-air patio to wash up, while the rest of the Rana clan ran down to the courtyard to pump water. Zelda had tried to help with the water run on her first day and almost dislocated her shoulder when she picked up one of the four buckets that were constantly being filled from the well below, and then lugged up five flights of stairs, several times a day. Like most Nepalese houses in this area, they had no running water; if they wanted to eat, shit, or shower, they had to pump water first. Zelda no longer envied Christine or her remote village; the young anthropologist's living situation had to be a lot worse than this.

The older children began shuffling downstairs without saying a word. Were they really going to do homework on a Friday night? Or were they hoping to sneak in some television, at least until their father's heavy footsteps were audible on the stairwell?

Zelda couldn't believe the family was dispersing and no one had asked her about her week. Other than a few curious glances and cautious smiles from the youngest children, the Rana clan pretty much ignored her tonight, just as they had at every meal thus far. It was as if they didn't care how she'd fared so far as a teacher or whether she was fitting in at the school. Zelda considered skipping the presents; if they couldn't bother to show the slightest interest in her, well then, forget them.

Telling herself to chill out, Zelda counted backwards from ten. Look at it from their perspective, try to walk in their shoes, as her grandmother always said. She exhaled noisily. Maybe *they* were pissed off at *her* for not giving them presents the first night, right after she arrived. Maybe *they* saw *her* as ungrateful. Well, she would show them tonight how much she appreciated them. Once they opened their gifts and saw everything she'd brought for them – all the way from America – they would look at her with new eyes and finally understand how happy she was to be here.

Flushed with excitement, Zelda cleared her throat loudly. "Hey everyone, before you go, I'd really like to give you something, as a sign of my appreciation for taking me in and feeding me."

Her new family members all stopped what they were doing and

looked over at her curiously. In faltering Nepali, she managed from memory, "I've brought you some presents from America." Murmurs of anticipation and delight followed. Her heart began to race. She hoped they would be happy with her choices and understand how much effort it had been to lug everything around all these weeks.

The father spoke up in English: "What have you brought for us?"

"Your gifts are downstairs, in my room. Why don't we all go down to the living room together? I'll bring them in there."

The father nodded appreciatively. The mother looked puzzled, until her oldest daughter translated Zelda's offer for her. The older woman smiled broadly upon hearing the news, warming Zelda's heart. *That must be it*, she thought, *they had expected something from me the first night!*

The Ranas filed downstairs, all nine of them squeezed into the tiny living room. Two fake leather couches and a pink love seat lined the walls, providing just enough room for everyone to sit. Zelda ran to her room, quickly returning laden with presents. She laid three packages onto the salon table in the middle of the room, exclaiming, "Wait, there's more!"

With a loud "ta-da," she dragged the large box of textbooks into the packed living room, thrilled to finally be free of its girth. The size of the box alone delighted her captive audience.

Zelda turned to her new family, all smiles, determined to break through this reservoir of reserved politeness. "So, thanks for coming downstairs. I brought you all some things from America, I sure hope you like them. You know, I really wanted to give them to you on the first night I arrived, but this week has been so crazy around here with Reecha's wedding plans and me becoming a teacher..." Blank stares. No one seemed to care about her progress after all. Fine. "Mother, this is for you."

Zelda held out a small package. The older woman smiled, taking it cautiously from Zelda's hands and turning it over twice before ripping off the colorful paper. Hypo-allergenic lipstick sat inside. The mother opened the top, twisting the tube so the color was visible. Her children reacted enthusiastically, oohing and aahing as she dabbed it onto her lips. Zelda realized in a flash that the color was wrong for her dark complexion, far too orangey. And besides, the woman wore lipstick every day; it was clearly not the luxury item Zelda had thought it would be. Still, the mother nodded her head in thanks before passing it on to her daughters to try as well.

"And these are for my brothers and sisters. I didn't realize there would be so many of you; hopefully you won't mind sharing. Please, here you go." She handed the other two gifts to the children closest to her, who tore them open without hesitation. After the giggles subsided, the older of the two held up the smaller object, daring to ask, "What is it?"

"That –" Zelda said, pointing to the bright pink object. "– is a yo-yo."

"How do you make it work?"

"It's all in the wrist!" She grabbed it out of her brother's hand and made it go up and down twice before it began spinning in a circle. "I've never been really good at it, but practice makes perfect."

"Pardon?" Reecha asked.

Zelda rolled her eyes; she had to be more careful about using American expressions here. "I mean, the more you practice, the better you'll get at it."

The children tried not to look too disappointed.

"But this –" Zelda grabbed the second gift, a basketball. "– I can show you how to play."

Her brothers and sisters glanced at each other, a few whispering and eyeing the ball suspiciously.

Finally Reecha piped up again, "But basketball is boring. We already know how to play. We prefer volleyball or badminton."

Zelda's grin remained frozen on her face. The nerve of these little brats! Why, most kids in America would be *thrilled* to have a basketball or a yo-yo, let alone both. She tried to laugh it off, emitting a thin bray.

"Well, let's see if this makes you happy," she said, dragging the box to her father's feet, grunting from the effort. "Please, this is for your library."

The father looked at her with a warm, yet confused, smile. "What library?"

"The school library. What's the word – *pustakālaya*?"

"Yes, yes, I know the word 'library.' But I do not understand. We do not have a library at this school. We tried it once long ago. The children take the books home but never bring them back. What good is a library if the books never come back?"

"But you could try again, with these books, seeing as they didn't cost you anything. I can make a signup sheet –"

"No, no. It is not possible. Perhaps the teachers can use them, during the lessons. I will ask Headmaster Padel. But the teachers will have to collect the books after each class."

Zelda pleaded with her father, refusing to give up so easily. "But my students seem really trustworthy, maybe…"

He shook his head gently, cutting her off with his words. "I am sorry, but these books will go into the headmaster's office, to be kept under lock and key."

Zelda wanted to throttle him. *Why did I drag all of this crap halfway around the world?* she fumed to herself. And not even one single thank you. What did she have to do to make this goddamn family happy? Did Mother Theresa or the Dalai Lama ever get rejected like this? It seemed as if people were always grateful to see *them*.

Zelda rose quickly, stretching her hands behind her back and yawning. "Well, thanks again for letting me stay here while I teach."

Her father nodded; the rest of the family sat staring at their new toys.

"I'm going to head to bed now."

Silence.

"Okay then, good night." She forced herself not to run.

Back in the safety of her bedroom, Zelda popped open her last can of warm beer smuggled in from Thamel and lit another cigarette, wondering why she'd bothered to come to Nepal at all.

CHAPTER TWENTY-THREE

Kicking hard off the cliff, Ian enjoyed a few seconds of flight before crashing back against the wall, sending a spray of red rock flying. His heart was still racing from the climb up. Raising his forearm slightly, he released the tension on his carabiner and slowly lowered his body half a meter down the cliff. He'd never rock-climbed before, but here in Krabi, it seemed to be the thing to do. And Veny's gang was up for anything and everything. Well, as long as it was expensive, he thought ruefully. They were a good group to hang out with, but his vacation money had been flowing like water since he'd met Veny and her mates.

Ian wished she and her friends didn't have such bloody expensive tastes. Snorkeling trips, rock-climbs, and kayak rentals were not cheap. And the hotels Veny and her friends fancied were at least ten times more expensive than the rooms he'd rented in Nepal. *Nobody's perfect*, he thought. And besides it was a small price to pay to be with her.

He double-checked his rope, making sure no knots had formed. Gazing down into the blue-green sea, he could make out rolling sand dunes just below the surface. It must have been some sort of optical illusion, but from Ian's high perch, the water suddenly appeared quite shallow. *Come on*, he chided himself, *Kylan just did it; of course the water's deep enough*. Taking a deep breath, he released the rope, free-falling into the warm sea below.

He bobbed up to the surface immediately, whooping with delight. "Did you see that?" he shouted.

Kylan paddled in closer, making room for Ian on the open-topped kayak. "Great job, man. I knew you could do it."

Pride and adrenaline surged through Ian's veins; he'd never experienced such an intense feeling of weightlessness as in those precious seconds of falling. He really had to give skydiving a go. After swimming over to his new mate, Ian pulled himself up onto the plastic boat. "Man, what a rush! I could do that all day long," he said, spitting up salt water.

Kylan handed him a pipe. Ian drew a long toke, erupting into a serious coughing fit. When he finally got control over his voice again, he rasped, "Maybe I better wait a minute. That fall knocked the wind out of me."

Taking a swig of bottled water, Ian studied the rock face above. "Man, I have *got* to do that again! You game?" It was one of the most popular climbing routes in Krabi – Ian knew if they didn't get back to the trailhead pretty soon, they'd be standing in line.

Kylan looked at him with half-closed eyes. "Naw, man, I'm good for today. I just want to get stoned, maybe grab some fried noodles. Wanna join me? The others are probably still on the hotel terrace."

"Sure, mate." No sense in arguing with him; he could always borrow the kayak and come back later if he really wanted to. He liked to let Veny and her friends make most of the decisions, seeing as he was tagging along on their holiday. These past two weeks had been the best of his whole life; if his new friend wanted to call it a day, no worries. Ian was in no rush.

Upon their triumphant return, Sigrid pecked Ian on the cheek, and Veny French-kissed him. The Norwegians were absorbed by the television screen mounted above the beach-front bar. A never-ending loop of Hollywood feature films had been playing since they arrived.

Ian stroked Veny's creamy skin and kissed her neck, breathing in her sweet scent. Her hair smelled like honey and fresh orchids. He still couldn't believe his luck. Not only was Veny drop-dead gorgeous, she was the most no-nonsense girl he had ever met. Even sex she regarded as nothing more important than a handshake; no shame about it, just a natural part of the human experience. Like breathing. Ian was quickly falling for her. He laid a hand on her thigh, but she only patted it automatically, clearly enthralled by the movie.

Kylan brought him a beer before struggling to light a banana-leaf joint. Kylan was trying to go local. By the time it made its way to Ian, the leaf was unraveling. He took a few puffs; clumps of red ash fell onto his T-shirt, instantly burning tiny black holes into his chest. He swatted at his torso, brushing off a few burning embers. He glanced around at Veny and her friends, but nobody seemed to notice him, they were all too absorbed in the film. Except for Kylan, the rest of the group had wanted to chill this morning. Ian didn't quite understand why. It had been nonstop action with Veny's crew since they'd met – that was one of the reasons Ian liked hanging out with them so much.

As soon as the credits started to roll, Veny jumped into his lap, spilling beer across his legs. "So how was the climb?" she asked, softly sucking on his earlobe, before caressing his neck with her soft lips.

Ian turned red with embarrassment. Sure, it felt great, but they were surrounded by her friends, and it was only two in the afternoon – Veny could hardly claim drunk and belligerent. He tried to control himself, thinking about anything but her tender mouth on his hungry skin.

Sigrid snapped at Veny in Norwegian. She stopped her kisses and shot Sigrid a dirty look before whispering in Ian's ear, "Would you like to go upstairs?"

"Yes," came the hoarse reply. Ian didn't care how pathetic he looked; he had to have her. They headed up, skipping stairs as they climbed. Veny was already stripping off her top and shorts. Ian gathered up her trail of clothes, barely able to keep himself from coming before he even got into their third-story room.

He took her from behind; as soon as the door slammed shut, he was inside her. What seemed like hours of passion ensued – actually only a few seconds – before he lost it completely, exploding inside her. Veny turned to him, grinning, wiping his cum off her ass with one hand, and fondling his balls with the other. Ian gently disengaged her hand from his nuts. "Sorry, darling, still a bit tender." Wrapping his hands around her, he laid them down on the bed together, spooning.

After a few unsuccessful attempts to restart Ian's motor, Veny pushed up onto one arm, staring down at him through her long blonde hair. He pushed her hair back and kissed her neck.

"We're going to Bangkok on Friday. Do you want to come with us?" she asked.

The kissing stopped. Ian pulled back, looking at her in disbelief, his euphoria vanishing instantly. "What? Going back to Bangkok? What do ya mean?" What day was it anyway? Ian had to think hard; they had arrived Saturday last and had been here for... "But that's in two days!" he exclaimed. His long-sought-after paradise was slipping away right before his eyes. Bangkok, as he'd learned his first night in Thailand, was absurdly expensive and overtouristed. Why would anyone trade in Krabi Beach for Khao San Road? Ian was happy where he was, but he was so taken by Veny and her friends he couldn't bear the thought of saying goodbye.

Veny seemed to sense his hesitation. "We won't be there for long," she said, patting his arm in reassurance. "Bangkok is an ugly city. So big and dirty. We're going to Pai to do a trek before we have to go back to Oslo. It was always our plan."

Bollocks. Ian wished he could understand Norwegian. They'd probably been talking about their plans right under his nose for days, and he hadn't had a clue.

"Please don't look so sad. You knew we were only going to be in

Thailand for five weeks, that this is just a short vacation for me and my friends," Veny said. She turned over onto her back, sighing wistfully. "I wish I could stay with you, backpacking around the world. It all sounds so romantic," she said, while caressing his cheek and tugging playfully on his beard stubble. "But university is waiting, and I graduate next year." She shrugged.

"But why Bangkok? You still have another two weeks of holiday, right?"

"Yes, but we have to book our trek," Veny said.

Ian looked at her blankly.

"Kylan and Ivar, that is why they came with us, to go to the Golden Triangle and hike through the opium fields. They are not beach people."

"Oh, I didn't notice," Ian said, sulking. Kylan especially seemed to be game for anything and everything; it had been his idea to rent the kayak and go rock-climbing today.

"Come, we need to dress." She jumped up and started to pull on her shorts. "The others are waiting for us. We have to buy our train tickets today. Will you join us?" Veny stared at him with those beautiful brown eyes. Ian wanted so desperately to say yes. But even a few nights in a four-star Bangkok hotel would blow his travel budget completely. And how much would this hike cost? He wouldn't be surprised if they wanted to fly up to Chang Mai as well.

But one look at those long legs and perfect ass, and Ian knew he had to find a way. Veny was everything he had ever hoped to find in a woman. He couldn't let her go, not now. Maybe his pa would lend him some money. How expensive could the hike be anyway? "Sure, yeah. Why not? I've not been to the north yet."

Veny smiled, clearly happy with his response, and kissed him gently on the mouth.

He laid her back onto the bed, fingers gliding lightly across her soft belly. "Your friends can wait a bit longer, right?"

She giggled, wrapping her creamy white arms around his bronze neck.

CHAPTER TWENTY-FOUR

Shivering, Zelda scrubbed at her back and arms, willing herself to finish what she'd started. As if to irritate her, a gust of cold autumn wind ripped in through the thin curtain blocking the doorway, adding to the frigidity of the experience. Even after two weeks of daily sponge baths, she still hadn't gotten used to bathing out of a bucket. *And probably never will*, she sighed to herself. The exotic charm of showering this way had vanished quickly.

Her Nepalese mother called out from the kitchen, yelling at Zelda to hurry up, the children were already arriving. Rubbing a thin towel briskly over her skin, she forced herself to think positive thoughts. It was a new day filled with new chances, she told herself. Closing her eyes and tilting her long neck back, she prayed to whoever was listening to please, *please* make it an interesting one.

Her older students had made it abundantly clear from the start that Zelda was merely one of the many volunteers who had been popping in and out of their lives since their school career began. A few humored her by asking questions about American films and music groups, but the vast majority of her pupils couldn't care less; they wanted to get through class as quickly and painlessly as possible so they could go outside and play. Ganesh, her trusty program coordinator, had done his very best to instill pride in all of his volunteers, making his recruits feel special and extraordinary. And it had worked. Zelda had thought she could change the world in a few months. Hearing the truth, especially uttered from an innocent-looking twelve-year-old in pigtails, hurt.

Would it be any different if she had joined the Peace Corps? At least then she would have been stationed in one community for two whole years. Maybe then she could have made a bigger impact, really made her presence known. Zelda sighed deeply, wondering whether time was the problem. Maybe she wasn't cut out for this kind of thing.

Her mother screamed at her again to get a move on. Zelda threw on a loose dressing gown and ran downstairs, offering her excuses as she flew by. Luckily she'd already mastered the art of putting on a sari; she could do it with her eyes closed now. After making a few adjustments in the mirror, she bolted downstairs to the courtyard, already full with children.

At least it wasn't raining, she thought.

On her left, the youngest children were diligently lining themselves up into rows. The older students held back, chitchatting conspiratorially amongst themselves like the teenagers they were. Zelda laughed to herself – it seemed no matter where you were in the world, when you got down to it, people were pretty much the same. That had been the most important lesson of her trip up until now – there were far, far more similarities between the peoples of Nepal and America than there were differences. She snorted in disgust, thinking to herself: *And that's precisely what makes this trip so boring.*

Had she made the wrong choice by coming to Nepal, rather than taking that full-time contract? That question had been haunting her all week. Or maybe she should have backpacked around the world on her own, instead of volunteering. Hell, that's what her friends in Seattle had done and what Ian was doing right now. Zelda couldn't help thinking about Ian in these darker moments, wondering what sort of glorious, crazy adventures he must be having. He *had* to be having more fun than she was, no doubt about it. Maybe he would email her one day and fill her in. But then she shouldn't hold out any false hopes. Ian must have met someone else by now, probably multiple someones; he was really cute in a rugged backpackery sort of way. And by now their brief encounter was certainly nothing more than a vague memory to him, and probably not one of the more interesting ones.

But no, so far no messages from Ian, only those from her friends and family back home. They all responded right away to her long, weekly email updates describing daily life in Nepal, telling her how much they wished they were in Kathmandu instead of slaving away behind their keyboards. Everyone told her how jealous they were, and how she must be having the time of her life. At first those emails were like virtual pats on the back and reinforced her decision to come to Kathmandu and be doing something *different*. But lately, they only served to remind her how little impact she had on her life back home and how easily she could vanish from her social circle. Life in Seattle seemed to be marching on, despite her disappearing act. And to her surprise and embarrassment, it really pissed her off.

Zelda slowly made her way towards her fellow educators. Mr. Baral was enthusiastically telling the other teachers of his latest plan to engage the students. It had something to do with colored flags and choosing names for each class – she still had difficulty following long conversations. The others listened carefully; only the two oldest teachers

140

hung back, smoking homemade cigarettes. They didn't seem to think much of Mr. Baral or his inspirations. But Zelda envied him, wondering how the young Nepalese educator continually came up with such great ideas, wishing she could be so creative.

Headmaster Padel strode out of his office, slamming the thick wooden door behind him. The rest of the children immediately fell into line, arranging themselves by class and age, the oldest students on the right and the youngest on the left. Zelda was responsible for teaching English to all of the students at some point during the week. She waved enthusiastically to the children; only a few dared to return the gesture.

Clearing his deep voice, Headmaster Padel lowered his reading glasses onto the tip of his nose and slowly looked up and down the rows of children. In a solemn voice, he delivered a short speech, of which Zelda understood nothing. The children squealed in delight. With two loud claps, the headmaster excused them all, sending streams of children and teachers rushing into their mud-walled classrooms. Wondering what the commotion was about, she started to ask Mr. Padel what exactly he had said, but his angry glare made her think twice. *I can always ask the kids*, she thought.

Zelda headed off to group one to begin her third week as their teacher. They were her youngest group, a class full of adorably rambunctious seven-year-olds. She spent most of the hour running around the room trying to stop them from hitting each other. She knew her younger students walked all over her, but Zelda didn't know how to command their attention and make them respect her – or at least listen to her – without resorting to violence.

Most of her precious charges were already fighting over seats and pulling on each other's hair. "Okay, children, what's on the agenda today?" she yelled over the rumble. The children didn't seem to notice she'd entered the room.

With a sinking heart, Zelda plopped into her chair and flipped open the old grammar primer she'd been using as a lesson planner, only acquired after much begging and pleading with Headmaster Padel. She was here to teach them, damn it, and that's what she was going to do.

"Hey, everybody, listen up! It looks like we left off on page –" Her class exploded with laughter, drowning her out. The kids were pointing at something behind her. She glanced around wildly, expecting a snake to be slithering towards her, or a bat waking up in the rafters. She'd learned the hard way that all sorts of creatures used the classrooms as bedrooms. But she didn't see anything amiss. However, the children's snickering only increased.

"What now?" she asked wearily, searching her students' faces for answers. "What did you do now?"

They were still giggling hysterically, covering their mouths and gesturing. Slowly Zelda realized that they were pointing *at* her, not behind her. Her eyes widened in alarm. She knew the younger kids loved to play disgusting pranks on each other, but she didn't think they were brazen enough to pull one on their teacher. Or were they?

Zelda shifted in her seat; it did feel softer than usual. As she sprung out of her chair, half-dried cow dung flew onto the chalkboard and wall behind her. The rest of the patty was smeared across her ass. She'd seen several of the younger kids throwing cow patties at each other – it seemed to be a favorite game after classes – but she never in a million years thought they would be brave enough to do *this* to *her*.

"You sons of bitches!" Zelda screamed at the top of her lungs. She had promised herself before coming that she would never, ever swear in front of the pupils, but this was going way too far. How dare they; she was their *teacher*.

Her reaction only intensified their laughter. "What in *the hell* do you think –"

A dark shadow passed over the open entryway. Headmaster Padel stood there with his large hands on his hips, staring down at her with a seriously perturbed look on his face.

"What do you think that *you* are doing, Miss Richardson?" he said curtly.

"I – they – look!" She turned around with indignation, pointing at her poop-covered sari. "Look at what they did – to their teacher." Zelda glared at the children, hatred oozing out her pores.

Headmaster Padel only shrugged his shoulders. "What do you expect? They clearly have no respect for you." He turned on his heel and stormed off.

She started to throw her textbook at his head, but thought twice, letting it drop onto her desk with a thud. "Hey, what did you mean by that?" She chased after him, catching up with the headmaster outside his office door.

"I mean," he growled, "that you are too lax with them. They can do whatever they want in your classroom and are never punished by you. It is like playtime hour. That is what I mean." He turned the handle, dismissing her with his actions.

"Wait a second. Just because I refuse to use a belt or ruler to beat them senseless does not mean they can't be taught to listen. I told you before, I do not believe in corporal punishment."

Headmaster Padel shrugged. "If you do not beat them once in a while, they will never respect you. It does not matter; you are only here for a very short time," he said, entering his office.

The first time Mr. Padel had said that to her, Zelda's world fell in. Now that it occurred on an almost daily basis, she could brush his hurtful remarks off more easily.

"What did you announce this morning anyway?" she demanded. *Or do I have to beat you with a ruler until you tell me?* she thought. *Please just ask me to.*

"Today is a half day. Mr. Rana and I have decided to add a second volleyball court to the playground. The children are to help dig it out this afternoon." He slammed his office door shut before she could respond.

"Give me a break," she grumbled. Volleyball and badminton were national obsessions here – when her siblings weren't doing homework or watching TV, they were outside, smacking a ball around. All day long – rain or shine – neighborhood kids and students congregated in the school's playground, nothing more than an unused field next to the Ranas' house with a torn net strung up in the middle.

But still, canceling classes to dig out a volleyball court was taking it a step too far, wasn't it? *Why am I here again?* Zelda asked herself. She turned back to her classroom and began trudging across the courtyard, head down.

From behind her, Zelda heard Headmaster Padel opening his door. She looked back as he called out in a too-loud voice, "Go change your sari. You look disgusting."

CHAPTER TWENTY-FIVE

It was all happening so quickly. As soon as they'd arrived in Bangkok, the gang headed to Khao San Road in search of the trekking company Kylan had read about online. It was only when they were huddled around the travel agent – Veny on his lap – that Ian realized he was screwed. His newfound gang of friends had their minds set on a seven-day luxury hike through the opium-filled fields of northern Thailand, departing from Chang Mai early the next morning. They'd have to fly up tonight if they wanted to join the forty other tourists waiting to be whisked through the jungles of the Golden Triangle on elephant-back. No problem, according to their travel agent, but they would have to pay more.

Ian stared at the pictures of happy westerners lining the travel agency's walls. Smiling whities were floating on bamboo-rafts, smoking long wooden pipes, playing with dirty children and eating bowls of god-knows-what. It looked so overtouristed. Ian could hardly believe Veny and her friends were so excited about going.

By the time he finally mustered up the courage to ask how much the flight, hotel, and trek were going to cost, his Norwegian friends had already whipped out their credit cards. Ian gulped audibly at hearing the price: almost a thousand Ozzie dollars. Veny had warned him on the train ride back that they were pulling out all the stops; this was Kylan's dream trek, and, unlike Ian, they didn't have months to kick back and enjoy.

But still – a thousand dollars for seven days. It seemed too ridiculous for words. Ian reckoned he could get by for two months on a thousand dollars if he counted his pennies. Not that he had that much left in the bank. But Veny... He stroked her leg. She pecked him on the cheek absently, totally absorbed in the colorful brochure their travel agent was showing them. He didn't want his time with her to end so soon. Even if his pa spotted him some cash – which his dad had already repeatedly said would only happen over his dead body; they had a farm to run, mate – taking this seven-day trip would mean the end of his travels. Now he understood why his friends had all gotten credit cards *before* hitting the backpacker trail.

Veny finally noticed he hadn't reached for his wallet. She whispered in his ear, "Is there something wrong?"

Ian scratched his head in embarrassment, not able to look her directly in the eyes. He definitely did not want to have *this* conversation in front of her mates. "Look, I, uh, the flight, this tour, it's all a bit out of my price range. I can't really afford to go without blowing the rest of me travel savings – literally." *And then some*, he added in his mind. "I really want to trek with you, but does it have to be this trip?" He began to stammer. "If we could book something a tad cheaper –" The travel agent scowled at him, clearing her throat noisily. "– then I could join you." Ian tried not to look as pathetic as he felt.

The shift in the room was palpable. Ian was suddenly no longer part of the gang.

Veny turned on him with cold eyes, speaking clearly and succinctly as if he was a two-year-old child misbehaving. "This is the trip Kylan wants to do. I told you already, this hike is why he came with us to Thailand. I cannot deny him this little pleasure." Her fair hair shivered as she shook her head, her face a frown.

Ian felt as if he had been slapped. He knew he was probably asking too much of her and her friends, but he hadn't expected such a mean response from his lover of three weeks. He mustered up a grin, trying to laugh off his suggestion. "Oh, of course. Sorry I asked."

The group *sans* Ian handed over their credit cards as if Ian and Veny's conversation never took place. He'd never felt like more of a heel in all of his life. Too dazed to get up and leave, he sat quietly with Veny still on his lap while the rest completed their transactions with their now beaming travel agent. With a deep bow, she handed over their tickets, and the group of happy Norwegians shuffled back outside, flush with the thrill of yet another upcoming adventure.

Ian sat in his chair, utterly dejected. Veny had skipped out with the rest, without even saying goodbye. It was as if he had disappeared from her vision and life in a span of a few seconds, simply because he wasn't as wealthy as she and her friends were. *Now that's love for ya*, he thought. Gathering up his broken heart and few worldly possessions, he dragged himself out onto the street, wondering what in the hell he should do now.

"There you are!"

Ian's heart skipped a beat as he looked up the street to see Veny racing back towards him. Her friends kept walking, chatting, and laughing with each other as they went. But here she was, running back to him. Ian dropped his bags, spreading his arms out wide to welcome her back. He wanted to hold her tight and never let go.

Veny ran up to him and briefly wrapped her long arms around his neck. She kissed him quickly, once on each cheek, before taking two steps backwards.

"Ian, it was really nice to have met you." Veny must have noticed the horrified look on his face – the recognition that his fantasy was now officially over. She smiled sweetly at him. "Oh, Ian, you know we are going back to Oslo after this hike. And the whole time we were together, you talked only of backpacking through the rest of Asia. It was a fun three weeks, but you didn't actually think we would ever see each other again, did you?"

He wanted to scream, "Of course, you bloody fool, I am totally and completely in love with you!" before pulling her head back and kissing her passionately. Make her stay in Asia with him for just a little bit longer or, better yet, come back to Darwin for a spell. But one look into her hazel eyes and he knew there was no point. She had already moved on and was fantasizing about Chang Mai and Pai like the rest of her mates.

Inhaling her honey-scented hair one last time, Ian kissed her once gently on the mouth. Veny pulled away slightly, but he ignored it, savoring the moment. "Enjoy your hike, Pai, the whole lot. Maybe you'll email me sometime?" He had already written his virtual address in her travel diary, in a moment of childish passion.

Veny smiled wearily. "Sure. You enjoy the rest of the world, Ian. I hope you find whatever it is you're looking for."

I already did, and she's walking away from me! Ian wanted to yell out. Instead he stood stiffly by while she turned away from him and ran up Khao San Road to find her friends.

As she disappeared into the crowded street, Ian could think of nothing better to do than get drunk and then get the hell out of Thailand. Purposefully walking in the opposite direction, he scanned the multitude of budget tours and flights on offer, searching for anything cheap. A boat ride to Laos caught his eye. It was only a hundred baht for a three-day cruise upriver. Perfect. Didn't one of his mates say you could shoot a rocket launcher at a cow there? All that old commie ammunition had to be good for something. At least in Laos he could squeeze a few more weeks out of his money before having to think about working for a living.

"Waiter, I said *double* whiskey; this one's got bloody ice cubes in it. Waiter!" Ian brought the worthless drink down hard onto the bar, spilling its contents onto the bloke sitting next to him.

"Look out, that's real leather," the man growled at him, grabbing handfuls of napkins and rubbing fanatically at his footwear.

"Sorry, mate. It's just the waiter doesn't seem to want to serve me a proper drink. Sorry about your shoes." At least that's what Ian tried to say; he was slurring his words so badly no one could understand him. He grabbed a few napkins off the bar and attempted to wipe the man's jacket off, missing him by centimeters and falling off his stool.

The man scowled at his Italian leather footwear, rubbing at his shoes for a full minute before helping Ian to his feet. As Ian righted himself, the man brushed off his shoulders and back. He stood in silence, awed by the man towering a good meter over him. Ian felt as if he was in the presence of a Greek god, Adonis come to life. The man's features weren't just sharp, they were chiseled. With his perfectly manicured eyebrows and coiffed hair, Ian could almost see the swimsuit models bouncing up behind him.

"It's okay. They are just shoes after all." Even his voice was magnificent, a low rumble that could easily summon Zeus.

The man looked down at Ian's backpack, now soaked in whiskey. "Are you alright? You look a bit down on your luck."

In a thick drunken slur, Ian informed his new acquaintance about the turn of events that had led him to this particular bar at this particular hour. "So after Veny ripped me heart out, I checked into this place just down the street, but when I lay down on the bed, it sounded like the walls were alive. I might be broke, but even I have my limits!" he exclaimed, rocking on the barstool.

The Greek god smiled slightly. So far he had said nothing, listening patiently while Ian spilled his guts. "Maybe I could help you find somewhere decent to stay, at least for tonight?" the stranger said.

Ian eyed the man unsteadily. The bloke was well dressed, perhaps too well dressed for a place like this. The man's clothes looked high end, tailor-made even. Why was he being so friendly? He couldn't imagine that this guy would want to roll *him*. But then why would he want to help him out? After a moment's silence, Ian blurted out, "I ain't no poof."

The stranger laughed. "Nor am I. Just someone who knows what it's like to be down on your luck. I guess I'm trying to help a brother in need."

Ian looked at his new friend with renewed interest. After all, the man did speak the universal language of human decency in a most sincere way. And besides, what did he really have to lose? The way he felt right now, if this bloke killed him, he might be doing him a favor. "What did you say your name was?" Ian asked.

"Harim," he said, offering Ian his hand. "It's a pleasure to meet you."

CHAPTER TWENTY-SIX

Tommy was being tossed back and forth by a couple of lumberjacks. He moaned in anguish as he thrashed about, trying to wake himself from this horrible dream. Voices were shouting all around him – at him – but he couldn't understand what they were saying. His whole body ached. As he struggled to rise, something hard pushed against his chest, forcing him back on the ground.

He opened his eyes slowly, letting them adjust to the dim light. Everything was blurring together. With difficulty, he focused on the metal tube pinning him down. It took him a few seconds to recognize it as the barrel of a rifle. He'd never seen one in real life before. He stared at it in fascination, vaguely aware he should be scared – it was pointed at his heart, after all. Shadowy figures surrounded him, speaking to each other in a hard clipped language, similar to Thai but not quite the same.

Tommy coughed. A light was shone in his face. Disembodied voices screamed at him again, but he couldn't make his lips move. His mouth felt like cracked wood; his tongue, sandpaper. In the distance, he could hear more shouting. The blinding flashlight began bobbing and weaving around the small crowd. Thanks to the flickering light, he could make out at least ten people dressed in military uniforms, maybe more. Thankfully Harim or his henchmen weren't among the onlookers. Behind the men were rows and rows of metal containers. The ground seemed to rock gently to and fro. They must be on a ship. On the fringes of his mind, Tommy realized he should be happy to be alive. He tried thanking his unknown saviors, his mouth opening and closing like a dying guppy, but no sound came out.

The barrel was removed from his chest, and Tommy was pulled roughly to his feet by two small men dressed in green camouflage. His legs felt soft and rubbery – they wouldn't support his weight. But Tommy didn't care, he felt so light and breezy. He managed to raise his head. A dark shape was moving closer. He smiled at it.

"I say, you're lucky to be alive," a crisp voice called out in heavily accented English. A small man with John Lennon glasses moved into the light. The shoulders of his green military uniform were adorned with red stripes and gold stars; a plethora of medals lined his chest. Tommy frowned. Did someone from the hotel call the military police? That seemed a bit excessive.

Tommy's attention was drawn to blood dripping slowly from his wrists. He watched with morbid fascination as the drops splashed onto the boat's deck and mixed with the sea salt. How in the devil did he get onto a ship any-hoo? Was there even a marina or harbor in Bangkok? Tommy didn't remember seeing one, but there were so many things he didn't know.

One thing he did know for certain was that flag on the man's chest – a field of red and blue, and, in the upper-left-hand corner, stars surrounded by husks of corn – was not Thai. Was that even the flag of a real country? It looked made up. But he had seen it before somewhere, in the news maybe? It was on the tip of his tongue. It was so hard to think; his head hurt like the dickens. How long had he been unconscious anyway?

The two men holding him up began dragging him towards the edge of the ship. Across the gangplank, he could see three military trucks and a few Jeeps, all with their lights on. His welcoming committee. But to where?

Tommy felt himself drifting back to sleep when a flash of memory jolted him out of his stupor. His last trip to the Golden Triangle. Their guide had gotten them lost. Everything was going fine until they came across a large sign nailed to a tree in the middle of nowhere. That was where he had seen that flag before. Whatever it was, it had really spooked their guide – they'd had to hightail it out of there. What was so special about that flag? Obviously it was that of a border country. Laos? No, wrong border – they had been hiking in the northwest of Thailand. As Tommy tried to recall his high school geography classes, a few maps slowly came back to him. His eyes went wide in recognition. Only then, after Tommy remembered whose flag it was, did he scream for the first time.

CHAPTER TWENTY-SEVEN

Everything was going so well. After the cow patty incident, Zelda resolved to be a pushover no more. She'd been studying her Nepali language books religiously, focusing on the words and phrases she needed to succeed at home and in the classroom. Her students were even responding to her new and improved teaching methods, if anybody could call them that. Since she'd begun threatening and cursing at her charges in Nepali, they were much better behaved. She wondered how long her shock-and-awe tactics would work.

And she'd made a point of chatting to her family in Nepali the past five weeks, exhausting her vocabulary and herself in the process. Her Nepalese siblings had clearly taken more of an interest in her because of it, spending time telling her about their classes, homework assignments, and what was going to be on the television later that night. They were even kind enough to speak somewhat slower so she had a greater chance of understanding them. She really felt as if she was starting to get somewhere with her Nepali, or at least was beginning to understand the underlying structure of the language.

Breathing in deeply, she reveled in the heavenly smell of frying bread as it sizzled and simmered on the hot iron plate. The family's helper scooped up two *roti*, slid them onto a porcelain plate, and handed it to the hungry westerner. Zelda nodded her head in thanks, tearing off a piece and popping it into her mouth.

"Yum, delicious," she said in Nepali while rubbing her stomach, pantomiming her pleasure. The woman smiled in satisfaction and returned to her chores, leaving her newborn baby to roll around on a blanket before Zelda.

Though she knew her renewed efforts were paying off, Zelda had to admit to herself that even the simplest of conversations were wearing her out. Learning a new language was mentally exhausting. But she was determined to keep trying, keep pushing forward. The results of her labors were already visible – she knew if she kept it up, she could leave her family and teaching post on a good note. Only one more week until school was out and she was done volunteering.

And who knew, if she got to be as fluent as Christine, maybe she could work as a translator. That would be an amazing way of making a living, Zelda thought, and surely more interesting than pushing pixels all day long. Did the United Nations need English-Nepali translators? She would have to look that up.

During these past five weeks of doing her best, Christine had become her role model. Zelda had even taken to carrying around a mini-dictionary and notebook. She'd finally given in to her Nepalese mother's demands and stopped trying to do everything for herself, allowing the family's helper to serve her every need. She'd ended up with a lot of free time on her hands as a result, most of which she spent observing. She flipped through the past few entries she'd made in her notebook. Her lengthy descriptions were less interesting to read than it had been to live through those agonizingly boring moments of basically hanging around. How did Christine get off on this?

Zelda made a face at the helper's baby, tickling its round belly. "He's a little Buddha boy, isn't he?" she said in English.

The family's helper – a devout Hindu – giggled politely, exposing her toothless smile. Zelda didn't think she could understand English, but after a long day of teaching, she was too tired to really care.

The kitchen door swung open, and Mr. Rana popped his head inside. "Oh, there you are."

He was speaking in English, so Zelda assumed he was talking to her. "Hi, *namaste*. Are you well?" She was quite surprised to see her Nepalese "father" home during daylight hours – he usually took off at the crack of dawn, returning home at 7 p.m. precisely, just as his wife was spooning up the evening's *dhal bhat*.

"Yes, yes. I am fine. I am looking for you. Are you done with your teaching duties for the day?"

"Yes, school finished an hour ago."

"Good, good. Please to come with me? I wish to have you meet a good friend of mine. He lives in Gorkha, a village close by. He likes to meet all of the volunteer teachers who honor us with their presence and skills."

Zelda blushed at the compliment, elated by his offer. After the cow shit incident, she was determined to do her utmost to be what the Ranas and Headmaster Padel wanted her to be. This was the first time her father had ever asked her to go anywhere with him. Come to think of it, this was the first time he had expressed any interest in spending time with her since she had arrived seven weeks ago. All of her efforts over the past few weeks had clearly paid off. Maybe she was cut out for this volunteer thing after all – she just had to show more interest in the local culture and language and accept it for what it was, instead of constantly comparing their way of life to her own.

Zelda looked gratefully up at Mr. Rana. "Sure, I mean, yes. It would be an honor for me as well. Let me grab my purse."

"So you see, we help many children here," said Mr. Koirala, the director of the orphanage, as he motioned to a hall on the left, full of tiny fold-up cots. They were walking along the third floor of an impressive complex of mud-brick buildings. The bare walls were made more colorful by children's drawings taped to most of the beds. Everything was so clean and tidy; Zelda could hardly believe that hundreds of children had been living here for the past eleven years. Everything looked brand new.

According to Mr. Koirala, most of the orphans were under the age of seven and came from villages all over Nepal. The orphanage director looked appropriately distressed when he told her how the girls were often left in his care because their families couldn't afford their dowries. Boys only arrived on his doorstep if they were sick or the parents were dead and no other relatives could care for them. Healthy boys were too useful to give away.

Zelda stared again at the long rows of little beds. It was so sad to see so many children in need. She wondered whether they could speak English yet. These orphans – girls mostly – needed every edge up they could get in this male-dominated society. She bristled just thinking about the times she was required to ask her nine-year-old brother to accompany her to the local market, only a few hundred yards from their house. She knew it was because she, as an unmarried woman, needed to be protected and sheltered by her family, but it seemed to be much ado about nothing. Her feministic streak had definitely been fired up since arriving in Nepal. Maybe this was her true calling, she thought, teaching orphaned girls English.

"When will the children be back?" Zelda asked. She couldn't wait to meet them, probably all dressed in matching school uniforms. She chuckled to herself; only a few months ago, the thought of being surrounded by hordes of excited children would have scared the crap out of her. But now she was looking forward to it.

"School does not end for another two hours. But please to come to my office for tea and lamb curry. Freshly made."

Freshly slaughtered, he meant. "How kind, thank you," she said.

Mr. Koirala led Zelda and her Nepalese father up to the rooftop of the main building. They were confronted by dramatic, sweeping views of terraced fields creeping up the valley's steep walls. The orphanage seemed to be a village in and of itself. To the right she could see the school – a collection of small buildings with children rushing between. To the left, a small medical clinic. A line of waiting women holding babies trailed onto the school's large courtyard, also home to three volleyball courts.

Headmaster Padel would be extremely jealous if he could see this, she thought. He had been pushing her – just as the rest of her Nepalese family had – to stay on at the school as a volunteer for at least another month. At first, Zelda didn't understand Mr. Padel's sudden change of heart; he had been anything but nice to her. But a few days ago, when one of her Nepalese sisters let slip that the next volunteer had canceled at the last minute, the pieces fell into place. Even she, the shitty teacher that she was, was better than no teacher at all.

Mr. Padel's transparent behavior irked her enormously. If only he had been *slightly* kind to her during the past seven weeks, she probably would have stayed on for another month or two, to help him and the Ranas out. But she was so tired of all these cultural mind games – she just wanted to get the hell out of her village. There was only one more week of classes before the school closed for its winter holiday. Then she was off to meet up with the rest of her group for their week-long trip to Chitwan National Park, marking the end of their volunteer experience. She was so looking forward to being a silly, carefree tourist for a change. She also couldn't wait to see her fellow volunteers and compare notes. How were they managing? Had their families and headmasters been kind to them? And most importantly, were they going to stay on longer or stop as planned?

No, even after a week of riding elephants and spotting rhinoceroses, Zelda couldn't imagine she would want to go back to her school and teach for another month, even if the rest were willing. She'd stuck it out and made it work without giving up early; she could be proud she'd accomplished what she'd set out to do. Only one more week playing teacher, then it was time to backpack around Asia, just like her friends Mary and Don had done. Her ticket was open-ended, and she still had plenty of money in the bank, enough for a few months of high-end backpacking anyway.

At least her family and students had come around. She may not have saved the world, but at least she could leave Nepal knowing there were no hard feelings. She smiled warmly at her father, trailing behind her and Mr. Koirala. Her father glanced up at her, then quickly down at the ground again. His friend must be an important man, Zelda thought. Her father had been jumpy and nervous ever since they'd arrived at the orphanage.

"Please to come inside," Mr. Koirala said, holding the door to his office open for his visitors.

With great reluctance, she tore herself away from the spectacular scenery and joined the other two at a round table in the center of his spacious office. Lacey doilies, the kind her grandmother used to make, covered almost every surface. Pictures of smiling children lined the cream-colored walls. A television and VCR were mounted on one wall. Mr. Koirala had arranged the chairs so his guests had an unobstructed view of the small screen.

"Please to sit. The tea will be here shortly. Did you enjoy your tour, Zelda?"

She nodded enthusiastically. "Oh, yes. It's amazing how you do so much with so few paid assistants." She could hardly believe a staff of twenty could feed, clothe, shelter, and teach up to four hundred kids. They must have the patience of saints, she thought, or use sticks.

Mr. Koirala beamed. Her father remained silent. "Please to allow me to show you a film we recently made for our supporters overseas. Perhaps you can tell me what you think of it? We can watch it together while we wait for lunch."

"Sure. I mean, yes. Great."

"Good, good." Mr. Koirala pressed play, and the small screen filled with happy brown children, dancing in a circle around a large group of older, wealthy-looking westerners. Zelda couldn't believe how adorable the girls were, all dolled up in heavy makeup and matching saris.

"Last year we organized a supporter's club convention to celebrate our ten-year anniversary. These are some of our most important members." Mr. Koirala fast-forwarded through the cultural dances and vocal performances, pausing the video occasionally to point out an important donor handing over a very large check. One by one, Mr. Koirala explained who each supporter was and how much he or she had donated to their "very worthy cause" over the years, the majority giving between ten and thirty thousand dollars per year. American.

Zelda started to shift around in her chair. Why exactly did her father bring her here?

"We have friends all over the world, even in the Pacific Northwest. We only need to raise a few hundred thousand dollars more, and we can build the next extension. You too can become a member of the orphanage support club. For only two thousand dollars, you can join and then make further donations every year." To Zelda's horror, Mr. Koirala pulled a full-color brochure out of the desk, spreading it open to reveal a donation form. "It would be an honor if you would join our cause. Did you bring your checkbook with you, or would you like to mail it to our post office box?"

What was happening? Zelda was too stunned to speak. Did this stranger really want – no, *expect* – her to give him *thousands* of dollars? And she'd thought Khamel and his family had screwed her over with the *thangkas*. "Look, I'm sorry, but there's obviously been some sort of misunderstanding. I can't give you any money because I don't have any more to give."

Mr. Koirala snorted. "But you are American. Your purse probably cost more than Mr. Rana makes in an entire year. No, no. Nepal is poor; we have nothing. In America you have everything; you are all rich."

Zelda couldn't believe her ears. Did she have a dollar sign tattooed on her forehead that only the Nepali could see? For the past two hours, Mr. Koirala had been nothing but smiles and love, the epitome of a selfless director of an orphanage. She figured he liked showing off to westerners, nothing more. Now all of a sudden he was a high-pressure salesman, and she was keeping him from his next appointment. Zelda, rich? Hah! In Seattle she was definitely the poorest of her friends, the only one in her social circle without company stock options. True, she had managed to save a lot of cash for this trip in just a few months' time, but only by keeping her spending to a bare minimum. And she was not about to give her hard-earned travel fund to this pushy stranger.

Apparently Mr. Koirala correctly interpreted her long silence as a no. "If you will do nothing for this orphanage, then at least you can support your father's school. He needs your help to make it larger and better."

Zelda's outrage boiled over. "How dare you! I *do* support him, by teaching classes at his school – free of charge – five days a week. And perhaps it slipped Mr. Rana's mind –" She glared at her "father," now cowering in his chair. "– but I also brought him seventy-two pounds of textbooks for his school and gifts for his children. What else do you two expect from me? Indentured servitude?"

"Money," Mr. Koirala retorted, his expression impassive. "Mr. Rana also wishes to expand his school. Kapil, did you not show her your plans?"

Zelda had never heard her father's first name, let alone anything about his plans for expanding the school. Her head was about to explode. "Jesus

156

Christ, I cannot believe this. I want to leave right now!" She jumped out of her chair, toppling it over.

"But your tea! Please to sit, Miss Zelda, the curry will be ready any moment now. And soon the children will return from school. Perhaps they can practice their English with you."

The nerve of this guy. He just didn't give up. "Sorry, but this is bullshit. I am leaving. *Now.*" She pushed past her father and Mr. Koirala, running down the stairs towards the Rana family's motorbike.

"Miss Zelda, you do not understand! Please to come back upstairs and talk," her father yelled after her.

Zelda whipped around to face him. "No way! Come on, *Kapil*, I don't want to spend another second in this place."

CHAPTER TWENTY-EIGHT

Yet another fantastic meal, a treat of his friend Harim. Ian sat back, sated. He could get used to this kind of life, he thought, though he could never afford it. This last week had flown by. Harim had taken him on a whirlwind tour of the finer side of Thailand's capital – heavenly massages at Wat Po, transvestite karaoke street parties, ringside seats at *May Thai* matches, and of course the infamous strip clubs of Pat Pong. And his new friend didn't want anything in return. Ian had never met a more generous man in his life.

Harim snapped his fingers together. A waiter dressed in long silk trousers and a high-collared shirt poured jasmine tea into tiny cups, then retreated from their table silently, bowing. "Ian, you seem like a decent guy, trustworthy. Frankly I don't meet many people like you these days. I've had a little problem at work – one of my employees let me down, and I had to let him go. That means I'm one man short this month. I could really use somebody reliable, like you, to take his place."

Ian didn't realize that Harim worked; he'd figured the bloke was a rich playboy on an extended holiday who tipped so well that everybody remembered him. It didn't matter where they were in Bangkok, people were constantly waving at him, calling out his name, sometimes even bowing to him.

But before he could continue, Ian began shaking his head. "Harim, you've been brilliant. I can't thank you enough for letting me stay at your apartment, showing me around, even feeding me. But I'm not looking for charity, and definitely not a full-time job."

His new friend smiled easily. "Please, it is nothing like that, I assure you. If you have just a few days to spare, you would be helping me out of a jam and earn some extra money to keep traveling, for minimal risk. You said you were running short of cash, right?"

Minimal risk? What was that supposed to mean? Ian's gut instinct told him to stand up, thank Harim for a fantastic week, and catch the next boat the hell out of here. He could still afford a few weeks in Laos. But as he glanced down at their empty plates, he reckoned he'd have to wash dishes for a week just to pay for their lunch. After all Harim had done for him, Ian could at least hear him out. He owed him that much.

"What exactly do you mean?" Ian asked.

"Simple transportation gig. You'd be heading to Kathmandu the day after tomorrow; my package needs to get there before the end of the week. You take it with you, give it to one of my associates, and he gives you four thousand American dollars. Then you walk away and have the vacation of a lifetime." Harim shrugged as if this was the most normal thing in the world. "Nothing more to it."

Four thousand dollars American! Ian's head was spinning. At today's exchange rate, that was almost as much as he'd saved up to begin with. *Bonzer!* It sounded so easy – a short plane trip and a handoff, that was it. Ian stopped midthought. A horrible idea crossed his mind. "Wait a second. What's the catch? I'm no drug mule," he whispered.

"Come on, get real. Why would I ask you to smuggle drugs into one of the biggest drug-producing lands in the world?" Harim laughed heartily, swinging his head from side to side as if it was the funniest thing he'd ever heard. "It's virtually risk-free. The only catch is that you have to show up on time and keep your mouth shut. That's it."

Ian laughed with him. Harim was right; why would someone want to smuggle hashish back into Nepal? "What would I be transporting then?"

Harim smiled. "Diamonds."

Ian was sure he'd misunderstood his companion. "Diamonds?"

"Yes, diamonds. Just a few small jewels. You can slip them into your shoe, a pack of cigarettes, or even your money belt. No worries about drug-sniffing dogs or X-ray machines. If you're stopped at the border, you say you thought they were fakes. Hell, look at you – no security guard in his right mind would believe you could afford to buy so many real ones," he said, lighting a cigar and passing it to Ian.

Ian puffed hard, careful not to inhale. Harim was right. A week without doing laundry in hot and smoggy Bangkok had taken its toll. He looked more like a strung-out hippie than the schoolteacher he was. And Harim was so relaxed, acting as if he was asking Ian to take a postcard or trinket back to his grandmother.

Four thousand American dollars for simply carrying a few gems across border control was nothing to sneeze at. Ian could easily turn that money into many more months of hedonistic pleasure, if he was careful. After all he'd wasted during his time with Veny and her friends, he wouldn't be so foolish again.

After a few contemplative puffs on his cigar, Ian finally asked, "And what would I do with the diamonds after I get to Kathmandu?"

Harim smiled.

CHAPTER TWENTY-NINE

Tommy had no idea how he'd gotten to be in Myanmar, but he couldn't seem to convince the men shoving his head into ice-cold water of that fact. They'd been questioning him for hours and hours, accusing him of all sorts of horrendous crimes. He'd begged them repeatedly to call the Canadian Embassy; they could surely explain to his torturers that he was a lost tourist and not a spy.

The man with round glasses and a Pinochet – General Khin – laughed his suggestion off. "How stupid do you think we are? A maple leaf flag sewn onto your jacket does not make you Canadian." Then he nodded to his henchmen, subjecting Tommy to another round of water-based torture.

They'd been in this windowless cell for hours, maybe even days. General Khin's men wouldn't let him sleep; every time his head started to nod, someone smacked him around. Tommy's whole body ached. He was sure his ribs were broken. What did Harim's men do to him? Tommy still didn't know.

It had only taken a few dips in the ice bucket to get Tommy's tongue wagging. He told them everything and anything that came into his foggy brain. His dysfunctional childhood in Canada, his run-ins with the local Toronto PD for shoplifting and petty theft, and finally fleeing to Thailand – anything to make them stop. But nothing he said seemed to satisfy his jailer.

Tommy's screams bubbled up to the surface. General Khin kept yelling at him, telling him to admit he was an American spy in Myanmar to help topple the legitimate communist government. He would have laughed at Khin's stupidity, if the man hadn't been a sadistic torturer. How could Tommy make him understand he really didn't know how he ended up bound and gagged inside a container on a ship now resting in Yangon Harbor? The last thing he could remember – as he repeatedly told his captors – was getting the shit beat out of him by a bunch of guys he owed money to, before being woken up by the barrel of an AK-47.

Where was his passport, identification, money, or plane tickets home? Tommy didn't know that either. Harim had walked out of his hotel room with all of his belongings slung over his shoulder, just before everything went black. But General Khin refused to believe him, asking the same questions, over and over again. Tommy tried to keep his answers simple and brief through chattering teeth; he had already learned his captor did not appreciate sarcasm.

"Tell me once more, how exactly did you come to be in Yangon Harbor?"

Tommy burst into tears. He had already gone through phases of anger, astonishment, and denial. "Please, I've already told you everything! I don't know what you want to hear. I just want to go home." Tommy *had* told General Khin about everything bad he'd done in his short life – everything, that is, except for the diamonds. *What do they do with smugglers here?* he wondered. If he told the truth, would he be facing jail time or the loss of a hand? The thought of rotting away in a Myanmar prison was just as bad as being mutilated for life; he couldn't decide which would be worse.

"I want the truth." His serene smile made Tommy shiver. "Before we begin to work on your genitals, make me understand: Why did we find you in Yangon Harbor without a shred of identification? Are you honestly telling me you don't know why you were tied up and left behind in that container? Someone must really not like you to have been so cruel. If the voyage had been much longer, you would have died from dehydration before you'd been found."

Tommy could feel the blood draining from his face. Suddenly everything fell into place. The Greek had hinted at how he took care of those who dared to cheat him, but Tommy was never sure whether it was boasting or empty threats. Now he knew: All the rumors about The Greek's cruelty were true. Instead of a bullet, he let you starve to death in a dark box, strapped to a ship where no one could hear you scream.

General Khin paced back and forth across the dingy cell, shaking his head. "No, Tommy, you are withholding information. I can feel it."

He didn't want to tell General Khin about the true nature of Harim's business; Tommy knew his own role as a smuggler would only get him into more hot water with his sadistic captor. But he was too scared to care anymore and too tired to lie his way out. If this crazy little man with glasses didn't kill him, Harim would, Tommy was sure of it. And if Khin's men did anything to his penis, well, he wouldn't want to live anymore anyway.

He cried out in frustration, "I'm not an American, and I'm certainly no spy! And yeah, okay, I'm a smuggler. But not drugs, man! Maybe I smuggled some stones here or there, but never drugs! And anyway I'm not the brains of the operation or anything, The Greek is. I'm just a mule. I…I am nothing!" Tommy began to cry unabashedly. He'd probably be dead within the hour; what did it all matter anyway?

For the first time since he'd entered the room, General Khin looked at him with real interest. "So these men you owe money to? Who are they? What exactly did you smuggle for them, Tommy?"

The change in the Asian man's tone pierced through his sobs. Tommy could hear in the man's voice there was only one way to keep his manhood intact: For the first time in his life, he would have to come clean. He could only hope that, after he'd told Khin the truth about one of the most active and widespread smuggling operations in Southeast Asia, the general would be lenient with him and send him home to Canada.

Without another second's hesitation, Tommy told them everything he knew about his months of transporting jewels for The Greek, who his contacts were, the most common pickup points, and even where he lived most of the year.

"What is this Greek's real name?"

"His first name is Harim. I don't know his last name. He's not Greek, either; he's Turkish. And one mean son of a bitch."

CHAPTER THIRTY

I haven't told the Ranas I am going yet, but after the way everyone has been acting, it might be best if I just disappear. I've become much more of an outcast than I ever could have expected. My "father" has refused to look at or talk to me for the past three days. The bastard has even taken to talking about me in Nepali while I'm in the room. He doesn't realize I understand Nepali quite well, even though I still can't converse in it.

He's even started locking the door to the main house so I only have access to the toilet and my own room. I only found that out tonight when I tried to make peace by watching the news with him. It seems to be his favorite thing to do if the electricity is working. I could hear him in the living room, even see him, but he refused to open up.

School's become next to impossible. The older kids know I'm leaving soon, and all they ask about is the new volunteer. Apparently no one's told them he canceled. Besides which, I haven't met the new recruits yet and have no idea whether Ganesh has managed to find another volunteer to take his place on such short notice. The younger ones still see me as their "playtime" teacher, who can easily be manipulated out of teaching real lessons. They've gone back to ignoring my feeble attempts at imparting knowledge, their little minds focused solely on the upcoming two-week vacation and all the candy and treats they'll get.

Coupled with my own realization that I haven't been able to teach them much, I am wondering why the hell I bothered to come to Nepal at all. Why didn't I just head down to Cabo for a few weeks, before committing three months of my life to doing something I know nothing about? At least I only have two more days of teaching. And then it's time to find a sandy white beach and chill out.

Three short raps on the door brought Zelda out of her latest journal entry. She opened the door slowly, dreading what she would find on the other side. Sure enough, chai tea and biscuits. Another breakfast alone. Since she'd gotten back from the orphanage three days ago, the family's helper had been bringing her breakfast to her room. Obviously she was no longer welcome to join the rest of the family in the kitchen upstairs.

With bitterness Zelda thought back to that terrible afternoon, only three days ago. As soon as they'd returned from Mr. Koirala's orphanage, she'd run into the living room and called her program coordinator. Of course Ganesh had been righteously pissed off, until he'd talked to her Nepalese father. "It must be some kind of cultural misunderstanding," he'd said, trying to soothe her injured feelings. "His friend just wanted to show you what they did at the orphanage, that's all. He thought you would be interested."

There was no misunderstanding, Zelda thought, cultural or otherwise. Her Nepali was far from perfect, sure, but she was certain her father had lied to Ganesh in order to save his own ass. Despite Headmaster Padel's attitude, his school did rely on the stream of volunteers Ganesh provided. There were probably plenty of other schools in the Kathmandu Valley that would be happy to have them, even for a few months. Why did she have to get stuck with this guy? Thanks to the locked door, she couldn't even call Ganesh to ask for advice; the only phone was in the living room. At least she'd see him next week, along with the other volunteers, at Chitwan National Park.

Even her upcoming jungle adventure had become a source of concern rather than joy. She couldn't stop thinking about what her father might have said to Ganesh. Lord only knows what kinds of stories the man had made up. Would her trusty program coordinator be mad at her? And what should she tell the other volunteers about her more recent experiences?

Ah, who was she kidding; all the volunteer families probably asked for money. How could they have a "rich" westerner living under their roof for so long and not be tempted? Although she was poor by Western standards, she had enough money in the bank to quit her job and fly to the other side of the world to "find herself." If she looked at the situation from their perspective, all of the volunteers were millionaires.

Never mind, only two more days of teaching and then she was free from her voluntary shackles. But there was still the matter of the weekend, she realized with a heavy heart. She wasn't meeting up with Ganesh and the other volunteers until Tuesday afternoon. Cultural misunderstanding or not, she was clearly no longer welcome in the Ranas' home. Did she really want to spend the weekend with them, after all that had happened this week?

Maybe it would be better for everyone if she left Saturday morning, after breakfast. Then she would have three days for herself before heading to Chitwan National Park with the others. She should do it tonight, tell her family she would be leaving in two days. They would probably be relieved to be rid of her, Zelda thought. She breathed a sigh of relief; it was as if a huge weight had been lifted from her shoulders. Just two more nights. She could hardly believe it. She had survived two months of teaching in a Nepali suburb without contracting any serious diseases or killing any of her students. And in less than seventy-two hours, it would all be over; she'd be back on her own again, ready for her next adventure.

Suddenly her predicament seemed bearable. With renewed enthusiasm, Zelda picked up her breakfast tray and dug in.

"What? But I have already arranged an interview with the local newspaper, in two weeks' time. Why did you not tell me sooner that you were not staying?" her father asked.

Zelda couldn't believe her ears. How could he have assumed she would stay another month, after all that had happened this past week? "If you are so happy to have me here, then why have you been locking the doors to the living room and kitchen?"

"Two of our neighbors have been burglarized. The television is inside the living room; we did not want it stolen. You had only to knock, and we would have let you in."

"I did knock and even shouted through the door. I could hear the television on, but no one got up to let me in."

"Oh, then the volume was too loud. We must not have heard you."

What a slick man, Zelda thought, *he's got an answer for everything.* She'd better try to find out what he had told Ganesh about her, otherwise Chitwan could be a nightmare ending to this increasingly hellish volunteer experience.

"If there were burglaries, why didn't you tell me so I could lock my door too?"

"We didn't think anyone would try to steal from your room. It's the television and propane they want." Though his words seemed to convince the rest of the family, he refused to look her in the eye. She knew he was lying.

"I do not understand. You have only just arrived in Nepal, and now you are going away again?" Mr. Rana asked innocently, shifting the blame back to her.

"Just arrived? I've been in Kathmandu for almost three months! And most of that time, with you," Zelda exclaimed.

"But why are you not coming back after the school holidays? What about the children? Your students need an English teacher."

"Look, I'm sorry that the next volunteer canceled on you at the last minute, but that is not my problem. I signed up for two months of teaching, and as of Friday – tomorrow – my two months are up. I think it is best for everyone if I left Saturday morning. Don't you agree?"

Her father shook his head sadly. "Please to go away now."

Zelda stood up with a huff, her plate of *daal bhat* barely touched. "Fine. I have to pack up anyway," she said, before running downstairs to her room.

CHAPTER THIRTY-ONE

General Khin knew he was dealing with an amateur. He had never seen anyone crack so quickly; twenty-seven minutes must be some sort of record. True, he'd already held Tommy in solitary for a day to loosen him up. But still. These westerners had no discipline.

His prisoner had clearly told them everything they needed to know; the general felt no need to interrogate him further. Besides, he didn't enjoy standing close to him; the Canadian really stank. Still, he couldn't resist ordering the shock cart to be brought into the room, just to see Tommy's reaction. He'd shit himself and passed out, as expected.

Afterwards, General Khin's men poured buckets of water over Tommy until he'd sputtered back awake. Thankfully most of the smell was gone too. On his orders, the guards gave their prisoner a clean set of clothes, then threw him into another windowless cell. The general had a few phone calls to make before he decided what to do with the Canadian intruder.

Returning to his plush office, General Khin relaxed on his red-velvet chaise lounge for a moment, lost in thought. He liked to keep his ear to the ground; you never knew when a random piece of information might come in handy. Years ago he'd learned just how profitable knowledge could be. Chuckling, he glanced around his private lair, filled with antique furnishings and priceless artifacts.

Rumors of a diamond smuggling operation headed by an unknown Turk had made its way to his office several months ago. General Khin was convinced Tommy's Harim was the diamond smuggler his Thai counterparts were searching for. Not that he owed the Thai anything. Still, it never hurt to have someone in his debt on the other side of the border.

He unlocked the top left-hand drawer of his Louis XVI mahogany desk and pulled out a bulky satellite telephone. It may not be fashionable, Khin thought, but it was definitely secure. There was no need for anyone else to get wind of this information, at least not yet. The guards who'd heard the Canadian's confession were still stationed below, well away from phones connected to the outside world. But he couldn't keep them downstairs forever. How long would it be before the information leaked out anyway? Fate had dropped Tommy into his lap; he had to make the most of this opportunity before it was too late.

Whoever he contacted would certainly have to be stationed outside of Bangkok. He couldn't believe Harim had been hiding in Thailand's capital for so long without the help of the city's finest. But who had enough clout to pull off the raid and make it worth his while?

He contemplated briefly which of his lucrative contacts would be the most receptive, then dialed.

CHAPTER THIRTY-TWO

Saturday morning arrived without incident. Zelda triple-checked her bedroom, but everything seemed to be packed up. One last breakfast with the family and then she was off, back to Thamel and the craziness of the tourist district. So much had gone through her mind since she'd told the Ranas she was leaving them. She felt as if she was flying out of Seattle all over again, tossing aside her safe haven for destinations unknown. Was she making the right choice? Would it really have killed her to play teacher for another month? Probably not. But the thought of being cooped up in her room for another four weeks nauseated her.

Who was she kidding? She wasn't cut out for this whole volunteer thing. She'd wanted so badly to make a difference but ended up feeling like one in a long line of temporary volunteers popping in and out of her students' lives. And not one of the better ones either.

And besides, her family would be happy to be rid of her; that was pretty damn clear. Since she'd told them she was leaving, her siblings had pretended not to see her when passing her on the stairs. Even the servant girl refused to acknowledge Zelda's *namaste*s. The whole clan had obviously held her responsible for the next volunteer bailing on them. But what did they expect her to do about it? It wasn't her fault; she didn't even know the guy. All the hours she'd spent trying to think up lesson plans that might engage her students, and all the weeks spent flipping through notecards to learn this stupid language. Not to mention the sore muscles from dragging those books and presents around for so long. And to top it all, she'd *paid* almost seven hundred dollars to be part of the volunteer program. How dare they treat her so shabbily just because she couldn't afford to give more financially.

Locked doors, secretive phone calls, and meals on trays – Zelda was sick of it all. Sick of not being able to walk around freely, tired of being surrounded by the dirt and poor sanitation, exhausted from hauling buckets of water up and down the stairs, and fed up with eating the same boring *daal bhat* twice a day. No, it was time to move on and try to salvage the rest of her trip.

She dragged herself upstairs, dreading the reception her family would give her. Would they even bother to show up at their last meal together?

169

Just in case, Zelda grabbed her camera so she could take a last few snapshots.

To her surprise, her family was waiting for her on the rooftop terrace, all decked out in their finest saris and silks. Only her father was conspicuously absent. Her siblings looked confused, not angry. And her mother was having trouble holding back her tears.

Taken aback by this unexpected display of emotion, Zelda stood speechless before them. She was so sure the Ranas would be thrilled she was finally leaving; this was not at all the reaction she had expected. Even if she could speak Nepali fluently, she wasn't sure what she was supposed to say. She hated goodbyes, false promises to write and visit, knowing as you utter them you will never see or hear from these people again.

Not that she had to worry about any of the school's staff wanting to stay in touch. Her last day as a teacher had made that apparent. The other teachers and Headmaster Padel ignored her completely, well aware she wasn't coming back after the winter holiday. The few older students whom she'd told she was leaving shook her hand and said goodbye as if they would see her next Monday. The younger children gazed back at her with blank stares. Didn't they understand she wasn't coming back after the holidays, or did they not care?

"Please. Before you go, my mother has a present for you. So you will never forget us," Reecha, Zelda's oldest sister, said in English.

The mother handed her a small package, bowing deeply.

"How could I ever forget you?" Zelda whispered. Hands shaking, she tore the wrapping open, revealing a framed photograph of a large stone shrine with a river flowing in the foreground. The Ranas stood on the water's edge, waving at the camera.

"This is Pashupatinath. It is very holy, the most holy Hindu temple in Nepal. We hoped to take you there next month for *Maha Shivaratri* to celebrate the birth of Shiva, but…" Her voice trailed off. Reecha wiped at her eyes, turning away. The rest of her siblings were avoiding her gaze as well, and their mother was sobbing unabashedly.

Zelda couldn't help but tear up herself. She still didn't know what to say or do. She knew from experience that hugs were taboo here. She studied the photograph, trying to think of the right words for the occasion. She recognized the temple vaguely from her guidebooks but hadn't had a chance to visit it. She'd certainly had no idea this place was so important to Hindus or the Ranas. In an instant, Zelda realized how much she still had to learn and see here, and how much more her family could have taught her, if only she'd spoken the language more fluently.

She turned the picture over. Next to her family's names was the date the picture was taken. Her jaw dropped as she realized it was the same day that she'd gone on a hike with Ganesh and the other volunteers. Why didn't the Ranas wait a day so she could have joined them?

Stung, Zelda realized this picture summed up her whole experience. Despite Ganesh's best intentions, she was never really a part of their family, simply one of the many foreigners studying them and their culture for a few months before moving on. And like the rest, she was always looking in from the outside and never part of what was going on all around her. Not that she or any of the other volunteers had the proper cultural background to understand it anyway.

A rush of emotion swept over her. Without thinking, Zelda grabbed her mother and squeezed her tightly. "Thank you so much for letting me stay here with you," she said in English, completely ready to get the hell out of there. She doubted the woman could understand her, but she didn't care anymore.

With one eye on her suitcases, she quickly shook hands with her brothers and sisters. When she reached her oldest sister, Reecha held onto her hand and met her gaze. "Would you write to us and send us pictures of America? Maybe one day you will want to come back and stay with us again?"

"Sure." Zelda kept her face and voice neutral, worried about a last-minute plea for money.

Reecha folded her hands in front of her and bowed deeply. "It was our honor to have you as a guest in our home. We hope you feel welcome to come back whenever you are in Nepal."

Touched by her words and actions, Zelda returned the gesture. "Thank you for your hospitality, letting me stay here, feeding me, all of it."

As soon as she straightened up, Zelda grabbed her bags and ran down to the courtyard. Suddenly her feet couldn't carry her fast enough away from this place. "Thanks again," she cried out, not daring to turn around.

Only after the house was out of sight did she stop, throw her bags onto the ground and bawl her eyes out. She'd never felt like such an egotistical bastard in her entire life.

For the past three days, all she could think about was leaving, regaining her freedom, exploring other parts of the world, but most of all – having *fun*. But as she ran away from her house for the last time, it finally hit her how much freedom she'd had the whole time. She'd *always* had the choice to leave. Nobody was forcing her to be there; she had *chosen* to come and be part of this program. But her Nepalese family was stuck here. This was it for them; this was their life. There was no dream vacation to Thailand or America in their future. Only rising propane prices, cold bucket showers, and on-again off-again electricity. The father would still take off every day to drink with his friends, the mother would still be stuck at home with her whiny sons and disinterested daughters, all with a never-ending supply of schoolwork to do.

Zelda didn't know whether to scream out in rage or cry in sympathy. She wanted to apologize for everything she had done and said, call "do over," press rewind, and start this whole adventure all over again.

But it was too late. She'd had her chance, and she'd blown it.

CHAPTER THIRTY-THREE

Ian wanted a few hours on his own before his flight left. One last trip down memory lane – or in this case Khao San Road. Harim needed time to organize a few last-minute details anyway. Frankly, Ian was looking forward to being on his own again – since he'd said yes to Harim, things had gotten very strange indeed. Take what happened the other night. They were at Harim's pad, getting ready to go clubbing. Ian was kicked back on the leather sofa, smoking a joint and feeling pretty good about their arrangement. Until his host demanded to see his passport and then proceeded to take several digital photos of it. And of Ian, snapped from all angles. For his own security, Harim said.

"You didn't think I would hand you thousands of dollars' worth of diamonds without some insurance, did you?" he asked, with a wink and a smile.

After an afternoon of serious drinking and smoking on sun-soaked terraces, Ian stumbled back to Harim's hotel. He was really going to miss Thailand. Well maybe not this stretch, he mused, gazing around at the flashing neon lights and swarms of stumbling tourists filling Khao San Road. On the islands, he'd truly found the hippie heaven he'd been searching for. But hey, he'd be back by the week's end. That thought alone had gotten him through the day and helped him to excuse Harim's erratic behavior. Ian had to keep his wits about him for a little bit longer. In two days, he'd be four thousand dollars richer, free to go and do what he pleased. He wasn't looking forward to going back to Kathmandu but knew it was a small price to pay. And as he was there anyway, it would be a laugh to see how Zelda Richardson was faring with her vow to change the world – one child at a time.

Harim was waiting for him on the hotel's terrace, sitting alone at a table for six, sipping tea like an English gentleman. Other guests were seated at tables scattered around the expansive cafe, but none close by. Only two largely built men in Hawaiian shirts sat a few meters away, chugging beers.

"Hey man, I've got to get going soon," Ian called out, tapping at his watch and adding loudly, "Can I get the stuff from you now, or are you coming with me to the airport?" He was later getting back to the hotel than planned. His flight left in four hours, and he didn't know how long it would take to get to the airport.

Harim went black with anger. Rising quickly from his table, he strode up the hotel's stairs, violently gesturing for Ian to follow.

What's bugging him this time? Ian wondered as he followed him up the wide staircase to the fifth-floor penthouse. Harim practically threw the door off its hinges. Before Ian could say a word, Harim grabbed him by the T-shirt and threw him inside, slamming the door behind them.

Ian, still surprised by his host's sudden change in moods, was caught totally off guard. He fell hard onto the marble floor, sliding into a black leather couch, headfirst. "What the hell?" he muttered slightly dazed. A golf ball was already forming on his forehead.

"What are you doing? I *live* here." Harim was towering above him, shaking his head in disappointment. "Is it too much to ask for a little discretion?" Harim turned towards the door, running his hands through his wavy hair. With his back to Ian he asked quietly, "You do understand that what I'm asking you to do is highly illegal, right? That is why you are being handsomely rewarded, for showing a dose of discretion."

Harim opened the top of his nightstand, pulled out a small bag and poured its glittery contents onto the bed. Twenty stones danced on the silken sheets. Grabbing the largest diamond – about the size of Ian's little toe – Harim scratched it across a mirror next to the door. The piercing sound of cracking glass filled the room.

Harim threw the stone at Ian; luckily his reflexes kicked in while it was still midair. The diamond shimmered in his palm in a way he'd never seen before. It seemed to be made of a million tiny sparkling rainbows. Ian pushed the tip of the gem into his hand, drawing a trickle of blood. Staring at the thin red line running down his palm, he suddenly realized he was in way over his head.

"Do you get it now, *man*?"

Ian's mind reeled with visions of spending the next five to fifteen years in a Nepali or Thai prison. Images of the Nepalese prisoners being unabashedly beaten by their jailors before the eyes of tourists danced through his head. He repressed the urge to ask Harim how much jail time he'd get if caught. How much money was his freedom worth anyway? Certainly more than four thousand dollars. He was just a teacher in a small Outback town, for Christ's sake, not a bloody smuggler. What had he gotten himself into? Was it too late to back out? Harim had a copy of his passport and had already booked a ticket and hotel room in Ian's name. No, he was in way too deep to back out now. And who knew how

Harim would react if he tried – the bloke was proving to be dangerously unpredictable at best.

Snatching the stone out of Ian's hand, Harim carefully placed all the diamonds back into their velvety home. He deposited the pouch onto Ian's open palm before the Australian could say a word.

Suddenly Harim kicked into salesman mode. "So what do you think? Little risk, big payoff. One run and you'll have enough money to turn your trip into the adventure of a lifetime." He closed Ian's limp fingers over the bag. "Here is your ticket. You'd better take a cab to the airport. It's Sunday, a busy day for flying, and we don't want you to miss your plane, now, do we?" When Ian didn't react, Harim continued, "Is Zelda Richardson picking you from the airport? Or are you going to meet up at her hotel – the Imperial Guesthouse, right? I can always email her and ask."

"What the...?" Ian felt cold all over. Of course, he'd used Harim's computer to email Zelda and tell her he was coming back to Nepal for a few days. In a drunken binge, he'd told Harim all about the silly American and her volunteer program. Such a fool.

Harim reached into his pocket and pulled out a few bills. "Here's an extra hundred for helping me out at the last minute."

Ian stood motionless. There was no getting out of this. He had to go through with his trip and appointment. Ian told himself to be realistic. As long as he showed up and handed over the jewels on time, Harim would have no reason to hurt anyone. He forced himself to forget about the risks and Harim's threats, focusing instead on the months of backpacking these three days of work – a few hours really – would finance. All of Southeast Asia was waiting to be explored. He'd have to watch out for shelia's on expensive holidays this time around, that's all.

Ian took the hundred from Harim's hand. "Why don't you take the diamonds to Nepal yourself?" he asked cautiously, beginning to understand that his host was used to getting his way, no matter what the costs.

"I do some of the runs. I've got to keep up my connections. Networking, you know." Suddenly the generous playboy Ian knew and loved resurfaced. His tone was so easygoing and his grin so reassuring. "But I'm too busy to be flying back and forth every week to some exotic location. But for someone like you, who's not tied down to a job, it's a great way to supplement your vacation allotment. Right? And who knows, maybe you'll like it. I'm always on the lookout for new blood." Harim laughed, spreading his arms wide open. "Endless possibilities, man. Endless possibilities."

CHAPTER THIRTY-FOUR

The roads seemed to be improving. At least Tommy thought he'd been getting thrown about a bit less, these past few kilometers. He wished his captors had at least taken off this damn hood before shoving him back here – he could barely breathe with it on. His legs were shackled and his hands cuffed; it wasn't like he was going anywhere. Was it daytime or night? For how many days had he been rotting away in that filthy cell? His sense of time had vanished completely. He hadn't seen the outside world since the Myanmar Army had woken him up on that cargo ship and dragged him into that god-awful jail.

Their transportation was slowing down. As they came to a stop, Tommy could hear high-pitched voices approaching. Doors creaked open. His heart skipped a beat. It was too surreal to be true; his mind refused to accept the inevitable. This was certainly not how he figured he was going to go out, dying in some stinking Asian jungle.

Tommy was forced to stand and then roughly shoved forward. He tripped and fell off a ledge, falling knees first onto hard ground. Somebody was grabbing at his hair, and suddenly white light blinded him. He tried to shield his face with his arms, but his hands were still bound. Oh, how his wrists ached.

Uniformed legs were moving towards him. Tommy sucked in the fresh air greedily. It didn't smell of salt anymore; the air here was mustier. His eyesight was readjusting quickly. Camouflaged vehicles were parked under a canopy of trees; only a few rays of the setting sun broke through the thick foliage. They must be in some sort of forest.

Tommy was forced to his feet. The thin Asian man before him was definitely military but wore a different type of uniform than General Khin. The man barely glanced at him before nodding to the soldiers surrounding Tommy and walking away.

Hands pushed against his back, forcing him forward. A gate blocking the road ahead of them opened as the men drew near. On the other side, a Jeep waited with its motor running. Tommy almost jumped for joy when he saw the big yellow sun and red field painted on the vehicle's doors. He was back in Thailand. Surely they had an extradition treaty with Canada. Maybe he wouldn't have to do any jail time at all, if he played his cards right. Right now he really didn't care; he just wanted to go home, in handcuffs if need be.

All of a sudden, Tommy felt dead tired. He'd been too terrified to sleep under General Khin's watch. Now that he knew Khin hadn't ordered a firing squad, but arranged a deal, Tommy could feel the terror draining out of him. There was still a chance he could get out of Asia alive. But what exactly would the Thai expect from him? Would he have to testify against Harim? Tommy was too exhausted to care.

The armed men pointed to the backseat of the Thai Jeep. Tommy's feet felt like lead weights. He struggled against his handcuffs as he climbed inside, finally pulling himself up onto the hard wooden seat. Before the guards could flank him, Tommy was fast asleep.

CHAPTER THIRTY-FIVE

Ian spent what felt like an eternity in the airport bathroom hiding and re-hiding the velvety satchel. Visions of cavity searches replaced those of banana-leaf joints and snorkeling trips. He didn't know what would be smarter, to flush the diamonds down the toilet and make a run for it, or go through with what he promised to do.

Suddenly everything Harim had said or done was tinged with sinister undertones. Ian could feel the bile rising in his throat again. Why did he ever say yes? He'd had a bloody brilliant three months in Asia; was another three really worth this hassle? How could he have been so stupid?

The airport announcement system crackled to life. Ian could just make out the final boarding call for his short flight back to Kathmandu. He dumped the loose stones into his money belt, spreading them out between the thick wad of dollars, baht, and rupees. Hopefully the gems would be less conspicuous there if he did get patted down. *Speaking of conspicuous*, Ian thought while glancing in the mirror; he looked like a sweaty mass murderer. His T-shirt and dreadlocks were plastered to his body. Dark bags loomed under his bloodshot eyes. Airport security would be crazy *not* to pick him out.

He toweled himself one last time, splashing water on his face in an attempt to lessen the blotchy redness of his skin. Donning his backpack, he charged off to his gate, a man on a mission. Concentrating on his dream of traveling around Asia, Ian put on his most relaxed "hey man, I just did Thailand" face and cruised through security without a hint of trouble. He boarded immediately, the airplane door closing behind him.

His heart was beating so fast that Ian swore he could see his chest moving up and down. As he searched for his place on the aircraft, sweat droplets cascaded down the pathway like breadcrumbs. Plopping himself into his aisle seat, he scanned left then right, not-so-inconspicuously. Images of Harim photographing his passport and laughing maniacally kept flashing through his mind. As he buckled himself in, a terrible thought occurred to him. Was he being set up? Had Harim called ahead and warned Nepalese border security to look out for a skinny, dreadlocked Australian? Is that why Harim had taken all those pictures of him? Were the Nepalese in on it as well?

Ian gripped the armrests with all his might as the plane's wheels left the ground. There was no turning back now; he would have to prepare for the worst. Nepalese jail cells couldn't be as bad as Zelda claimed they were – could they?

Déjà vu, back in Tribhuvan Airport again. Ian prayed this stay would not be permanent. He slapped his perspiration-soaked rupees onto the visa clerk's small desk. The Nepalese man only raised his eyebrows slightly when picking up the bills but didn't say anything. Maybe Ian's sheepish grin was enough. After double-checking his authenticity, the clerk stamped his passport and waved him through.

Crossing between armed guards on his way to the baggage claim, Ian forced himself to casually stroll downstairs and into the waiting chaos below. He wanted to whoop with delight; Harim *hadn't* set him up. At least one of his nightmares hadn't come true.

Feeling elated, Ian made his way to the taxi stand. Harim had given him the name of a hotel close to Durbar Square. After he checked in, a message would be delivered to his room. The note would tell him where Harim's "friend" would meet him the next morning. Ian would hand over the jewels to this person, receive four thousand American dollars for his troubles, and then they would part ways, mutually satisfied. He would enjoy Kathmandu for a day or two, and then head on back to beautiful Thailand, or wherever else he chose to go.

Ian had played this scene over and over in his head during the flight. It all sounded so easy and straightforward. Now all he had to do was get to the hotel and check in.

CHAPTER THIRTY-SIX

Someone was jostling Tommy on the shoulder. "Come on, mom, just ten more minutes."

Cold water rushed over his head and shoulders, snapping him out of his sleepy state. "I'm up, I'm up!" he yelled, looking around in confusion. He was in a white room, handcuffed to a folding chair, placed next to a metal table. Two armed guards were standing on either side of him. Across from him was a middle-aged Asian woman; a sketch pad and pencils were laid out in front of her. To her left was a video camera mounted onto a tripod and aimed directly at him, its red record light already lit up. The man from the Jeep was seated next to her, straddling the chair cowboy-style. Tommy tried to sit up straight, but the handcuffs prevented him from doing so.

"What's going on?" he asked, still a bit foggy. He looked down at his body, now clothed in white pajamas. He had no recollection of changing into them.

"That's what I was hoping to ask you. Thomas Braintree, correct?"

Tommy looked up at the man vaguely, then glanced around the room. Where in the heck was he now?

"Do not worry. You are in safe hands now. The Myanmar Army does not look so kindly on those who arrive, let us say, unannounced?" the man from the Jeep said, leaning his face forward into Tommy's own as he grinned broadly. Thinking about General Khin and his men sent shivers up his spine.

"So, Tommy, are you going to be helpful to us, like you were with General Khin? That is the first question we need to consider."

Tommy nodded his head vigorously. "Please, I will tell you anything you want to know. Anything! I just want to go home."

"Good. But let me make this very clear before we begin: You have admitted to smuggling diamonds between Thailand and Nepal. You were also caught trying to enter Myanmar illegally. If you lie to me, I will personally see to it that you spend the rest of your days in a Thai jail cell."

"Trust me, I was *not* trying to enter Myanmar!" Tommy screamed in indignation. He was found chained to a chair inside a locked container; why on God's green earth did they think he had anything to say about his destination?

The man from the Jeep raised one finger to his lips, shaking his head gently. Tommy didn't need his captor to spell it out for him; he watched the news. He knew perfectly well that prisons in Thailand were nothing more than disease-ridden, open-air pens. He had to get himself extradited back home. Tommy took a deep breath and told himself to calm down. He needed this man on his side. If the Thai authorities didn't arrest Harim, he would be on the run for the rest of his life. He had no choice but to tell them everything and pray they could capture the slippery bastard.

"If you cooperate, we might be able to, how do you say, 'cut a deal.' Extradition to Canada could be arranged."

Tommy nodded enthusiastically, glad he and his Thai captor were on the same page.

"Tell me about this smuggler. What is his name?"

"I call him The Greek. But his real name is Harim. I thought it was Antonio for a long time, but then I heard someone else call him Harim." Tommy knew he was babbling, but he didn't want to leave out any of the details. He wanted to get it right the first time.

After he got out, he was going straight. No more screwing around with half-baked schemes or grandiose plans. It was time to find some mind-numbing nine-to-five job in Schmucksville and settle down. Make weekly visits to his mother and listen to her bitch about how things used to be better. Maybe he could even make it right with Chantal. They could have fat kids together, two cars, a house in the suburbs with a picket fence – the whole goddamned lot. Only a few days ago, that kind of life would have bored the fuck out of him, but right now, keeping up with the Joneses sounded like heaven on earth.

"And where did you meet up with this Harim?"

"We met on a terrace, in front of his hotel. He lives in the penthouse."

"And where is this hotel?"

"In Bangkok, walking distance from Khao San Road. It's on a side street. There's a courtyard with big banana trees on either side of the main entrance."

"And the address?"

"I don't know; please don't hurt me." Tommy crouched down into the chair, sure he was going to get beat up again.

"Can you show me the street on a map?"

"I think so," he whimpered.

The man from the Jeep pushed his chair back and stood up. "Okay

Tommy. Now you will tell her –" he pointed at the woman with the sketch pad "– exactly what Harim looks like."

Within twenty minutes, the sketch artist had created a portrait of Harim that was his spitting image. The likeness was so great, simply looking at it gave Tommy the chills; she'd reproduced his piercing eyes and menacing gaze perfectly. He'd even been able to point out Harim's hotel on a map. The man from the Jeep seemed satisfied.

Tommy was taken to another cell – somewhat cleaner – and given proper clothes and a bowl of soup. He slurped the warm broth down in two gulps, then threw himself onto the bed, still in his pajamas. It was a thin foam mattress covered in thick burlap. At least this cell had a bed. His mind was racing. What more could the Thai authorities want from him? Had he told them all that they wanted to hear? Was it enough to get him extradited back to Canada?

CHAPTER THIRTY-SEVEN

Within an hour of arriving in Kathmandu, Ian was standing in the lobby of the four-star Kali Guesthouse. As he climbed the wide marble staircase to the third floor, he remembered Zelda telling him Kali was the god of revenge. He hoped the choice of hotels wasn't some perverse joke on Harim's part.

His light-filled room was huge and tastefully decorated in muted yellows and reds. The bed alone was as big as the first hotel room he'd rented in Kathmandu, only a few kilometers away. From his private balcony, he had an unobstructed view of the manicured hotel gardens. Peacocks strutted around the wide lawn while leashed monkeys gobbled up papaya slices thrown to them by hotel guests sitting on the cobblestone terrace. He dropped his bags and went downstairs for a beer.

Sitting quietly in the hotel garden with only the hoots of primates to disturb him, Ian could feel the adrenaline of the past few hours seeping out of his body. Just a bit of work, he told himself, and he was back on the road again. Maybe it would be better to start afresh and see someplace new, instead of going back to Thailand. Someplace like Laos or Vietnam maybe. They certainly seemed to be cheap countries to backpack around. Besides, he didn't want to run into Harim again. The money was good, but Ian didn't think he could handle doing another run – his nerves weren't up to it.

Shortly after he'd ordered his third round, a bellboy approached unobtrusively, handing him a sealed envelope in the most discreet of manners. Ian stuffed the note into his pants, downed his beer, then hurried upstairs.

Back in the safety of his own room, Ian sat on the bed and opened the envelope with shaky hands. It was brief and to the point: "Basmati Brothers Jewelers, corner of Ganga Path and Freak Street, 10 a.m. Ask for Bishal."

The handwriting was neat and tidy; there was no indication of who had written it or where it had come from. Was someone on the hotel staff in on it? Most certainly; there was no address or room number on the envelope, not even his name.

Ian reread the instructions, puzzled by the address. Was the sender serious? Those couldn't be real street names, could they? He would have to get a map, see whether someone was messing with him. There would certainly be street maps in the lobby.

Ian grabbed his smoking kit and sprinted downstairs. Plucking a map off the counter, he scanned the street index, hardly believing his eyes when he found both names listed. *This must be some sort of sign*, he thought, *the good kind*. With a grin on his face, he headed out to find the Ganga Path before hitting the bars.

After many wrong turns, he finally found the jewelry store, now closed. He repeatedly retraced his steps to his hotel until he found a more direct route. After committing the path to memory, he headed off to find his little drug dealer. Would the boy in the Jimi Hendrix shirt remember him, two months later? Ian hoped so – his hash was out of this world.

The next morning, Ian had tea sent to his room, rather than heading down to the gardens for breakfast. He'd been tossing and turning all night, worrying about the delivery, and was not in the mood for food or company. What if this Bishal bloke tried to shortchange him, or pulled a knife? He should have asked the Sherpa Club's owner to go with him when he'd had the chance last night. He'd considered it briefly but decided against confiding in Raju. If he told him what he was up to, the bloke would probably expect a cut of Ian's share. No, he was just going to have to get tough, do it on his own. Just a few minutes' work for a few months of pleasure. No worries.

He finished his drink and glanced at his watch, surprised to see it was only half past eight. Plenty of time to smoke a joint. It would certainly help calm his nerves. From his balcony, he scanned the hotel garden below. Out here he'd be too exposed, he reckoned; too many guests were still eating their breakfast. And this was definitely a posh hotel; who knew how the staff would react to illegal drugs. Probably not too kindly.

Ian went into the tile-covered bathroom and pulled the door shut. He wet a bath towel and shoved it into the crack beneath the door. Flipping on the high-powered fan, he waited for the ventilation system to kick in. The fan seemed pretty strong; he reckoned this would do.

Setting his daypack on the edge of the porcelain sink, he rooted around for his smoking kit. He could feel the small wooden box at the bottom of his bag, but it was caught on something. With a rough jerk, he pulled it free. But instead of just the box, the velvet satchel also flew up into the air, its thin cord tangled around his smoking kit.

As the satchel hit the edge of the sink, he saw several stones shoot out of the velvet bag and ricochet off porcelain and mirrored glass, before disappearing. Ian grabbed at his chest. "You've got to be joking!" he screamed.

He felt around the white tile floor for the transparent gems. Three were spread around the sink in front of him; his fingers closed greedily around their cool surfaces. He held the diamonds up to the light; no cracks or splits as far as he could see. With a huge sigh of relief, he carefully placed the stones back into the bag, hoping that was all of them. Only one way to be sure. He poured the contents of the velvet satchel onto a hand towel and counted the gems. Only eighteen; two other diamonds were still somewhere in this room. He frantically crawled around, feeling every millimeter with his fingertips, but to no avail. The renegade gems had definitely not landed on the floor. With a gulp, Ian realized that left only one place to look.

He dug around his backpack for his pen light, shining its thin beam into the sink's drain. Just centimeters away, Ian could see a tiny ray of light refracting off the stones. They were definitely in the drainpipe, seemingly caught up in a blob of hair.

Bollocks! He tore open his backpack, dumping its contents onto the floor. He grabbed his Swiss Army knife and tried to unscrew the drain cap. But the screw seemed to be disintegrating the more he turned. The pipes – red from rust – had apparently not been replaced during the hotel's major renovation last year. Try as he might, the drain would not budge. *If I had a hammer*, he reckoned, *I might be able to pop it off.*

He looked around his room for a heavy enough object, settling on a stone statue of the Hindi god Kali, the hotel's demonic namesake. He angled the screwdriver's flat blade under the drain's edge and heaved with all of his might. The statue shattered into hundreds of pieces, but the drain remained firmly in place.

"Shit!"

He kicked aside the shards and returned to the contents of his backpack. There had to be another way. *Think, mate, think!* The chewing gum and pen lying on the tile floor gave him an idea. Maybe, just maybe. He popped the last two pieces into his mouth, chewing as hard and fast as he could. When the Nepalese gum finally softened, he wrapped it around the pen and slid it carefully through the wide slits and into the pipe below.

Slowly, oh so slowly, Ian edged the pen closer and closer to the stone. He couldn't see what kind of crap was stuck to the insides of the pipe and didn't want to accidentally knock the stones further down, away from his reach. The pen was just long enough. With the slightest of pressure, Ian nudged the gum into the first stone, willing it to stick. Holding his breath, he raised the diamond ever so slightly. The gum seemed to be holding. Ian tried to keep his hand steady as he raised it carefully towards the light.

As he approached the drain opening, the stone began to wobble. Ian held in his breath – he was so close. He repositioned the light to see whether it was trapped on something else, when the stone lost its battle with gravity and disappeared into the darkness with a loud plunk.

"NO!" Ian yelled at the top of his lungs. He kicked the pipe hard, taking his frustrations out on it, only to be rewarded by hearing a second splash.

"No, no, no, no, no! This was not how it was supposed to go!" The pipe made a ninety-degree angle before it disappeared into the wall; the stones must be down there, he reckoned. Ian tugged on the pipe with both hands, screaming curses at it, trying to yank it from the wall. It wouldn't budge. He attacked it with the pliers on his Swiss Army knife, but the bloody thing was too wide for his traveler's tools. If only he had an actual wrench and a hammer.

Panting from exhaustion, Ian told himself to calm down. What if he called housekeeping and said he dropped his contacts? Would they take the pipe out for him? Even if they did, how could he explain the two diamonds trapped inside? Nobody here at this hotel would believe he could afford to buy real diamonds, especially ones this big. They would call the police right away or pocket them.

"Calm down, Ian, there has to be a way out of this," he told himself rationally. If he could find a big enough wrench, he should be able to remove the L-shaped segment himself and recover his lost wares. So where could he get his hands on such a tool? Wracking his brain, he tried to remember whether he'd even seen a tool store in Thamel. He'd only really been interested in the bars and head shops during his wanderings. Would the hotel staff help him find the tools he needed without wanting to know why he required them first? No, he couldn't ask the hotel staff for help; there were too many unanswerable questions.

He contemplated searching the hotel for their maintenance room but figured he would raise too much suspicion if he got caught opening random doors. Though he suspected somebody working here was Harim's inside man, he had no idea who it could be. If only he knew, Ian raged, they would have to help him out of this mess. But he couldn't risk asking the wrong bloke; the risks were too high. Ian wanted to avoid seeing the inside of a Nepalese jail firsthand, if at all possible.

No, he had to sort this out on his own, or at least without the help of the hotel staff. But who else did he know that had the right tools at their disposal? In a flash, Ian knew who he could turn to: Raju, the owner of the Sherpa Club. Of course. The bloke was always there. The bar was huge; he must have the proper tools to make repairs now and again.

Ian glanced at his watch – almost 9 a.m. His meeting was in one hour. There was still time, if he hurried. He checked that the rest of the diamonds were really in their satchel before securing the cord tightly this time and placing it into his money belt. Throwing the "Do not Disturb" sign on the door, he ran down to the lobby.

"Oi! What's the quickest way to Thamel from here?" Ian rasped.

"It is quite far – perhaps it would be better to take a taxi. Please to let me call one for you," the man behind the front desk offered.

"Cheers, mate. I am in a bit of a hurry."

Twenty minutes later, Ian was standing in front of the Sherpa Club's entrance, the adrenaline rush making him sweaty and out of breath. The taxi was indeed a lot faster than walking. For once, he didn't hear any music playing inside. *Shit!* When he'd stumbled out of here at 2 a.m. – just a few short hours ago – the bar was still full. The owner and his staff were probably fast asleep. Well, he was here and in a jam, might as well see whether the door was unlocked. Ian tried the handle. The door creaked open.

He entered slowly, hesitantly calling out, "G'day? Anybody awake?"

No response. The place smelled like stale beer and old cigarettes; the staff must not have left any of the windows open. Ian closed the door softly behind him, hoping not to wake any sleeping staff, at least not suddenly. He didn't want to get confused for a burglar. No sense getting himself shot up or stabbed; the day was already going badly enough. If he could just borrow a wrench and hammer, he could get the pipe open, fish out the diamonds, and still make his meeting at 10 o'clock. He'd paid the taxi driver extra to wait for him.

He knew the office was in the back, behind the bar. That must be where the owner kept his tools, he reckoned. Walking slowly through the cavernous club, he listened closely for any sounds of life. He knew the owner lived somewhere in the building, but not exactly where.

As Ian reached the bar, the hairs on his forearms stood on end. What was that? Did he hear someone yelling?

He listened carefully, tempted to call out again, but something inside told him to keep quiet. Maybe he wasn't alone after all. Was it the owner? Or had he interrupted a robbery in progress? That would just be his luck today. He was pretty sure the office door was in the next room – if there were robbers present, that's where they would be.

Maybe he should split, get out of here while he still could. But then what? Harim didn't seem like the type of guy who tolerated screw-ups. The thought of the two diamonds stuck in his hotel bathroom's drainpipe forced him to at least sneak a peek. He'd come this far. If he didn't see anything suspicious, he would pop into the office and see whether he could locate any tools. Quickly and quietly.

Ian poked his head around the corner and spotted three doors lining the far wall. One of those had to be Raju's office. The door in the middle was slightly ajar; a thin shaft of light spilt out onto the hallway floor. As he tiptoed towards the narrow opening, another round of yelling ensued. Ian lay down on his belly and stuck his head inside.

The smell of feces and sweat was overwhelming. He could see down the staircase and into a poorly lit room filled with bunk beds. Raju stood in the middle, surrounded by large group of dirty children. Ian scanned the crowd and spotted his drug dealer amongst them. Raju was taking money from the kids, cursing and slapping them when they didn't hand over the rupees fast enough. When one boy resisted, trying to hold a few bills back, Ian's "friend" took a leather strap and whipped him mercilessly, obviously as a warning to the rest.

As Raju raised his whip again, Ian started to rise with it. None of those kids looked to be older than twelve, around the same age as his students back in Darwin. How could Raju beat children like that? But before Ian could get to his knees, he lay back down. What could he really say or do? Tackle the bar owner and explain the wickedness of his ways? He was easily twice Ian's size and clearly loved to fight. Ian doubted the bloke would let him just walk out of there. He forced himself to stay down while Raju continued his tirade.

After he'd collected money from all of the kids, Raju tore open a sack of bread and threw it up into the air. The children scrambled towards the crumbs, scratching and clawing at each other for the largest pieces. Ian's blood boiled; he could feel bile rising in his throat. These were children for Christ's sake. Not animals. Clamping one hand firmly over his mouth, he forced himself to move silently towards the entrance before his anger got the better of him.

When Raju turned towards the stairs, Ian was already running out of the club.

CHAPTER THIRTY-EIGHT

After several wrong turns, Ian finally found the street his hotel was on. His breathing was ragged from jogging most of the way. By the time he'd stumbled out of the Sherpa Club and onto the street, his taxi had split or given up on him. In either case, it was gone. Ian kicked himself for being so stupid – he should have known better than to have paid the taxi driver in advance to wait for him. Yet another shitty bit of luck.

He still felt anger and shame coursing through his veins. But mostly it was disgust with himself for not doing or saying anything to stop the bar owner from abusing those children. The faces of his students – happy, well-fed children – kept flashing through his mind. He felt like such a coward. Yet he still didn't know what he could have done without risking serious bodily injury. Would having gotten himself beaten up or even killed have helped those boys? Probably not. What could he do about it now? Go to the police? Who would get in more trouble, the respectable bar owner or drug-dealing street kids?

He whacked his fists against his head, forcing himself to push the image of Raju degrading those kids out of his mind. Right now he had a bigger – or at least more immediate – problem on his hands. He had to get himself out of this mess with Harim.

As Ian approached his hotel's gated drive, he glanced at his watch again, stopping midstep and staring in disbelief. It was already a quarter to eleven; he was officially forty-five minutes late for his appointment. *Bollocks!* He *had* to find a way to get the diamonds out of that bloody pipe and get himself down to Harim's jeweler as quickly as possible. Even if that meant asking the hotel staff for help. He'd exhausted all other options, and right now making noise or arousing their suspicions seemed unimportant in the face of Harim's wrath.

Either way he sliced it, Harim was going to be pissed. That Grecian god didn't seem like the type who was used to dealing with problems tolerantly and rationally. Ian *had* to find a way to get those stones back and Harim out of his life. Was there another way out of this, he mused. Perhaps he could pay for the two gems he'd lost. He snorted at the thought. Though he had no idea what the going rate for one of Harim's diamonds was, Ian was sure two of them were worth more than his pa's overextended farm back in Darwin.

He nodded distractedly to the two porters holding the hotel doors open for him, still lost in thought. As he entered the lobby, he tripped over a pile of suitcases stacked up next to the door and wacked his head on a potted palm tree, yelping as he fell. Ian felt his forehead gingerly. Though a golf-ball-sized knot was quickly forming, the fall had not broken skin. He waved at the two stunned porters to let them know he was okay.

Ian started to push himself back up when he noticed two large men in Hawaiian shirts standing next to the front desk looking around for the yelp's source. Their eyes crisscrossed the lobby diligently but, in the hustle and bustle of guests checking in and out, Ian remained unseen. After a few moments of searching, they resumed their conversation with the hotel manager.

Ian's whole body started to tremble. His gut told him to stay low. He'd seen those blokes before, but didn't know where. Wherever it was, it wasn't a happy place. All he wanted to do was get up to his hotel room and start destroying his room's drainage system. But the only entrance to the hotel's guest rooms was via an inner staircase located directly next to the front desk. He'd have to walk right past those blokes. Something inside was telling him that was a very bad idea. He wouldn't be able to get up to his room until those two moved on.

Could they be working for Harim? Ian's mind skipped forward to the worst-case scenario. *Calm down, get ahold of yourself,* he told himself, *you're being paranoid*. The men were probably just overweight ex-rugby players, talked into a cultural tour of Nepal by their wives. His meeting with the jeweler was scarcely a half-hour ago; if they were working for Harim, then they must have driven to the hotel as soon as he didn't show. Unlikely, he reckoned. He figured the jeweler would have given him a bit of leeway before sending in the big guns. Naw, they weren't working for Harim. He was most likely working himself up about nothing.

But still, his legs refused to move. With all the comings and goings, he couldn't hear what the men were discussing from his current position, crouched down below a large potted palm tree, located in the middle of the hotel's sizeable lobby. To be on the safe side – and before he announced his presence to those blokes by running up the staircase – he had to get closer and find out who these jokers were, before deciding what to do next.

Ian waited for another wave of new arrivals to enter the hotel lobby, then sprang up and sprinted towards one of several high-backed chairs placed only a meter from the front desk. He reckoned from here he'd be able to hear a bit more of their conversation without being seen. As he tuned his ears to the men's voices, Ian prayed they were just a couple rednecks complaining to the manager about a shortage of towels or bad coffee, and not thugs working for Harim.

With much trepidation, he stretched out his neck, curving his ear around the soft velvet of the chair's winged back. There were so many people checking in, he had trouble homing in on their conversation. It took him a second to work out the hotel manager's strongly accented English. Ian was pretty sure he heard him say, "No, he still has not shown up yet."

"How can you be sure?" asked one of the thick-necked men.

"This is the only entrance to the rooms, and I have been on shift all day, since he left this morning anyway. He was in a real hurry. I had to call him a cab to Thamel."

"Where in Thamel?"

"I don't know. He told the driver to 'step on it' as soon as he jumped inside. He didn't say where he was going."

"Did he have his luggage with him?"

"No, nothing but a small daypack. He had more luggage when he checked in."

"Okay. Are you sure no one has seen him since then? Maybe he slipped past you and went back to his room? He didn't show for his appointment, and none of our guys have seen him wandering around the area. We thought he might have gotten lost."

"That is what I have been trying to tell you," the manager said, exasperated. "After he left in such a hurry, I checked his room to see whether the rest of his luggage was still there. It looks like there has been a struggle. A statue is broken on the floor, towels and bedsheets strewn everywhere, and all the drawers are open. Someone else must have searched the room already. I do not know how somebody else could have gotten up there and then fled without me seeing them. Was it one of yours? Or is someone else involved?" the manager asked, concern apparent in his tone.

Ian went red and softly groaned in despair. He'd done that damage himself while trying to find something he could fashion a tool out of to break open the pipe. Now they'd think he'd gotten robbed and had taken off. How would Harim react when he heard that news?

Harim's thugs exchanged worried glances. "And now he's disappeared?" the larger of the two asked.

"Here, you take the key and look for yourself. Room fifteen, on the left. Maybe the stones are still hidden there, somewhere. I will stay at the front desk, in case he comes back."

Both men nodded before waddling their way up the staircase leading straight to his room.

Ian's whole body was shaking so badly that the chair he was sitting in seemed to be dancing. The bloody hotel manager. Ian should have known he was in on it. Who knew how many other employees were working for Harim, too. Harim or whoever he worked for apparently had deep pockets and lots of friends. If only he'd known beforehand, he could have explained what had happened and gotten help. Pissing off the manager would have been vastly preferable to losing the diamonds. But it didn't matter now, he realized with a heavy heart. He could forget about rescuing the last two gems – he was no match for Harim's hired help. Ian doubted that his thugs would give him the chance to explain where the gems were before breaking his kneecaps. And even if they did, would either one of them believe the two missing stones were probably already swirling around Kathmandu's drainage system?

The sudden realization of how much shit he was in hit home hard. Ian let his head drop into his hands. How could he have been so stupid? Why had he ever said yes to Harim? Was his physical well-being worth a measly four thousand dollars? He thought not. He would do anything to make things right, but he couldn't see any way out. He couldn't get to the last two stones or pay for them. He was alone, broke, and guilty as charged. If Harim ever found him, he was dead. Period. Game over.

Ian used his T-shirt to wipe away the tears forming in his eyes. When his sight cleared, he noticed an older couple dressed in matching khaki shorts and white tank tops. Baseball caps sporting the American flag completed the ensemble. They'd plopped down onto the couch across from him and were pointing and gesturing at him, obviously engaged in some kind of argument. Ian leaned back into his chair and closed his eyes, pretending to drift off to sleep.

"Harold, do you think that guy is actually a guest here?" the older woman whispered not-so-softly into her husband's ear. "If he is, we'd better talk to the tour operator."

"Don't be so melodramatic, Claudine. Look around you already. The hotel's lobby is fabulous, and the guidebook gave it four and a half stars. Can't we just relax and enjoy ourselves for once?"

"Harold, look at him! He looks like a beggar who hasn't showered for months. He's probably a drug addict too. How can you be so casual about sleeping under the same roof as someone like him?"

"Shush already, stop raising your voice. Let's ask the manager whether the guy's even a guest here before you go and spoil our whole trip, okay? If he's not, I'm sure hotel security will get rid of him for you."

Before Harold could rise, Ian jumped up and pushed his way through a pack of arriving guests, racing top speed along the gravel driveway, back into the welcoming chaos of downtown Kathmandu.

CHAPTER THIRTY-NINE

Zelda woke groggily. It sounded like someone was banging on the door. Who could that be? Did one of the other volunteers leave their homes early too? Her group was meeting Ganesh downstairs in her hotel's lobby in two days, just a few hours before their bus departed for Chitwan National Park. As she hadn't had the courage to call her program coordinator and tell him she'd already left the Ranas' house, no one knew she was here. Before she could snuggle back down under the covers, the pounding resumed. There was definitely someone out there trying to get her attention.

Zelda looked at the clock. It was already noon. She pulled a pillow over her head and moaned. She'd wallowed in self-pity last night, managing to drink herself into oblivion. All she wanted to do right now was sleep off this hangover and forget about being a volunteer. "Go away," she mumbled, trying to drift back to sleep. But the thuds didn't stop, only grew more insistent. It sounded like someone was yelling through the door. In her half-dream state, she couldn't understand what they were saying. Was there a fire or something? She sniffed the air suspiciously but didn't smell smoke. What was the word for "fire" in Nepali again?

She pulled on boxer shorts and a T-shirt, calling out, "Okay already, I'm coming!"

The pounding didn't cease. Throwing open the door, she bellowed at her unwelcome, unknown visitor, "What's the emergency?"

Zelda stopped short, in shock. "Ian?" was all she could manage.

He pulled her into a big bear hug, squeezing hard. "Thank God you're all right!" His clothes smelled like he'd slept in them. "May I please come inside?"

"Yeah, sure." Zelda released his embrace and stepped out of the doorway, letting him pass. "What the heck's going on, Ian? What are you doing in Kathmandu?" She pinched her hand; a jolt of pain shot up her arm. Yes, she was awake.

"Sorry to burst in on you like this, but I've gotten us into a jam. You've got to get out of here, and I mean now." Ian picked her suitcase up off the floor, threw it onto the spare bed, and began tossing all of her belongings inside. "Can you please get dressed?"

Zelda was too shocked to react. "Wait, you got *us* into a jam?"

"Unless you have ten thousand dollars or so lying around, we have to get out of here and fast. Harim's men know about this hotel."

Her pulse rose instantly. "Who the hell is Harim, and why do you need ten thousand dollars?"

"I promise to tell you everything, absolutely everything, but right now I need you to get dressed. Can you do that? *Please*?" he pleaded, tossing a pair of pants at her.

Zelda started to speak, but one look at her friend told her he wasn't pulling her leg. Wordlessly she speed-dressed as he closed up her suitcase and pulled on her backpack. He opened the door while she buckled her sandals, looking both ways before waving for her to join him.

As soon as they were in the hallway, Zelda turned towards the main staircase leading down to the lobby two flights below. Ian grabbed her arm and whispered, "Is there another way out of here?"

She looked at him, puzzled. "I'm supposed to turn the room key in to the front desk when I leave. They don't like us taking them out of the hotel, in case I get robbed on the street."

Ian tightened his grip, hurting her arm. "Just this once, I'm asking you to break the rules. Is there another way out of here or not?" The urgency in his voice scared the crap out of her. This wasn't some sick joke; he was truly frightened.

"The back stairs will take us down to the gardens. The middle path leads to the main road."

"Good, let's go."

As they fled down the stairs, Zelda's mind raced with disaster scenarios. Did he rob someone named Harim? Get caught with his wife or buying dope from him? And most importantly, why had he gotten her involved?

Once they'd made it to the hotel's courtyard, Ian poked his head out to make sure they were alone before pulling Zelda out of the stairwell and shoving her behind a large shrub. "Wait here; try to stay out of sight." Her eyes grew large, but she said nothing, doing what he'd asked. "I'll be right back."

Ian snuck up the path to the hotel's lobby, peeking around the corner. Two large men were standing by the front desk, watching the staircase. As one turned to speak to the other, his tunic shifted slightly and Ian saw the butt of a gun sticking out of his belt, right next to a particularly large knife.

He raced back to Zelda, his tanned face temporarily as white as a sheet. "We have to go *now*." He grabbed her suitcase and hand, pulling her through the garden and into the busy streets of Thamel until he'd found the tourist-filled sanctuary known as the English Bookstore.

They had to wait for a table in the shop's small cafe, filled to the brim with western tourists in Nepal to hike or explore. Ian still refused to look at her. His eyes kept darting around, his body twisting and turning as he checked out the patrons entering the building. When the waiter showed them to their table, Ian immediately positioned himself with his back against the wall so he had a full view of the store and cafe. Only after they'd received their chai teas and dumplings did Ian finally return her gaze. "I am so sorry; so very, very sorry, Zelda."

Fed up with his cloak-and-dagger routine, Zelda leaned over the table and asked through clenched teeth, "What did you get me into, Ian?"

Over the next thirty minutes, he told his tale in hushed tones, starting with his last few weeks in Thailand and ending with the morning's events, leaving nothing out. Despite the hustle and bustle all around them, Ian kept a vigilant watch of the main entrance, staring down each and every new visitor entering the shop.

As she listened, Zelda took sips of her tea and wondered what she'd done so wrong that she deserved to be dragged into Ian's diamond-smuggling scheme. Was this her payback for not volunteering longer? Did karma work that fast?

When he finished his tale, Ian looked at her expectantly.

"How could you?" was all she could muster.

"It seemed like easy money. I clearly wasn't thinking straight," he muttered.

"Damn right," she snapped, poking at the cold dumplings on her plate with her fork. She didn't take a bite; her hunger had disappeared as soon as Ian started talking. "But why did you get me involved?"

"I didn't mean to. We were talking about people we'd met during our travels, and I told him about you volunteering here. You have to believe me; if I'd have known what a psychopath Harim was, I never would have mentioned you, let alone have said yes to him," Ian pleaded, trying to make her understand. "I never meant to get you mixed up in this. But I did. And now we have to figure out how to get of this mess."

"Are you sure the stones are gone?"

"Like I said before, by the time I got back to my hotel, two of Harim's men were already talking to the hotel manager. He thought someone else had torn up my room looking for the diamonds and that I'd done a runner. Since I reckon Harim's buyer wouldn't have been happy with eighteen out of twenty – especially after sending his welcoming committee to the hotel so quickly – I haven't gone back to the jewelry store."

Zelda stared at him through narrowing eyes, letting his words sink in before kicking his shins as hard as she could. This was real; there really were scary thugs wandering around the city looking for them both. "You idiot! You fucking idiot!" she screamed as she realized how much shit Ian had gotten her into. She wanted to jump up and strangle him, but the cafe full of gaping tourists kept her seated. Zelda settled for another shin slam before burying her face in her hands.

"If only I'd waited to roll that joint until after my meeting at the jeweler's, then none of this would be happening." Ian tore at his dreadlocks. "I'm a schoolteacher, not a smuggler! I'm in way over my head, Zelda. You've gotta help me."

"So far I only hear problems and no solutions," she hissed, unimpressed with his emotional pleas. He was the one stupid enough to say yes to Harim, not her. Men like that didn't pay strangers four thousand dollars to do something legal – Ian should have known better. "Well, I can't conjure up the diamonds for you. What are your suggestions for getting us out of this? Can we buy Harim off?"

Ian started to scoff, but one look at Zelda's face and he held his tongue. Instead he leaned back in his chair, contemplating her words. Suddenly he sat up straight, almost toppling over. "Actually, money might be our way out of this mess. And I may know how we could get ahold of enough of it." He contemplated his idea for a second, then slumped back down. "No, that's even more dangerous than disappointing Harim."

"What? Spit it out," Zelda yelled, hoping the other tourists would take their conversation for a lovers' tiff.

Ian leaned over the table and whispered, "Raju at the Sherpa Club has to be making a fortune off of those kids. He must store the profits in his office somewhere. If we could break in, find the safe, and crack it, we could pay off Harim. But Raju's always there, and my teacher's certificate program didn't include lessons in picking locks."

Zelda smoldered, not happy with his attempt at a joke. "Okay, so we have eighteen diamonds, ready for delivery. Two are missing, presumed flushed, value unknown. And one rich bar owner, guilty of exploiting minors." She gazed around her, unseeing, thinking back to her first two weeks of classes with Ganesh and the other volunteers. In addition to describing all the communicable diseases one could get in Nepal, he had also shared the darker side of living in one of the poorest nations in the world: indentured servitude, arranged marriages for financial gain, sexual inequality, child prostitution, necessary thievery, and drug mules. She'd witnessed firsthand the first three in her Nepalese homes and had found those situations hard enough to bear witness to. However, Ganesh had also told them about various volunteer organizations that helped homeless and abused children escape their often intolerable living conditions. He must know someone who could rescue the Sherpa Club's gang of thieves and dealers and get them into an orphanage where they belonged.

She shook the thought out of her head, realizing there were more pressing matters at hand. What about the diamonds? How could they get the eighteen stones to Harim's jeweler without his thugs hurting Ian or herself? And how in God's name could they ever pay Harim back for the missing two? Ian was right; neither one of them was qualified to break in or crack Raju's safe.

Zelda glared at her table companion, now fidgeting with his cup and looking around nervously. His dreadlocks were sticking to his neck; a sheen of sweat covered his body. With his stretched-out T-shirt and army-print Bermuda shorts, he looked like every other ganga-smoking trekker in this place. A dim idea came into her head. Maybe they didn't have to rob anyone. "How down and out were you when you met Harim?"

"Desperately drunk. I even spilled a drink on his shoes. That's how we got to talking."

"And he knows you have a habit of getting yourself into predicaments?"

"Well, I wouldn't go that far."

"Okay, but if you told Harim that you'd gone to the Sherpa Club your first night back, gotten drunk, and in your nervousness about the exchange, you babbled everything to the owner? And that Raju then stole the diamonds from you – would Harim believe you?"

"What are you getting at, Zelda?"

"I think I know how to get us out of this mess without having to rob anybody. I just have to make a phone call about the kids first. I saw a pay phone by the front door."

"Noble of you, but we have another, more urgent problem, don't you think?"

Zelda smiled mysteriously. "It'll be important to have a backup plan, in case Harim doesn't take the bait."

As soon as Zelda returned to their table, Ian pounced. "Did you get their contact information? Does Ganesh think they'll raid the place?"

"I did, and he does. We just have to call it in, when we're ready. Apparently their team reacts pretty quickly. So tell me, if your friend Raju had eighteen of the stones when Harim's men came calling, do you think they would believe him, that he never had the other two?"

Ian shook his head resolutely. "I seriously doubt it, especially as he'll deny having stolen them from me in the first place."

Zelda nodded. She was unbelievably nervous about going through with her plan but saw no other way out. It was the best they could come up with on such short notice. And with Harim's men looking everywhere for them, they had no time to think up a better one. Their lives – or at least imminent futures – were dependent on both their individual successes in the coming hours.

Ian signaled to the waiter, signing for him to bring the bill. "With a little luck, Harim's men will still be there when the police raid the place," he said.

"So long as Harim believes Raju stole all of the diamonds from you, it won't matter who gets there first. Either way, we should be in the clear."

Ian nodded in understanding. "Harim would never know whether it was the police or Raju who'd screwed him over."

CHAPTER FORTY

"No, no, no. Ian, you are going to have to be *way* more convincing than that. If you don't come across as the most pathetic sap on the face of the planet, he will *never* believe you. Try again. Let me see your best 'she just dumped me' look."

He thought about Veny and how he'd felt watching her walk away from him. His eyes welled up instantly.

"Wow, that's perfect! Do that – yeah, that face. Jeez, you don't have to actually cry." Zelda slapped him on the shoulder. "I have faith in you, man. You can do this!"

He responded by downing his sixth beer of the afternoon.

"You've really got to sober up. We need you in top form tonight, Ian."

Ian certainly didn't feel in top form. He wanted this whole thing to be over. For the millionth time since he'd left Bangkok, he wondered why he'd ever said yes to Harim the diamond smuggler.

"Are you sure about all this, Zelda?" he slurred.

"We have to call their bluff. From everything you've said, it sure sounds like Harim and the hotel staff are in cahoots."

"But what if they're not?"

Zelda threw her hands on her hips. "Do you have a better idea?"

"No," he mumbled in shame.

"Look, if everything goes well, we'll both be out of Kathmandu before Harim could possibly find us. Let's try to stay positive, okay?"

"But what if…"

"Ian, you got me into this. Now man up and help get us both out of this."

Another wave of guilt washed over him. "Okay, you're right."

"Can you stand up?" Zelda asked, tugging on his arm.

Ian glared up at her and then passed out on the table.

"Hey, Raju. How's it going?" Ian's head was pounding, his dreadlocks still wet from the bucket of water Zelda had dumped over his head. He tried hard to focus on his goal and stay in character. Tonight he was just a stoner hippie, backpacking around the world, unaware of who Raju really was. He *had* to block out what he had seen and felt this morning. This meeting wasn't about payback, Ian reminded himself; this was probably the only chance he had to get both himself and Zelda out of this mess.

"Ian, already time for another safety break?" The owner of the Sherpa Club came around the counter and hugged him.

Ian suppressed the urge to punch the man, instead returning his embrace. "I am sorry I did not get to talk with you last night. It is good you are back. But tell me, why the long face? Sit, sit. Tell Raju all your problems."

"It's a long story, mate." Ian sighed heavily, taking a seat at the bar. "Could I get a vodka first, then I'll tell you all about it."

"No problem, matey."

"Cheers."

Ian sipped his drink slowly. "It's my girl. Stupid sheila was supposed to meet me in Kathmandu tomorrow. Emails me a few weeks ago when I was still in Thailand, telling me how she was going crazy without me and was jealous as hell. I'd been emailing her little updates of my adventures, you know. So she tells me how she wants to trek the Annapurnas with me. I couldn't believe it – after months of slagging my travels off, she wants to join me. I fly straight back here so I can arrange the hike. I even splurged and got her a brilliant present in Thailand. Then this morning, I get another email from her saying she's decided not to come. Some new bloke in her office takes her salsa dancing a few times, and all of a sudden it's true love! We'd been together two years, and she dumps me in a bloody email." Ian pounded his fist on the bar, bit his lip, and looked away quickly, trusting his performance would add to his illusion of pain. He hoped he could keep all the details straight – he hadn't exactly been sober when Zelda had explained her plan to him.

"Oh, what a stupid girl, indeed. Sheila does not know what she has lost."

Ian sucked in his breath. It was now or never. "That's right. And now what am I supposed to do with these? Cost me a bloody fortune, they did." He tossed the velvet bag onto the counter, shaking it until a few of the stones fell onto the bar. "It's supposed to be the best cubic zirconium they make. They look like real diamonds to me. I was going to get them set into a necklace here in Kathmandu and surprise my girl with it when she arrived. Bloody waste of money now." Ian sucked back the rest of his drink. He tried to casually wipe away the beads of sweat rapidly forming on his forehead. Raju was too busy eyeing the diamonds to notice.

"May I take a closer look?" he asked.

203

Ian shrugged indifferently.

The bar's owner picked up one stone and held it up to the light. Even from where Ian was sitting, he could see tiny prisms forming. Raju was so excited he almost dropped it. After placing the diamond carefully back onto the countertop, Raju pulled his bong out from under the bar. His hands were shaking so badly, it took him a full minute to light the bowl.

Ian pulled a pre-rolled sticky out of his bag and lit up. He had come prepared, knowing he could never roll a proper joint with this pressure. The bar's owner took a few more hits off his bong before finally breaking the silence.

"That is one dumb girl. If she only knew what you had done for her…" Raju said, nodding towards the velvet satchel. "Where did you buy them?"

"From some blanket merchant in downtown Chang Mai. The whole city's one big outdoor market. You can find anything there if you look long enough. When I saw these, I thought, ya, these are perfect for my girl. But they only sold loose stones, none in a setting. That's why I was going to see about getting them made into a necklace, but there isn't much point now, is there?" Ian said, stabbing his spent joint into the ashtray. He pushed away from the bar and stood up. "Can I get another one of those? Gotta go to the loo."

Ian forced himself to walk slowly and take his time in the bathroom, giving Raju time to consider his situation. Splashing water on his face, he tried to calm himself down. *Just a few more minutes with this slimeball and you're in the clear.*

When he finally returned, Raju had still not made his drink. Instead he was twisting one of the diamonds under the lamp, watching it sparkle. When he heard Ian approaching, the bar's owner put the stone down and began pouring vodka. "This one is on me," he said.

"Cheers for that."

"You spent a lot of money on this girl, yes?"

Ian nodded.

"Perhaps I can help you?"

Ian shrugged, as if the whole situation was hopeless. "Look, mate, I'd like to flush the bloody things down the toilet, I'm so sick of looking at them. But they cost too much. Do you know anybody who might be interested in buying them? I just want to get me money back and get the hell out of Nepal."

The man grinned mischievously, "Well, it is my mother's birthday next week. She would surely love a necklace made with these stones."

Ian could hardly believe his ears. Or how easy that had gone. Zelda was right; greed was universal. He forced himself not to smile. Raju had fallen for the first trap; he didn't want to muck it up now. "Ya, and you don't have to tell her they're fakes," he added.

Raju's face clouded over momentarily in confusion before laughing nervously. "Yes, yes. Of course. Fake diamonds. No, no, I will not tell her." He kept giggling, handing Ian the bong. "Tell me, how much did you pay for these, umm, stones?"

Ian coughed up a lung full of marijuana smoke. The moment of truth had arrived. "A hundred for each, I bought all eighteen." He tipped the satchel's contents onto the counter. It was like he'd switched on a disco ball. "I know it's a lot of money, but I really loved her, man. I just wanted to make her happy." He pretended to wipe away a tear.

"Oh my gods." Raju looked like he was going to shit himself. He was muttering under his breath, his eyes transfixed by the eighteen gems gleaming on the bar.

"They're good quality, eh?" Ian said. "That's what attracted me to them in the first place, their sparkliness. My girl would have loved them." He thought again of Veny's perfectly tanned legs as she turned to join her friends, disappearing from his life forever, and let himself get caught up in the emotion. Real tears began to stream down his cheeks.

"This girl caused you a lot of trouble and heartache, yes?"

Ian nodded.

"It is terrible to see you in such pain. You are a very good customer to the Sherpa Club. It is not fair some girl can destroy your vacation plans so heartlessly. Please to let me buy them from you. I can give you your eighteen hundred dollars back."

Ian's jaw fell open, drink frozen in midair. He couldn't believe Raju had taken the bait – hook, line and sinker. "Oi, mate, are you serious? You don't know how much you're helping me out. Cheers!" Ian held up his drink in mock salute, trying hard not to overdo his enthusiasm.

"Please to stay there." Raju was running towards his office. Ian gulped back his vodka, dribbling some down his chin. *Keep it together, mate, you're almost out of here*, he told himself.

Raju returned quickly, carefully counting eighteen hundred-dollar bills – American – onto the bar between them. Hand poised over the velvet satchel, he looked at Ian questioningly. "Yes?"

Ian smiled slightly, trying to add a tinge of sadness for Raju's sake. He'd meant Australian dollars.

Raju shoved the sack of diamonds into the pocket of his pants.

"Now I can get the hell out of Nepal – no offense, I mean."

The bar's owner shook his head as he chuckled. "I would want to leave too, if I was in your situation. Do you want another drink – on the house?"

"No thanks, I'm off to the travel agencies to see about getting a flight out of here."

"Good, good. But first, please to tell me, do you have any more of these diamonds – I mean, *fake* diamonds – with you?"

"Naw, you've got them all."

Raju smiled broadly. "Have a nice trip."

Ian stood up, zipped his newly acquired cash into his money belt and walked casually to the door. Raju followed closely behind. As soon as Ian was out in the stairwell, he heard the deadbolt clicking shut. He walked down the stairs slowly at first, desperately trying to remain in character. But by the time his feet hit the ground floor, he was flying towards the light. Ian could only think of his young drug dealer. And the fact he'd just given a child-exploiting bastard thousands of dollars in real jewels. He prayed Zelda's plan would work and they could get out of Nepal before Harim found them. And that somehow Raju would get his due.

Chapter Forty-One

As the cab pulled up to the front entrance, Zelda smoothed down her best sari once more. Her knees wouldn't stop shaking.

"Can you wait for me, please? I'll just be a minute," she croaked. Her voice box wasn't working properly.

The cab driver nodded.

Exhaling slowly, Zelda mentally prepared herself for her next move. She hoped Ian was holding his nerve better than she was. Whatever he was going through was a hell of a lot worse than what she was about to do. She couldn't image having to face that bar owner without going ballistic. *Come on, Zelda, get it together*, she told herself. Ian was relying on her to deliver this note. She hoped for both of their sakes that her crazy plan would work.

She stepped out of the cab and gasped in admiration as the hotel doors were opened simultaneously by uniformed porters. Potted orchids and palm trees dotted the waiting area; a bamboo waterfall gurgled in the background. Zelda wondered how much a room would cost per night. She wove her way through the overstuffed chairs and golden statues towards the front desk, all smiles.

"Hello, madam. Welcome to the Kali Guesthouse. How may I be of service?"

"I need to speak to your manager."

The front desk clerk smiled broadly. "Is there a problem with your room or luggage? I will be happy to assist you."

"No, nothing of the sort. I just need to speak to the hotel manager personally, right now."

The man shot her a puzzled look before bowing deeply and disappearing behind a locked door. A few moments later, an older man emerged. His name badge said "manager." Perfect. "Hello, *namaste*," Zelda said, bowing graciously. "I believe we have a mutual friend."

"Pardon?"

"The man who was staying in room fifteen last night, an Australian with dreadlocks?" The hotel manager's face was a mask of neutrality. Zelda kept her smile plastered on, hoping and praying her gut instinct hadn't led her astray. "He was very careless with a package he was carrying. Very careless indeed."

"A thousand pardons, madam. I do not understand," the manager said, frowning slightly.

Oh shit! He genuinely didn't seem to know whom or what she was talking about. But there was no time to second-guess herself; she had to push forward. Their freedom depended on it. Ian didn't have any other way to make contact – neither of them dared to go to Harim's jeweler, sure they would walk right into an ambush. If the hotel manager didn't lead them to Harim, no one else could.

"Oh, that's too bad. You see, the Australian got into some trouble with a local bar owner and lost a package he was carrying, for a person you may know in Bangkok named Harim? Quite an expensive package as well. This local bar owner is extremely impressed with the merchandise. He would very much like to talk to Harim about it. Directly, personally." Zelda placed a piece of folded paper onto the counter.

The man's client-friendly attitude vanished. "Madam, I do not know who this Australian is or what you are talking about. If you do not wish to book a room, I must ask you to leave. Now."

Zelda threw up her hands. "Oh well, my bad. Have a nice day anyway." She turned and walked slowly through the lobby, praying the manager would take the bait.

As she reached the door, Zelda looked back over her shoulder to see him unfold the note. They'd argued for an hour before she and Ian finally settled on: "Our mutual friend was careless. If you want your package back, come to the Sherpa Club and bring one hundred thousand American dollars. You have twenty-four hours." If that didn't get Harim's attention, she didn't know what would.

The hotel manager's eyes widened in horror as he read Zelda's neat handwriting. With an unsteady hand, he grabbed the lobby telephone and dialed from memory.

Zelda raced towards her cab, grinning from ear to ear.

CHAPTER FORTY-TWO

"Where are we going?" Tommy yelled out. His shackles rattled loudly as the van swung left, throwing him hard against the side. "Ow," he cried out, rubbing at his wrists. The ten policemen surrounding him – all dressed in matching riot gear – didn't even twitch.

The man from the Jeep smiled at him through a small opening in the back of the cab. "Almost there."

Through the windows in the rear door, Tommy could see they had turned off Khao San Road onto a small side street. Seconds later the van came to a rolling stop in front of a sprawling five-story hotel surrounded by a tree-filled courtyard. The man from the Jeep looked back for confirmation.

Tommy nodded. "Yeah, this is it," he squeaked, praying he didn't shit himself before this was over. The man from the Jeep shouted a command in Thai, and Tommy's backseat companions jumped from the van and spread out to surround the building.

Even with the back door open, Tommy couldn't see much from the bench he was chained to. He closed his eyes and tried to picture how the arrest would go down. Would The Greek's men put up a fight, giving their boss time to escape? If he did make a break for it, would the cops shoot him dead, or did they have orders to take him alive?

Before Tommy's imagination could kick into overdrive, screams of anger and indignation echoed through the courtyard. He gulped hard; it was definitely his former boss being dragged towards the van. Now Harim would know for sure it was Tommy who'd ratted him out.

The yelling intensified as the armed police dragged one of Asia's most notorious smugglers towards the vehicle's open rear door.

"No, no, NOOOO!" Harim cried, his face a mask of pure rage and hatred. "You're supposed to be dead; your bloated corpse on its way to North Korea!"

Harim's hair was dripping wet, his body covered only in a silk bathrobe. *That's why they were able to arrest him so quickly*, Tommy thought, *he was in the shower*. Somehow seeing his former boss handcuffed and half-naked gave him a surge of confidence. "Guess your goons picked the wrong container ship."

Harim kicked against the door of the van, rocking the vehicle from side to side. "I am going to kill you myself! As soon as my lawyers get me out, you are a dead man, Thomas Braintree! Dead!"

Tommy cowered inside, for the first time in his life thankful for police protection. He watched in amazement as the officers dragged Harim – kicking and screaming – to a marked police car and threw him in the backseat. Like a common criminal.

After Harim's car and several armored police escorts pulled away, the man from the Jeep popped his head inside the van, a grin spread from ear to ear. He whipped out a tape recorder and held it up to Tommy's mouth. "For the record, is that the man you know as Harim, the same man for whom you smuggled diamonds to Kathmandu?"

Tommy nodded enthusiastically. "Yes, yes it is."

"Good." The man from the Jeep stopped the recording and began closing the door when Tommy called out, "Please, wait!"

His captor paused, a questioning look on his face.

"Can he really get out on bail?" Tommy asked, a tremor in his voice.

"Not a chance. Thanks to your testimony, he will never be a free man again," the man from the Jeep responded, obviously jazzed up by his big score. He slammed the rear door shut and climbed back into the passenger seat.

Tommy could hardly believe his ears. An unknown rush of pride surged through his veins. He, Thomas Oscar Braintree, was singlehandedly responsible for the downfall of one of the most dangerous smugglers working in Asia today. He was a real-life hero. Suddenly he wanted to tell the whole world what he had done, warts and all. It didn't matter if he went to jail; he just wanted everyone to *know*.

Would his extradition make the papers back home? Tommy closed his eyes, gleefully visualizing a mob of press awaiting his arrival. He knew he would spend the next ten to fifteen years in jail, but at least it would be a Canadian one. Would Chantal come and visit him, once she read what he'd done? Did Canadian prisons even allow conjugal visits? Tommy would have to find out. "Hey, mister, when is Harim's arrest going to be in the papers?"

The man from the Jeep shone like a peacock. "Tomorrow morning, on the front page." Tommy's captor pounded on the dashboard, capturing the driver's attention. "To the airport!"

CHAPTER FORTY-THREE

"Say, Zelda, you think Harim will find him? Raju, I mean? Or did we just give a child abuser thousands of dollars' worth of diamonds?" Ian asked as he snapped his newspaper shut.

"Do you really want to be responsible for the stones, after everything you've been through these past few days?"

"No, of course not. But it would be nice to know if Harim gets his diamonds back. I figure if he does, then my family is safe. I don't want them to have to keep looking over their shoulders because of something I've done."

"Maybe you should have thought of that before you agreed to smuggle diamonds for him," Zelda blurted out, immediately regretting her outburst. She knew Ian felt stupid for getting sucked into Harim's crazy scheme and putting them all – herself included – at grave risk.

Ian started to respond but held his tongue. Instead, he took a long sip of beer and stared off into the distance. Zelda's eyes followed his gaze across the resort's spacious lawn to the dense jungle rising up behind the manicured rhododendrons. They'd taken the first bus they could to Chitwan National Park, boarding only minutes after calling Ganesh's NGO contact and telling him everything they knew about Raju and the Sherpa Club. With any luck, the children he'd been exploiting would be freed before the day's end, the man assured them. As long as Raju didn't get tipped off first.

That was two days ago. They'd been scouring the hotel's generous selection of local and international newspapers during breakfast, looking for any references to the Sherpa Club, but to no avail. *Maybe they should check the obituaries?* Zelda pondered. Neither of them knew what Harim's men would do to Raju, especially if he didn't hand over the diamonds right away.

"Blokes like Harim and Raju never really get what they deserve, though, do they?" Ian almost whispered.

It took her a second to work out what he'd said. "I don't know about that. The hotel manager was on the phone before I was out the door. By now Harim must know about our note and where his diamonds are. I guess as long as he gets his shipment back – or thinks the police have them – there's no reason for him to turn up on your doorstep in Darwin."

Ian looked over at Zelda, concern etched on his face. "However it works out, Harim should have no reason to come after either one of us. But I still don't think you should travel to Southeast Asia right away; that's his backyard. I know I'll feel better if you don't. India's nice this time of year, why don't you check out Goa first?"

"Like I've said a hundred times already, after Chitwan I'm going to Vietnam. Period." Zelda couldn't believe she'd remain a target once she'd left Nepal. It wasn't as if she and Ian were lovers or even good friends – Harim couldn't use her to get to him after they'd parted company.

"Look, it's bad enough we're here, Zelda. Everyone working at your hotel knew your volunteer group was heading to this national park for a week; all Harim's men had to do was ask. And I'm sure that's what they did, once they figured out we'd snuck out of your room via the back stairs. Until we know how this all plays out, I think you should stay away from your group."

Despite his constant pleading, Zelda had refused to bail out on her volunteer group's week-long trip to Chitwan, opting instead to leave Kathmandu two days earlier than the rest and book her own room at a different hotel on the other side of the vast national park. She couldn't believe Harim would be so desperate to find Ian that he'd dare kidnap her while she was with the others. But she didn't want to endanger her fellow volunteers either. As she wouldn't cancel, Ian demanded he tag along as bodyguard; it was his fault after all.

"Yeah, yeah. Whatever, Ian. My group checked in to their hotel last night. I promised Ganesh I would meet them there so we can all go on our first excursion together. Are you coming?"

"Did you hear anything I said?"

"Ian, this trip is my reward for giving up two months of my life to teach, and I'll be damned if your stupidity is going to ruin that for me. So help me be a tourist for a few days, will you? If you feel the need to tag along, I'll see whether Ganesh can squeeze you into our group. But it's really you Harim's after; maybe you should stay behind."

"No way, I'm here to protect you. Besides, I didn't shave my head for fun. I should be able to get the jump on his men if they do try anything."

Zelda had to admit she'd barely recognized him after his visit to a curbside barbershop during their five-hour bus layover. In combination with his newly purchased polo and Bermuda shorts, he looked more like the schoolteacher he was than the stoner-hippie he wanted to be. "Okay, let's go then."

When they arrived at her group's hotel a half-hour later, Ganesh was waiting by the main entrance. "Thank the gods that you arrived safely!" He bowed deeply before Zelda, then asked, "Is this your friend Ian?"

"Indeed, the teacher I told you about." As far as her program coordinator was concerned, Ian was an old friend in Nepal to hike. She'd told Ganesh on the phone that during a night out, Ian happened to see Raju locking kids into a room inside his club and told her about it the next day.

"Ah, yes." Ganesh bowed again. "If you ever want to teach here, you are most welcome. Please to come inside, I have exciting news for you both." He led them through the hotel's small lobby to a patio filled with tables and ordered a pot of chai tea by snapping his fingers. "Two hours ago, my friend called to tell me the owner of the Sherpa Club was arrested yesterday morning. Fifty-six children were locked up inside his bar. They are all being placed in local orphanages, much like the one your father showed you, Zelda."

She thought back to the orphanage she'd visited, hoping the kids were lucky enough to end up somewhere like that. She reddened in shame as she remembered how mad she'd gotten when the director had asked her for money to expand. Now she understood how necessary both foreign help and an abundance of orphanages were in a country where children were often seen as financial burdens or objects to be exploited. She still had their folder in her suitcase – she'd have to send them a check once she was working again.

"That is bloody fantastic news!" Ian exclaimed.

"And the owner? Was he arrested? Or did he get away before the police arrived?" Zelda asked.

Ganesh's smiled dimmed slightly. "The owner of the club was found unconscious on the floor of his office, his safe open and empty. He had been badly beaten and some of his toenails removed. It was all very messy." He wrinkled his nose in disgust, as if he'd been telling them about getting poop on his shoes.

Ian and Zelda exchanged glances, both suppressing smiles. Harim's men must have taken back the eighteen diamonds and stolen Raju's drug profits while they were at it. Whatever was in that safe must have been enough to satisfy Harim; otherwise Raju wouldn't be alive.

Ganesh continued, oblivious to Ian and Zelda's improved moods. "The police suspect he had been robbed shortly before they arrived, but so far Mr. Pokharel has refused to tell them what had happened. He was taken into custody and will face charges for exploiting those children and

– according to the records my friend's organization found in his office – many others."

A wave of relief and satisfaction washed over her. Not only were she and Ian safe, so were all those kids.

Ganesh slapped his palms on his thighs and rose. "Come, the other volunteers are waiting for us in the breakfast hall. It is time for our first excursion, an elephant ride through Chitwan National Park. It was not a problem adding Mr. Ian to our group; there is room enough for everyone!" he exclaimed, perky as ever. He started to lead them back towards the hotel's entrance when he stopped, concern crossing over his face. "The others know nothing about what has happened in the Sherpa Club, and I would ask that you do not discuss it with them."

Both Zelda and Ian nodded their heads enthusiastically. "No problem," she said, having no desire to discuss what had happened with anyone, ever. All she cared about was knowing Harim got his gems back. Now she and Ian could relax and enjoy the scenery, knowing there was little chance Harim or anyone in his gang would be chasing after either one of them.

"Good. Please to follow me."

CHAPTER FORTY-FOUR

As they walked back to their hotel, a plethora of stars sparkling over the mustard fields, Zelda wrapped an arm around Ian's waist and leaned her head onto his shoulder.

"What are you thinking about?" he asked, kissing her lightly on the forehead.

"How nice it is to be a tourist," she lisped, leaning heavily on Ian for support. She was slightly drunk and sore from the long elephant ride, but psyched they'd gotten so close to a family of rhinos. She was still shocked by how big and bulky they were and how fast they could run when disturbed.

After their ride through the wildlife park, they'd all returned to the volunteers' hotel and lounged around in the sun, drinking beers and swapping war stories. Ganesh had discreetly excused himself, leaving the others to exchange accounts of their experiences without his fatherly presence.

"Oh God, yes! My family started in the very first night I arrived about a remodeling they were planning. And with my help they could get going the very next day," Doris smirked, in response to Zelda's careful attempt to find out whether any of the others had been hit up for cash.

"My mom kept stealing my underwear," Sarah piped up.

"What?" Zelda and Doris both cried out.

"I swear, I finally caught her doing it. Every time I washed my clothes, a pair would disappear. She said it was the wind, but I finally caught her red-handed putting her latest acquisition away in her bedroom, next to six others she'd already stolen. She refused to give them back; can you believe the gall of that woman? I had Ganesh move me to another school straight away."

Zelda shook her head in disgust. She'd had no idea how bad it had been for the others. She was righteously pissed, but also secretly glad it wasn't just she who had been treated like a pariah when she didn't donate to any of her family's causes. "I didn't know. I wish I did."

"None of us knew what was going on with the others. Ganesh kept us apart on purpose, I suspect. He doesn't seem to like to dwell on the negative," Doris observed. Zelda nodded in agreement, thinking about how he'd asked her not to mention the Sherpa Club.

"Well, my family hasn't asked me for anything," Christine stated. Up until now she'd been suspiciously quiet while the others talked of less pleasant things. "In fact, we've gotten along so well, I'm going to stay on another three months."

No wonder, Zelda thought, *they're just waiting until Christine is well and truly done volunteering before hitting her up for money.* Not that she could blame any of their placement families for trying to wheedle cash out of them. Coming into contact with "rich" westerners was probably the main reason most of them agreed to participate in the program in the first place.

As Zelda lay back in the wooden sun chair and let the others' stories sink in, she thought back to the idealistic goals she and the other volunteers had shared at the beginning of their adventure. Despite their best efforts, none of them had really made a lasting impact on their villages or schools, or "found themselves" while living rough. Only Christine seemed to have gotten what she wanted out of the experience, though the girl was clear from the start that she was only here to get into her university's anthropology program; she never had the illusion she was saving the world or discovering her true self.

Maybe that's my problem, Zelda realized. *I'd put too much pressure on myself from the start.* But did that mean she'd wasted her time by coming here? In all honesty, she wasn't any closer to figuring out what she wanted to do with the rest of her life than before she'd left Seattle. Though she was pretty sure being a teacher or anthropologist was out of the question.

Rather than sinking into a depression, Zelda reflected on all the hardships she'd faced since arriving in Nepal. She had survived continuous electrical blackouts, a lack of running water, and using a hole in the ground as a lavatory and her hand as toilet paper. Cows running through the streets and goats losing their heads were everyday occurrences. She'd managed not to beat the living hell out of her students – as much as she'd really, really wanted to sometimes. And she'd even gotten the hang of wearing a sari properly. She'd clearly gotten a firsthand look into the daily life of the Nepali, more than most backpackers anyway. She *had* experienced Nepal in a way few foreigners ever would. And here she was, three months later, still standing.

A smile began to spread across her face. *She had done it!* She was more resilient than she realized she could be, wrapped up in her expensive cocoon of a life back in Seattle. So she wasn't the best teacher ever, and the Peace Corps probably wasn't in her future, but she'd given it her best shot and hadn't given up. And that's all anybody could have asked of her.

CHAPTER FORTY-FIVE

Zelda relaxed into her hammock, rocking gently in the warm midafternoon sun. Only the sounds of rustling bamboo and the hoots of monkeys broke the silence. After an excursion-filled week, it felt good to sleep in late and chill out for a while by herself in the garden of her hotel. As soon as Ian was done showering and packing up, she'd have to get her own bags together and check out.

She listened to the monkeys calling to each other for a moment before returning her attention to this morning's *Kathmandu English Times*, relishing every word of the article detailing Harim's extensive band of smugglers, specializing in diamonds and gold. The capture of Harim and his international gang had been the front-page news story for three days running, even here in Nepal. Before Ian's mess-up, Zelda never knew these kinds of things happened in real life.

Thanks to Thomas Braintree, she could backpack around Asia without worry, and Ian could rest easy knowing his family was safe. With Harim locked up in a Thai prison for the rest of his life, none of them had to fear his wrath anymore. At first neither of them could believe it was the same man Ian was working for who was behind bars, until pictures of his arrest and booking were released to the press. Ian was absolutely sure; photos don't lie. Zelda knew Ian had already bought a ticket back home, but with all her group's cultural excursions and nature walks, they'd had almost no time to themselves. She had no idea what his plans were once he got back.

Before she could finish today's article, Ian bounced into view, freshly shaven, backpacks in hand.

"I already ordered us beers. Figured you could use one before your cab arrives."

"Cheers for that!" Ian said, taking a long pull before sitting down in a chair across from her.

"So what are you going to do next?" she asked.

"My plane's headed for Darwin, but I've still got another three months of sabbatical. A cousin of mine opened a surfer bar on Bondi Beach last year. I reckon I'll give him a call, see whether he needs some help for the summer. That seems like enough adventure for me for a while." He sighed wistfully.

"Summer's still a ways off," she said with a frown.

"It's summer in Australia now. *Southern* hemisphere, remember?"

"Oh, right." Zelda reddened; she had no idea December was summertime Down Under. She'd simply never thought about it.

"If nothing else, I can stay with my cousin for a few weeks and build up me tan. Pull a few beers between waves." Ian winked with his whole face, his right hand forming the hang-loose sign.

"Awesome, dude," she teased back.

The clanking sound of a poorly tuned engine approaching made them turn. A rusty Honda was chugging its way up their hotel's long driveway.

"That must be my ride."

After the taxi driver had forced his gear into the tiny trunk, Zelda kissed Ian once more on the lips. "Be safe."

He started to chuckle.

"Yeah, well, I guess now that Harim and most of his associates are behind bars, we both should be," she added with a grin.

Ian wrapped his arms around her, squeezing her tight. "Good luck to you too, Zelda. I hope you find whatever it is you're looking for."

"Me too."

He climbed in and blew her one last kiss before turning to face forward, already looking ahead to his next escapade.

She watched as Ian's taxi slowly made its way down the drive of the hotel, knowing he wouldn't look back but waving until her arm hurt anyway. After the emotional strain of the past few weeks, she'd expected a rush of tears to accompany his departure, but they didn't materialize. *It was nice meeting Ian*, Zelda thought. But she didn't imagine she'd ever see him again, let alone keep in touch. And there were definitely other adventures in store, for both of them.

THE END

Thank you for reading my book.
If you enjoyed it, please take a moment to leave a review on your favorite retailer's website or Goodreads. I appreciate it!
- Jennifer S. Alderson

ACKNOWLEDGEMENTS

This book was born in fictionalized form during an Arvon writing retreat held in Moniack Mhor in 2007. My sincerest thanks to my fellow fledgling writers and our wise tutors for their invaluable input and in particular the kindhearted Val McDermid for asking the right questions at the right time.

My own experiences volunteering in Nepal and traveling around Thailand and Vietnam in 1999 and 2000 provided the basis for this story. Thanks to all the individuals and families who looked after a very naive and idealistic me during my fantastic journey.

I am indebted to everyone who read earlier versions of this manuscript and provided the feedback necessary to get it finished, as well as my editor Jane Dean for her numerous catches and excellent suggestions.

Down and Out in Kathmandu is dedicated to my wonderfully understanding parents for supporting me no matter how crazy my upcoming adventures seemed to be, and trusting me when I said everything was going to work out fine. Somehow it always did.

To my darling husband, Philip, for encouraging me to keep writing and for creating the cover artwork. And our beautiful son for reminding me there's more to life than sitting behind a computer screen.

ABOUT THE AUTHOR

Jennifer S. Alderson (1972) worked as a journalist and website developer in Seattle, Washington, USA, before trading her financial security for a backpack. After traveling extensively around Asia and Central America, she moved to Darwin, Australia, before finally settling in the Netherlands. There she earned degrees in art history and museum studies. Home is now Amsterdam, where she lives with her Dutch husband and young son.

Jennifer's travels and experiences color and inform her internationally oriented mystery series, the *Adventures of Zelda Richardson*. *The Lover's Portrait: An Art Mystery* is a suspenseful "whodunit?" that transports readers to wartime and present-day Amsterdam. Art, religion, and anthropology collide in *Rituals of the Dead*, a thrilling artifact mystery set in Papua New Guinea and the Netherlands. Her free short story set in Panama and Costa Rica, *Holiday Gone Wrong*, will help fans better understand this unintentional amateur sleuth's decision to study art history and give new readers a taste of her tantalizing misadventures.

Her travelogue, *Notes of a Naive Traveler*, is a must read for those interested in learning more about – or wishing to – travel to Nepal and Thailand.

For more information about the author and her novels, please visit http://www.JenniferSAlderson.com.

The Lover's Portrait
An Art Mystery

Book two in the *Adventures of Zelda Richardson* series

"Gripping mystery…the suspense is intensely magnetic and the characters equally captivating" – BookLife Prize for Fiction 2016, No. 14 in Mystery category

"Well worth reading for what the main character discovers—not just about the portrait mentioned in the title, but also the sobering dangers of Amsterdam during World War II." – IndieReader

"*The Lover's Portrait* is a well-written mystery with engaging characters and a lot of heart. The perfect novel for those who love art and mysteries!" – Reader's Favorite, 5 star medal

When a Dutch art dealer hides the stock from his gallery – rather than turn it over to his Nazi blackmailer – he pays with his life, leaving a treasure trove of modern masterpieces buried somewhere in Amsterdam, presumably lost forever. That is, until American art history student Zelda Richardson sticks her nose in.

After studying for a year in the Netherlands, Zelda scores an internship at the prestigious Amsterdam Historical Museum, where she works on an exhibition of paintings and sculptures once stolen by the Nazis, lying unclaimed in Dutch museum depots almost seventy years later.

When two women claim the same painting, the portrait of a young girl titled *Irises*, Zelda is tasked with investigating the painting's history and soon finds evidence that one of the two women must be lying about her past. Before she can figure out which one and why, Zelda learns about the Dutch art dealer's concealed collection – and that *Irises* is the key to finding it.

Her discoveries make her a target of someone willing to steal – and even kill – to find the missing paintings. As the list of suspects grows, Zelda realizes she has to track down the lost collection and unmask a killer if she wants to survive.

Available as paperback, eBook, and audiobook at your favorite online retailer.

Find direct links to buy *The Lover's Portrait: An Art Mystery* at: http://www.JenniferSAlderson.com.

Turn the page to read an exciting excerpt from Zelda's next adventure in Amsterdam...

CHAPTER ONE

June 26, 1942

Just two more crates, then our work is finally done, Arjan reminded himself as he bent down to grasp the thick twine handles, his back muscles already yelping in protest. Drops of sweat were burning his eyes, blurring his vision. "You can do this," he said softly, heaving the heavy oak box upwards with an audible grunt.

Philip nodded once, then did the same. Together they lugged their loads across the moonlit room, down the metal stairs and into the cool subterranean space below. After hoisting the last two crates onto a stack close to the ladder, Arjan smiled in satisfaction, slapping Philip on the back as he regarded their work. One hundred and fifty-two crates holding his most treasured objects, and those of so many of his friends, were finally safe. Relief briefly overcame the panic and dread he'd been feeling for longer than he could remember. Preparing the space and artwork had taken more time than he'd hoped it would, but they'd done it. Now he could leave Amsterdam knowing he'd stayed true to his word. Arjan glanced over at Philip, glad that he'd trusted him. He stretched out a hand towards the older man. "They fit perfectly."

Philip answered with a hasty handshake and a tight smile before nodding towards the ladder. "Shall we?"

He was right, Arjan thought, there was still so much to do. They climbed back up into the small shed and closed the heavy metal lid, careful to cushion its fall. They didn't want to give the neighbors an excuse to call the Gestapo. Not when they were so close to being finished.

Philip picked up a shovel and scooped sand onto the floor, letting Arjan rake it out evenly before adding more. When the sand was an inch thick, they shifted the first layer of heavy cement tiles into place, careful to fit them snug up against each other.

As they heaved and pushed, Arjan allowed himself to think about the future for the first time in weeks. Hiding the artwork was only the first step; he still had a long road to go before he could stop looking over his shoulder. First, back to his place to collect their suitcases. Then a short walk to Central Station where second-class train tickets to Venlo were waiting. Finally, a taxi ride to the Belgian border where his contact would provide him with falsified travel documents and a chauffeur-driven Mercedes-Benz. The five Rembrandt etchings in his suitcase would guarantee safe passage to Switzerland. From Genève he should be able to make his way through the Demilitarized Zone to Lyon, then down to Marseille. All he had to do was keep a few steps ahead of Oswald Drechsler.

Just thinking about the hawk-nosed Nazi made him work faster. So far he'd been able to clear out his house and storage spaces without Drechsler noticing. Their last load, the canvases stowed in his gallery, was the riskiest, but he'd had no choice. His friends trusted him – no, counted on him – to keep their treasures safe. He couldn't let them down now. Not after all he'd done wrong.

*   *   *

Rituals of the Dead
An Artifact Mystery

Book three in the *Adventures of Zelda Richardson* series

"Excellent story, interesting twists. I really love *The Lover's Portrait* but *Rituals of the Dead* is a step up." – beta reader

Zelda Richardson's back and embroiled in another exciting art mystery. This time she's working at the Tropenmuseum in Amsterdam on an exhibition of *bis poles* from the Asmat region of Papua New Guinea – the same area where a famous American anthropologist disappeared in 1962. When his journals are found inside one of the *bis poles*, Zelda is tasked with finding out about the man's last days and his connection to these ritual objects.

Zelda finds herself pulled into a world of shady anthropologists, missionaries, art collectors, gallery owners, and smugglers, where the only certainty is that sins of the past are never fully erased.

Join Zelda on her next quest as she grapples with the anthropologist's mysterious disappearance fifty years earlier and a present-day murderer who will do everything to prevent her from discovering the truth.

Art, religion, and anthropology collide in Alderson's upcoming art mystery thriller, Rituals of the Dead, Book Three of the *Adventures of Zelda Richardson* series.

Expected release date April 6, 2018. Available as paperback and eBook.

Pre-order *Rituals of the Dead* now at your favorite retailer.
Find direct links at: http://www.JenniferSAlderson.com.

Notes of a Naive Traveler: Nepal and Thailand
A Travelogue

"I recommend it for anyone thinking about taking a trip … anywhere."
5 stars - Author Rebecca Carter

"*Notes of a Naive Traveler* is a heart filled journey through the eyes of a young nomad who had the courage to exchange Starbucks for Stupas. So pack your bags and enjoy your trip. Just be sure to bring hand sanitizer."
5 stars - Libro Illustrato by Kyra, Book Blog

"I never thought I would have reason to say to someone, "Sorry I'm late, it took longer to dismember the goat than originally planned."

Part guidebook on culture and travel, part journey of self-discovery, this travelogue takes you on a backpacking adventure through Nepal and Thailand and provides a firsthand account of one volunteer's experience teaching in a Nepali school and living with a devout Brahmin family.

Trek with me through the bamboo forests and terraced mountaintops of eastern Nepal, take a wild river-rafting ride in class IV waters, go on an elephant ride and encounter a charging rhinoceros on jungle walks in Chitwan National Park, sea-kayak the surreal waters of Krabi, and snorkel in the Gulf of Thailand. Join me on some of the scariest bus rides you could imagine, explore beautiful and intriguing temples, experience religious rituals unknown to most Westerners, and visit mind-blowing places not mentioned in your typical travel guides.

Notes of a Naive Traveler is a must-read for those interested in learning more about – or wishing to travel to – Nepal and Thailand. I hope it inspires you to see these amazing countries for yourself.

Available as paperback and eBook at your favorite online retailer.

Find direct links to buy *Notes of a Naive Traveler* at:
http://www.JenniferSAlderson.com.

Made in the USA
Middletown, DE
16 November 2018